Charles Edgar Lewis Wingate

Shakespeare's Heroes on the Stage

Charles Edgar Lewis Wingate

Shakespeare's Heroes on the Stage

ISBN/EAN: 9783337214098

Printed in Europe, USA, Canada, Australia, Japan

Cover: Foto ©Andreas Hilbeck / pixelio.de

More available books at **www.hansebooks.com**

JUNIUS BRUTUS BOOTH AS KING RICHARD III.

SHAKESPEARE'S HEROES
ON THE STAGE

BY

CHARLES E. L. WINGATE

AUTHOR OF SHAKESPEARE'S HEROINES ON THE STAGE, PLAY-GOERS'
YEAR BOOK, ETC., AND ASSOCIATE EDITOR OF FAMOUS
AMERICAN ACTORS OF TO-DAY

WITH

ILLUSTRATIONS

From Photographs and Rare Prints

NEW YORK: 46 EAST FOURTEENTH STREET

THOMAS Y. CROWELL & COMPANY

BOSTON: 100 PURCHASE STREET

PREFACE.

IN the kindly notices, by the critics, of " Shakespeare's Heroines on the Stage," the suggestion was made, in a number of instances, that a companion volume, treating of remaining plays and of the Heroes, might prove a useful accompaniment ; and for that reason this volume (entirely distinct from the other, and dealing almost entirely with another series of Shakespeare's plays) has been written.

This book, like the " Heroines," is not intended exclusively for the professed lovers of theatrical literature. It is written with the hope of entertaining the masses of people who read Shakespeare's works and see them played, and who would naturally feel interested in knowing how the great actors of the past and present, in England and in America, have interpreted the famous characters on the stage.

Scores of books have been written about Shakespeare's plays, and about theatrical performers; but no book has been published to show how the plays were presented by those performers, and what incidents accompanied the presentations. A field, therefore, has been open to a book of this kind. So far as it fails to fill that field, the fault lies with the author.

The old-time pictures are, for the most part, from the collection of Mr. John Bouvé Clapp of Boston, and in a number of cases reproduce rare prints.

C. E. L. W.

CONTENTS.

vii

LIST OF ILLUSTRATIONS.

ix

OTHELLO AND IAGO.

"Until four years ago," quoth Edmund Kean, as he held high in air a glass of brandy and water, "I could play Othello with no need of this. Now I can't do without it."

Too true it was of that magnificent but ill-taught genius.

He uttered the words only a few months before his pathetic farewell to the stage,—a farewell that seemed almost a death-scene. On the 25th of March, 1833, for the first and only time in their lives, Edmund Kean and Charles Kean stood upon the London stage together. The father was clothed in the robes of Othello; the son was clad in wily Iago's garb. Though but six-and-forty years of age, the once inspiring, vigorous hero of the greatest plays of Shakespeare was now so weakened by debauchery as scarcely to be able to lift his arms through the sleeves of the Moor's robes.

1

All knew beforehand that this dread scene must come. Even at earlier performances, when the people in front surmised little of the terrible struggle for strength within the slight body upon the stage, friends between the wings had noted the pathetic efforts of the actor.

Ah, "that helpless, speechless, fainting mass," as Dr. Doran saw him when "Othello" had been performed a short time before the farewell! Nothing but frequent doses of strong brandy and water then kept alive the once noble Moor. "Ay, and still noble," declared Doran, aroused to enthusiasm at the recollection; "for when his time came, he looked about as from a dream, and sighed, and painfully got to his feet, swayed like a column in an earthquake, and in not more time than is required for the telling of it, was before the audience, as strong and as intellectually beautiful as of old — but only happy in the applause which gave him a little breathing-space, and saved him from falling dead upon the stage."

And yet how the audiences in that earlier season of 1827–1828 adored the player! That night when Dr. Doran was present, the Iago was Young, the Desdemona was Miss Jarman, and the Cassio was Charles Kemble. So great was the crowd that weak men fainted, and strong men saved themselves from suffocation only by climbing over the boxes into vacant places where they could breathe. In vain the stately Kemble argued with the crowd. They wanted nothing of the graceful player then; they worshipped at the shrine of the great tragedian whose presence could move them to tears or to silence as he willed.

This admiration for Kean at one time alone had weakened. Then the little man drew himself within the dignity of his own self-consciousness of genius, and bade the people defiance. It was just after his home had been broken up by the scandal with a neighbor's wife, to the great sorrow of faithful Mary Chambers Kean, the devoted helpmate who gave to the erratic actor her love and care in starving misfortune as well as in luxurious prosperity. The pittites thundered about him their disapprobation, voicing condemnation in harshest terms. He met them with ferocious courage and lofty contempt. In their turn they tried one night an insult, by giving all the applause to the ranting Iago, the minor actor, Cobham. Nettled though the famous Othello was, he broke no faith with the management, but played the character steadily through to the end. Then, however, when the audience howled for

Kean to appear before the curtain, the swarthy player, stepping boldly to the front, demanded, "What do you want?"

"You! you!" they cried in one acclaim.

"Very well!" he said; "let me tell you that though I have played in every civilized country where English is the language of the people, I never acted to an audience of such unmitigated brutes as you are!" and then he stalked slowly off.

Again, in the very last year of his career, the tumult in the house disturbed him. "Go you, sir," he cried to the manager, "and bid those fellows be quiet within five minutes, or I'll quit the house." And, having heard his message repeated, he walked upon the stage, sat down before the footlights, and with watch in hand waited for the noise to cease. Long before the five minutes had passed, the house was peaceful and repentant.

Last scene of all! The wretched, wasted body and the nerveless, weakened brain giving way when most men are in the fulness of their strength! On that fateful night in March, 1833, Edmund Kean, feeble and shaking, pouring down brandy after brandy to give fictitious courage and strength, whispered to his son that he must constantly keep at hand, for life seemed ebbing away.

EDMUND KEAN.

Yet safely the play went on until the third act was reached.

"Farewell! Othello's occupation's gone!" the actor cried, with such pathetic emphasis that the house applauded to the very echo. Even as they cheered, the poor man's chin dropped upon his breast, the eyes grew dull, and for a moment it seemed as if slumber had suddenly come upon him. But more than sleep was at hand. Pitifully reaching out his hands, as if to ward off the invisible calamity, he fell with a moan into the arms of his son.

"I am dying, Charles," he stammered; "I am dying — speak to them — tell them I cannot go on."

Down fell the curtain forever on Edmund Kean. For a while he lingered, nursed by that forgiving wife, who at his call of anguish had hastened home to his side; but on the subsequent 15th of May, with an old play tag upon his tongue, the actor's suffering ended.

Still another tragedy in life was there during a performance of "Othello." On a night when Thomas Sheridan was acting the Moor in Dublin, his Iago was Layfield, a very clever and highly esteemed performer. They gave their respective parts in excellent style, meeting with frequent applause, until the crucial scene of the third act, when, to Sheridan's astonishment, Iago entirely misquoted the lines, exclaiming: —

> "Oh, beware, my Lord, of jealousy!
> It is the green-eyed *Lobster*" —

The audience roared. They thought it was immensely funny. Poor Layfield! No one knew until later that that strange and ludicrous misquoting was the first indication of the approach of incurable madness. It was with him the beginning of the end.

But to go back to the beginning of our Othellos.

It was the year 1602 that the tragedy was first represented upon the stage; and the original interpreter of Othello was Richard Burbage. Probably Joseph Taylor was the original Iago. Of Burbage's Moor we have a reference in his funeral eulogy, reading: —

> "But let me not forget one chiefest part,
> Wherein, beyond the rest, he moved the heart;
> The grieved Moor, made jealous by a slave,
> Who sent his wife to fill a timeless grave,
> Then slew himself upon the bloody bed.
> All these and many more are with him dead."

Othello, however, proved too strong a character to be buried in the tomb. Soon after the theatres

had reopened, when the clouds of the Revolution had cleared away, Burt, who then assumed the *rôle*, though an actor far beneath Burbage in rank, must have carried out the last scene with realistic vigor, judging by the words of the gossiping diarist, Mr. Pepys. On the 11th of October, 1660, he wrote in his private book:—

"Here in the Park, we met Mr. Salisbury, who took Mr. Creed and me to the Cockpit to see the Moor of Venice, which was very well done. Burt acted the Moor. By the same token, a very pretty lady that sat by me called out to see Desdemona smothered."

Again Pepys saw Burt in the character on the 6th of February, 1669, and in his brief record has room not only to criticise the acting, but to add two important facts: First, that he saw in an upper box Colonel Poynton and Doll Stacey, "who is very fine, and by her wedding-ring I suppose he hath married her at last;" and second, that on his way home the bolt on the fore axle broke, and the horse dashed away, leaving our perplexed friend with his coachman staring down the highway in temporary dismay. Had the accident been more serious, we never should have known at this day how badly played was "Othello" on that night, — Mohun, much to Pepys's surprise, "not acting Iago's part

by much so well as Clun used to do; nor another
Hart's which was Cassio; nor indeed Burt doing
the Moor so well as I once thought he did."

Clun's Iago had, in fact, been the most famous
in his _répertoire;_ but it had not long delighted Mr.
Pepys, for, five years before this last record was
made by the dramatist, the actor, while on his way
home after a midnight carousal with friends, was attacked by robbers, wounded in the arm, and thrown
into a ditch to bleed to death.

Though our good friend Pepys was occasionally
interested in Shakespeare, yet he frankly admits
that on reading "Othello" he decided it to be "a
mean thing." But then, the cause of this rare
judgment lay in "The Adventure of Five Houres,"
which remarkable work he found so vastly superior to Shakespeare's tragedy as to lead him to
rank "Othello" in the lower class. We must
grieve that the open-eyed recorder did not see the
performance of Dec. 8, 1660; for that was the
night when for the first time any English woman
(Mrs. Hughes as Desdemona) appeared upon the
stage, the female _rôles_ having previously been
played by boys. What interesting comments Pepys
might have made, had he been there and "i' the
mood"!

One of the most famous boy actresses of the early days of the theatre, Hart, was the successor of Burt in the title *rôle* of the tragedy of jealousy.

As for Betterton, — the great Betterton, — who played Othello with success some seventeen years before the beginning of the eighteenth century, and who played the part with equal success seven years after the century had been ushered in — his was a splendid impersonation. It was several times well set off by the Iago of Sandford, and by the Iago of Verbruggen. Sandford, indeed, was such a consummate actor of villains' *rôles* that, though personally a most amiable man, he was so completely identified by the public with infamous parts, that they would not accept him in an honest character. On one occasion they actually damned the play as an imposition on their patience when the author brought Sandford's *rôle* to an upright ending.

The *Tatler*, just after Betterton's remains were interred in Westminster Abbey, in 1710, said, " I have hardly a notion that any performer of antiquity could surpass the action of Mr. Betterton in any of the occasions in which he has appeared on our stage. The wonderful agony which he appeared in when he examined the circumstance of the

handkerchief in 'Othello,' the mixture of love
that intruded upon his mind upon the innocent
answers Desdemona makes, betrayed in his gesture such a variety and vicissitude of passions as
would admonish a man to be afraid of his own
heart, and perfectly convince him that it is to
stab it to admit that worst of daggers, — jealousy.
Whoever reads in his closet this admirable scene
will find that he cannot, except he has as warm an
imagination as Shakespeare himself, find any but
dry, incoherent, and broken sentences; but a reader
that has seen Betterton act it observes there could
not be a word added; that longer speech had been
unnatural, nay, impossible, in Othello's circumstances. The charming passage in the same tragedy where he tells the manner of winning the
affections of his mistress was urged with so moving and graceful an energy, that while I walked
in the cloisters I thought of him with the same
concern as if I waited for the remains of a person
who had, in real life, done all that I had seen him
represent.''

So, in regard to Betterton's successor, the *Tatler*
has an interesting word to say. It was in June,
1710, when Wilks first played the Moor at the
benefit of Colley Cibber, and our friend had stolen

in, incognito, to see the performance, that, out of curiosity, he might observe how Wilks and Cibber came out in the parts where Betterton and Sandford so highly excelled. Wilks, like the witty mimic Foote, — who, under the misconception that he was a tragedian instead of a comedian, made his *début* as Othello, — was famous in the humorous *rôles*, and, besides imitating Betterton in the great tragedy, laid himself open to popular misunderstanding throughout. Thus the *Tatler* points out this fact: "There is a fault in the audience which interrupts their satisfaction very much; that is, the figuring to themselves the actor in some part wherein they particularly liked him, and not attending to the part he is at that time performing. Thus, whatever Wilks, who is the strictest follower of nature, is acting, the vulgar spectators turn their thoughts upon Sir Henry Wildair."

In Cibber' Iago, if Tom Davies saw aright, Othello would have discerned the villain written plainly on his brow, Cibber's style was so plainly hypocritical, and so affected in its drawling.

Old Colley himself declared Wilks's Othello a failure; while to Barton Booth, of whom Wilks was extremely jealous, he gave warm praise. Yet not every spectator saw Booth at his best; for a

bad supper or a small house would make him too
often indifferent of his reputation. Yet when he
knew his auditors he was ready to act to the height
of his power rather than drop in their favor.

The story is told that one night, when there were
few people in the theatre and Othello had simply
been walking through his part, suddenly, to the astonishment of his fellow-actors, he roused every
energy in his mind and body, and gave a magnificent interpretation of the final acts.

" What does this mean, Booth?" queried a friend
in the green-room, as the great actor, flushed with
his own triumphant exertion, entered after a glorious
performance of his part in the great scene of the
third act. " Why this sudden change?"

" There's a man in the pit," Booth replied with
enthusiasm, " an Oxford man, whose judgment is
worth having. I saw him there, and for his criticism I have more regard than for that of all the
rest of the audience."

The graceful air, the manly sweetness of countenance, the harmonious voice, the picturesque posturing,—these attributes of Booth were strongly in
contrast with the appearance, utterance, and bearing
of another Othello of those early years of the eighteenth century. Desdemona, they thought in those

days, would hardly fall in love with James Quin, whose "declamation was as heavy as his person, his tones monotonous, his passions bellowing, his emphasis affected, and his understrokes growling." But yet Quin, strong, vigorous actor that he was, could hold his own against many a handsome player of his day — till Garrick came. In Othello, indeed, he could lead even his little rival; for Davy, though contesting with the veteran when the latter was in his last years of stage-life, yet could meet with not enough success to warrant attempting the *rôle* more than twice thereafter.

However, in the general run of play-acting David Garrick was by far the leader, and his triumphs soon made old Quin disgruntled and ugly. Off the gray-haired actor hurried to Bath, there to sulk in his tent. This avocation, however, soon grew monotonous, and the yearnings for the vanity-pleasing applause of the pittites at last broke down the obstinate resolution of the veteran. He determined to drop a hint of his relenting to Rich, the manager. Hence the following laconic, but suggestive, message was posted by stage to the metropolis: —

JOHN RICH, *London.*

I am at Bath.

Yours,

JAMES QUIN.

Bluff Manager Rich's reply was equally suggestive, and thoroughly unexpected: —

> James Quin, *Bath*.
> Stay there, and be d——d.
> Yours,
> John Rich.

But difficulties were patched up before long; and Quin came back to play in "Othello" for a charity benefit, and, with generous disposition, to act without a penny of charge.

Queerly costumed were the Othellos of both of the leaders of the two opposing styles of acting, — the theatrical, grandiloquent school, and the easy, natural school. Quin, with a mammoth, heavily powdered wig crowning his black face, "made such a magpie appearance of his head as tended greatly to laughter." For dress, this Othello appeared in the English soldier's uniform of the actor's own period. Garrick put on flowing Eastern robes, and thus brought down upon his devoted head the comparison with the little turbaned colored boys who, fashion then decreed, should bring in tea at private receptions.

"Aha!" cried envious old Quin to Bishop Hoadley's son, as the two sat in the pit on the night of the stage Whitefield's first appearance in the tragedy,

"Here's Pompey, sure. Where's the lamp and the teakettle?" The apt but cruel allusion to Hogarth's black boy set everybody around into a laugh.

Sly Davy, however, in his very size — or, rather, lack of size — had one point of advantage, as he thought, over his stalwart rival. Into "Othello" he could introduce the scene of epilepsy with no fear of comparison with the corpulent Quin, to whom a fall would have been clumsy, if not injurious.

Handsome Spranger Barry could look the character, and could act it. Garrick might contest his Romeo and his Lear, but he did not dare to oppose his Othello; though, indeed, in 1749, the little man played Iago to Spranger's Moor. The latter "happily exhibited the hero, the lover, and the distracted husband," says the same playgoer who so roughly handled Quin; "he rose through all the passions to the utmost extent of critical imagination, yet still appeared to leave an unexhausted fund of expression behind. His rage and tenderness were equally interesting. . . . His figure was a good apology for Desdemona's attachment . . . and the harmony of his voice to tell such a tale as he describes must have raised favorable prejudice in any one who had an ear or heart to feel."

While the gallant fellow could win the audience
as well as the senate by his tender, insinuating plea,
and could touch the hearts by his pathetic utterance
of " No, not much moved," he could also give to the
words, " I'll tear her all to pieces," such frightful
fierceness as to cause ladies in the galleries to shriek
with terror, and could so impress the experienced
John Bernard as to drive sleep from that veteran's
eyes for a whole night after witnessing " Othello."

" It was wonderful," declared Bernard, describing
the scene next day to his friends. "I sat there
watching him prepare for a volcanic burst with the
lines, ' I'll tear her all to pieces.' His muscles
began to stiffen, the veins extended, and the red
blood actually boiled through the dark skin, so
earnest was his feeling, until at length his passion
bore down all barriers, sweeping love, reason, and
mercy before the thunder of his rage."

An odd costume Spranger Barry wore, — odd in
the sense of to-day's correct dressing of the great
plays. Picture him, if you will, before the grave
and reverend signiors, a gentleman in a scarlet
suit, well covered with gold lace, and tapering off
with knee-breeches that could cover but not con-
ceal, in later years, a pair of rather gouty legs, and
see the same hero touching to the people of Cy-

prus his little cocked hat, — and you have Barry's Othello. His wife, when she played Desdemona, was somewhat nearer to the ideal, since she wore a captivating Italian dress.

Unlucky woman! Her second husband was no such actor or gentleman as her first. Two years after Barry's death she married the rascally young Irish lawyer Crawford, and tried to educate him for the stage. He, in his contemptible way, not only spent her money, but on his part showed a most niggardly spirit. When he tried to manage a theatre he so disgusted play-goers and play-actors, that the former would not patronize him, and the latter were obliged to strike for their pay. To such an extreme was he driven one night, that he was compelled, dressed as he was for the *rôle* of Othello, to go down into the orchestra's seats, and play the violin alone for the overture, the entire band of musicians having suddenly deserted him.

With Spranger Barry, Othello had been the first character to be played in London when, coming over from Ireland, he dared enter the tourney against the great Roscius of England. It was a venturesome act for the erstwhile silversmith, now barely in his twenty-seventh year, and with his mere four and twenty months' experience on the stage; but with rough old Macklin to play the hypocrite so naturally that the spectators actually cursed him, and with Mrs. Rideout to act the suffering Desdemona, Barry showed the London set, on that night of Oct. 4, 1746, what grandeur there was in the great tragedy.

Garrick trembled on his throne.

A shrewd fellow was Macklin, on as well as off the stage. You remember the trick that Macready and Phelps tried to play on Helen Faucit, holding themselves a little in the rear of her, so that they could face the spectators while she had to show her back to her friends before the footlights? Macklin and Sheridan were both adepts at this trick; and one night, when playing the leading parts in "Othello," they worked so hard to turn each other round, as to bring themselves, before they knew it, both plump up against the back scene.

This backing scheme was a game that Edmund Kean also tried. Gallant Spranger Barry never would attempt it.

Another production in which Macklin was interested would have delighted the heart of nobility-loving Pepys, had he lived to see it. That was the performance of the 7th of March, 1751, when the auditorium, even to the footmen's gallery, was filled with dukes and princes, duchesses and princesses. On the stage, under Macklin's direction, a company of amateurs, all of noble birth, was acting "Othello," Sir Francis Delavel playing the Moor; John (afterwards Lord) Delavel, Iago; Captain Stephens, Roderigo; Mrs. Stephens, Emilia; and Mrs. Quon, a sister of Sir Francis, and afterwards Lady Mexborough, Desdemona. Walpole best describes the furor this production aroused, — a furor never equalled before or since that day: "The rage was so great to see the performance," he says, "that the House of Commons literally adjourned at three o'clock on purpose. The footmen's gallery was strung with blue ribands. What a wise people! What an august senate! Yet my Lord Granville once told the prince, — I forget on occasion of what folly, — 'Sir, indeed your royal highness is in the wrong to act thus; the English are a grave nation.'" Of the players themselves Walpole says, "They really acted so well, that it is astonishing they should not have had sense enough not to act at all."

Nine months after this amateur performance, on the 26th of December, 1751, there came the first production of "Othello" in America, Robert Upton, the traitorous advance agent of Hallam's Company

playing the Moor, his wife playing Desdemona, and
Tremain, Iago. Thus they forestalled the initial
production by Hallam's actors when Malone acted
Othello, and Rigby Iago, to the Desdemona of Mrs.
Hallam, at the Williamsburg, Va., performance of
Nov. 9, 1752.

Hallam's successor as manager of the first organized American company, David Douglass, essayed
the Moor at Annapolis in April, 1760, Palmer sustaining Iago's character, and the Williamsburg Desdemona, now Mrs. Douglass, again impersonating
the faithful wife. When New York first saw the
tragedy, April 11, 1768, Douglass still held the
title *rôle;* but young Hallam, the son of the organ-
izer of the company, had been promoted from Cassio
to Iago, and Miss Cheer had supplanted the now
elderly heroine of the earlier performances. The
first Philadelphia production, Jan. 27, 1773, saw
Hallam and Douglass reversing their New York
rôles, while still another Desdemona, Mrs. Henry,
had come upon the stage.

In the spring of 1769, at the John Street
Theatre in New York, appeared a Moor who later
was to attain a wider fame in other lines; this
was Major Moncrief, the British officer. He was an
amateur actor of much merit, and had consented

to act one night in order to help the players out of the pecuniary embarrassments then troubling them. On the bills he was announced simply as "a gentleman," his identity being entirely concealed.

In the days when Sir Henry Clinton's army locked itself up in New York City, after evacuating Philadelphia and retreating by night from Washington's army, the British soldiery found nothing to employ their minds except play-acting, gaming, and social entertainments. With enthusiasm the officers of the crown produced at the abandoned theatres every play on which they could lay their hands. In fact, their performances were so varied that before long they had exhausted their stock of dramatic literature, and were compelled to advertise in the papers for printed play-books. On the programs they said that the performances were for sweet charity's sake; but each officer drew regularly a dollar for his night's performance, — and with necessaries as well as luxuries demanding high prices, probably found his stipend very acceptable. These same programs, furthermore (in one season at least), solemnly announced: "No children in laps will be admitted."

Major Moncrief and Major Lowther Pennington, of the Guards, apparently monopolized the char-

acter of Othello, while Dr. Hammond Beaumont
acted Iago. Major André in those days (1778)
was a gay young aide of Clinton, and undoubtedly joined the actors at the playhouse; for, as
we know, in Philadelphia shortly before this time
he had become sufficiently interested in the sport
to paint sets of scenery for the amateur stage.

Messrs. Heard and Ryan as Othello and Iago, and
Mrs. Robinson as Desdemona (with Mr. Shakespeare as Cassio), were the names printed upon the
bills of 1782 at the first Baltimore production of
the tragedy; while the first New York performance
after the Revolution brought back Mr. Hallam to
the cast, though now as Iago to the Othello of the
tall, handsome Mr. Henry and the Desdemona of
Mrs. Henry. This Othello, pronounced by Dunlap,
the old historian, the best up to that time, crowned
a jet black face with woolly hair, and wore a British officer's uniform. Later, in Baltimore, Fennell.
Green, and Mrs. Morris sustained the leading *rôles*.

Dissipated, rattlebrained Fennell was always fond
of his Othello; perhaps because it was the character
in which he had made his *début*, in 1787, in Edinburgh. He was not handsome in face; but he was
massive in form, his superb figure measuring full
six feet.

"Yes," cried Cooper one day, noticing his associate pacing up the street, "here comes two yards of a very proper man!" So, too, thought the Annapolis planter when, admiring vastly the intelligence of Fennell's Moor, he sent the managers an offer of five hundred dollars for the negro!

Naturally, Fennell's spendthrift ways at last resulted in poverty; but even though so reduced as to be imprisoned for debt, he did not lose his high spirits or sell himself as a negro. When, in his distress, an old friend, Mr. Leigh Waring, presented him with a surtout, the classically educated gentleman in a spirit of fun dashed off the following expression of gratitude:—

"Dear Sir, your surtout
Is a present to suit,
While fortune to me is so sparing.
It's been worn, it is true,
But your kindness makes new
What can ne'er lose its value from Waring."

As Robert Treat Paine, son of the signer of the Declaration of Independence, sat on the rough seats of the old Boston playhouse, and listened to Fennell's Iago, and then, a few nights later, saw Cooper in the character, he declared with emphasis that the latter was the superior by reason of his

bolder, stronger coloring of the character. But all
did not agree in this, for Fennell at that time was
in full glory.

Cooper had made his *début* in New York on the
28th of February, 1798. At once the public favored
him, admiring his handsome face and noble person,
marking his mingled dignity and grace of movement,
and listening with pleasure to his forcible yet melodious recitation of the text. At that time Fennell
was playing Othello as a thorough negro so far as
color was concerned, — absolutely black. Cooper,
essaying to rival the favorite actor, made his Moor
more nearly the color of a mulatto.

Many a story is told of the inaccuracies of the
new player as regards the text of his author. It is
said, for instance, that in "Othello." instead of
giving the words, " Yet I'll not shed her blood nor
scar that whiter skin of hers than snow and smooth
as monumental alabaster." he exclaimed, "nor scar
that beauteous form as white as snow and hard as
monumental alabaster!"

And Rees declares it is a fact that the eccentric
Higgins, a stock actor of that day. when playing
the Duke in "Othello." would not be outdone in
originality by Cooper. and so substituted for the
line, "Take up this mangled matter at the best."

the absurd words, " Take up the Star Spangled Banner, and carry it off to the West."

At the time Cooper began starring, his pay was but a twelfth of Fennell's remuneration. In a few years he was getting far more money, so rapid was his rise.

On the night of Dec. 19, 1825, when the English-born player was acting in " Othello " at the Boston Theatre, the announcement was made that Edmund Kean would return to the city to apologize for his former show of disrespect to the Boston audiences, and to appeal once more to their judgment and favor. There was applause and there were hisses over the announcement; for Kean's impetuous anger was not entirely forgotten. As we shall see in the tale of Richard, more troubles were to follow this renewed engagement.

Before returning to Kean, let us glance at a few more of the stage heroes who connected the two centuries with their impersonations. When Hodgkinson, the comedian, acted the Moor in Philadelphia during his first season here (1792–1793), he played so successfully as to be termed " The American Kemble." " His address to the senate," said the *Federal Gazette*, " was spoken with judgment; the whole of the acting where Iago so carefully

excites his jealousy was very natural; the heaving
of his breast, the expression of his countenance,
and the rage which Iago causes when he determines
to kill Desdemona, was a masterly piece of acting."
Hallam as Iago "performed to admiration," while
Miss Tuke as Desdemona "pleased the audience."
The graceful young actress, we are told, possessed in
this character "a natural diffidence truly engaging."

John Brown Williamson, son of a London sad-
dler, and a popular actor at the Haymarket in
London, came to America in the latter part of the
eighteenth century, and on the 25th of January,
1796, made his *début* at the opening performance of
the season at the Boston Theatre. The play was
"Othello." The *débutant* acted the Moor; Iago
fell to the lot of Mr. Harper, and Desdemona to
Mrs. Snelling Powell. Later on, Williamson, as
actor and manager, was to become a prominent figure in American theatrical history.

More than a passing notice must be given the
Iago of George Frederick Cooke. Conceited, irre-
sponsible, liquor-loving Cooke could rival John
Kemble, — "Hark ye, Black Jack," he had angrily
cried to the elder actor, "hang me, if I don't make
you tremble in your pumps one day yet!" — and
could stand with Cooper; but by himself he could

GEORGE FREDERICK COOKE AS IAGO.

fall, disgraced and ruined, into a drunkard's grave ten years after he had started on what seemed to be a glorious career, and before "Black Jack," as he termed him, had begun his final performances.

Cooke played the Moor to great applause, with the viceregal court in Dublin as audience, and then, after the performance, drinking himself into a beast, in a wild fit enlisted as a soldier. His friends paid for his discharge, and before long (1801) Cooke and Kemble were dangerous rivals in London town. But his "indispositions" continued, and deservedly brought public disapprobation.

When Cooke first played Iago in London, he had only the recollection of Henderson to combat; for Kemble, up to that date (Nov. 28, 1800), had not essayed the *rôle* of the Ancient. His triumph was pronounced. Some of the audience said that he betrayed so much of the workings of deceit in Iago's mind, that it was strange Othello should be deceived by him; but all agreed that the impersonation was extremely interesting and strong. The jealousy scene must, indeed, have been thrilling. Grasping Kemble's left hand with his own, Cooke would rest his right hand like a claw upon the shoulder of the Moor, and, holding him rigid in that position, would draw himself, after the manner of a snake, close up to the swarthy face of his wickedly charmed victim, while he thrust out the poisoned words with fang-like rapidity. Writhing and twisting, Kemble would strive to work himself away, pressing tightly, meanwhile, with his freed hand his throbbing temples.

"It was a wonderful sight," said Washington Irving, after witnessing the great scene on the Covent Garden stage. And simple George III. maintained that Cooke must be a very bad man at heart, otherwise he could not so well act out such fearful villany.

But now the years pass by until, in 1785, the majestic, superb Kemble assumes the *rôle* of the jealous soldier to the Desdemona of his stately sister, Mrs. Siddons. It seems as hard to imagine the one making a success of the fiery, impetuous husband, as to conceive the other achieving fame as the sweet, gentle wife. However, it is probable that Mrs. Siddons gave to the crucial scenes more impassioned acting than did her brother, since, as she herself says in speaking of their styles, "John, in his most impetuous bursts, is always careful to avoid any discomposure of his dress or deportment; but in the whirlwind of passion I lose all thought of such matters."

Possibly Kemble's biographer, Boaden, correctly

described the player in "Othello" as wrapping "that great and ardent being in a mantle of mysterious solemnity, awfully predictive of his fate;" but it is more likely that Macready better pictured his acting when he wrote: "The majestic figure of John Kemble, in Moorish costume, with a slow and stately step advanced from the side wing. A more august presence could scarcely be imagined. His darkened complexion detracted but little from the stern beauty of his commanding features, and the infolding drapery of his Moorish mantle hung gracefully on his erect and noble form. The silent picture he presented compelled admiration. . . . I must suppose he was out of humor, for, to my exceeding regret, he literally walked through the play. My attention was riveted upon him through the night in hope of some start of energy, some burst of passion, lighting up the dreary dulness of his cold recitation; but all was one gloomy, unbroken level — actually not better than a school repetition. In the line, 'Not a jot! not a jot!' there was a tearful tremor upon his voice that had pathos in it; with that one exception not a single passage was uttered that excited the audience to sympathy, or that gave evidence of artistic power. His voice was monotonously husky, and every word was enun-

ciated with labored distinctness. His readings were
faultless; but there was no spark of feeling that
could enable us to get a glimpse of the 'constant,
loving, noble nature' of Othello. . . . The play
went through without one round of applause. . . .
The curtain fell in silence, and I left the theatre
with the conviction that I had not yet seen
Kemble."

This was written of Kemble in 1816, when he
was bidding farewell forever to Dublin, and was
within one year of his retirement from the stage.
Kean had bounded forward into the public favor,
and at this time was so potent a factor as to contribute not a little, through the remembrance of
his fiery acting, to the small houses attendant upon
the older player.

Othello ranked among the best of Edmund Kean's
impersonations. The very year Kemble was heavily
plodding through the lines in Dublin, Hazlitt was
pronouncing the Othello of the wiry little dark-
skinned wonder, "the highest effort of genius on
the stage." He may have looked too much the
gypsy, and too little the soldierly Moor; he may
have lacked imagination, and may have carried his
character too often and too long pitched "in the
highest key of passion;" yet his overwhelming en-

ergy and his burning vehemence gave extraordinary force to his scenes of jealousy. As for the latter part of the third act, that, said Hazlitt, was "a masterpiece of profound pathos and exquisite conception, and its effect on the house was electrical."

Even John Kemble in honesty had to say of Kean's Othello, "If the justness of its conception had been but equal to the brilliancy of execution, it would have been perfect." But naturally the stately actor thought the young man's fiery bursts were erroneous. "The whole thing is a mistake," he declared, "the fact being that Othello was a slow man."

OTHELLO AND IAGO.

It seems strange that Kean's Iago never equalled in favor his Othello; for usually Kean was unsurpassable in picturing concealed hypocrisy. Moreover, his Ancient was original and unconventional, in that the customary "villain" of the stage was thrown to one side, and Iago was presented in an easy and natural vein.

Byron admired Kean's Iago. "Was not Iago perfection?" the poet wrote to Moore, "particularly the last look? I was close to him in the orchestra, and never saw an English countenance half so expressive." Hazlitt cried out in praising words, "The accomplished hypocrite was never perhaps so finely, so adroitly, portrayed, — a gay, light-hearted monster, a careless, cordial, comfortable villain."

These men genuinely admired the actor's work. For the fawning, pretending admirers, the hot-tem-

33

pered son of wandering Nance Carey had his own method of punishment. He illustrated it with Raymond, the stage-manager of Drury Lane, who, at the rehearsals before Kean made his London *début*, had spoken discouraging and insulting words, but who after the player's success strove in every way to thrust flattery upon him.

"Come to my room," said the gypsy player, the night his Othello had been received with a thousand plaudits; "I have a fine hot punch for you."

He had it there, indeed, in a bowl of very generous size.

With smiles and bows the manager began another series of fulsome compliments, when Kean, fiercely interrupting him, exclaimed, "Look you, sir! now I'm drawing money to your treasury, you find out I'm a fine actor. You told me when I rehearsed Shylock it would be a failure. Then I was a poor man, without a friend, and you did your best to keep me down. Now you smother me with compliments. 'T is right I should make some return. Sir, to the devil with your fine speeches! Take that"—and the angry play-actor literally gave the manager the punch, bowl and all, throwing it over his head and body. "Now, sir, you can have satisfaction if you desire," cried the little man, as he promptly stripped off his coat and rolled up his sleeves.

But the manager deemed discretion the better part of valor, and declined the combat.

Few men could stand up before the wiry, undisciplined, impetuous actor, on or off the stage. All remembered the experience of Junius Brutus Booth when he came from Covent Garden to Drury Lane to test supremacy with the flashing actor whose look in tragedy, Southey declared, was like Michael Angelo's rebellious archangel, and whose matchless eyes could charm even while they excited. The future great leader of the American stage was fairly driven from his engagement by his complete defeat. The trial play was "Othello," with Booth as Iago, and Kean as the Moor. Barry Cornwall described the scene as it appeared to him : —

"Booth at first appeared to shrink from the combat. He eventually, however, overcame his fear, and went through the part of Iago manfully. But Kean ! — no sooner did the interest of the story begin, and the passion of the part justify his fervor, than he seemed to expand from the small, quick, resolute figure which had previously been moving about the stage, and to assume the vigor and dimensions of a giant. He glared down upon the now diminutive Iago ; he seized and tossed him aside with frightful and irresistible vehemence. Till then we had seen Othello and Iago as it were

together; now the Moor seemed to occupy the stage alone.
Up and down, to and fro, he went, facing about like the
chased lion who has received his fatal hurt, but whose strength
is still undiminished. The fury and whirlwind of the passions seemed to have endowed him with supernatural strength.
His eye was glittering and bloodshot, his veins were swollen,
and his whole figure restless and violent. It seemed dangerous to cross his path, and death to assault him. There is no
doubt but that Kean was excited on this occasion in a most
extraordinary degree, as much as though he had been maddened by wine. The impression which he made upon the
audience has, perhaps, never been equalled in theatrical annals.
Even the actors, hardened in their art, were moved. One
comedian, a veteran of forty years' standing, told us that
when Kean rushed off the stage in the third act, he (the narrator) felt all his face deluged in tears — 'a thing I give you
my word, sir, that has not happened to me since I was a
crack thus high.' "

Other critics said that "Kean had floored Booth,
and walked over him completely." Booth himself, years later, speaking of his experience to the
famous Falstaff, Hackett, declared "Kean's Othello
smothered Desdemona and my Iago too."

Like his followers, Macready and Phelps, Kean
had a good idea of the value of the "centre of
the stage." One night he seemed to be playing
Othello with more than usual intensity.

"You were great to-night," said a friend, as the

two met on the street after the performance. "I
never saw you so magnificent in the third act.
I really thought you would have choked Iago, you
seemed so tremendously in earnest."

"In earnest," repeated the tragedian, flushing up,
"well, I should think so! Hang the fellow! he
was trying to keep me out of the focus of the
light!"

Bitterly could Kean fight his rivals, and yet
honestly could he recognize their merits.

"How much longer must I act to the Iago of
that Jesuit, Young," he exclaimed contemptuously,
when appearing with one of the most gentlemanly
and talented players of the time, and one, too, who
could with rightfulness claim attention by the side
of the great tragedian.

The two were to have alternated Othello and
Iago during that exciting histrionic contest of
1822; but the impetuous Othello of the first night
refused to give his finely formed, noble-voiced
rival opportunity to play the Moor, as previously
agreed. "No," cried Kean; "I would rather throw
up my engagement. I had never seen Young act.
Every one had told me he could not hold a far-
thing rushlight to me, but he can. He *is* an actor;
and though I flatter myself he could not act

Othello as well as I, yet what chance have I in Iago after him, with his confounded musical voice? I tell you what, Young is not only an actor such as I did not dream him to be, but he is a gentleman. Go to him; tell him, then, for me, that if he will allow me to keep Othello and Jaffier, I shall esteem it a personal obligation. Tell him he has made as great a hit in Iago as ever I did in Othello."

That Kean did wise to avoid the comparison is certain, even if Young was not great enough to "light up an era." The reality of Othello to the handsome gentleman's son was a remarkable indication of his high-strung sensibility as well as his nervous absorption of character. So genuine did the love and jealousy of Othello seem to Young, that, as he once told a friend, many a time after smothering his Desdemona he had flung himself upon the bed in a paroxysm of tearful remorse, from which he was aroused to a realization of its unreality by the thundering applause of the audience.

Kean and Young, during this engagement at Drury Lane, each received two hundred and fifty dollars a night. So great was the public interest that seats were sold six weeks in advance.

Macready, playing with Kean in the latter's declining years, could show only a fair degree of comparison. His looseness of figure rather suited the flexibility of the character, in the opinion of such an eminent critic as Hazlitt; but there were no massy movements in his action, no sweeping outlines to overwhelm the spectators. Moreover, there was an effeminate tone to his Moor, and an inclination to be "whimpering and lacrymose" in the pathetic passages. His Othello was an out-and-out negro, queerly dressed, irritable in his passion, and lacking grandeur in his agony.

That jealous actor, Fredericks, whom Macready had annoyed by dictatorial ways at rehearsal, declared with cynical scorn, when asked his opinion of the long-gowned, dark-painted star, "I have nothing to say about the man's acting; but he looked like an elderly negress of evil repute going to a fancy ball."

Yet in Paris the Frenchmen were so pleased with this Othello, that when they could not, by their plaudits, force him to accept a call, on account of a stringent police edict forbidding actors to appear before the curtain, they rushed into his dressing-room, dragged him, not unwilling, around to the auditorium, and then bodily lifted his tall

form over the footlights, so that they might pay
him the desired compliment, and yet keep within
the letter of the law.

Macready's Iago was a success. When he played
the part to Young as the Moor, the latter seemed
to the auditors like a great humming-top, with
Macready as the mischievous boy whipping it.

"Yes," growled one of the actors, "when Macready plays Othello he compels Iago to be nowhere, making the Ancient a mere stoker to feed
fuel to the Moor's passion ; but when Macready plays
Iago, presto! it's all changed. Then Othello must
be a mere puppet, a pipe for Iago to play upon."
In other words, the shrewd actor turned every scene
to his own advancement, whatever his character.

As for Charles Kean's Othello, he himself illustrated its difference from the Moor of his father
by an anecdote he once told his fellow-actor,
Herman Vezin. A gentleman called upon the
younger Kean during a Liverpool engagement, and
said, "I am going to see your Othello to-night,
to compare it with your father's."

That night the actor, knowing the situation,
played to the height of his ability. "What say
you, sir?" he cried to his new acquaintance when
they met the next day.

" Well, Mr. Kean," was the slow response, " I was very much pleased with your performance, very much, sir; but — you are not your father."

" That I know perfectly well," said the young man, smiling; " but to what difference do you particularly refer? "

" To this," continued the friendly critic; " your pathos, Mr. Kean, comes from here," placing his hand on his heart.

" Ah!" exclaimed Kean with pleasure, " you could hardly pay me a better compliment."

" But your father's pathos," quickly added the other gentleman, " that came from here," and he slapped the sole of his foot.

" He was right," declared Charles Kean emphatically, when narrating the anecdote to Vezin.

Nor did Samuel Phelps make his Othello or his Iago more than a creditable, painstaking performance. The Moor he showed so tender and pathetic as even to be tearful. Charles Dillon, too, constructed Othello in the same line of delineation; in fact, it was said that " he painted the character with such doting tenderness, and deplored the supposed betrayal of his love with such moderate resentment, that it was surprising he should have revenged it."

Fechter, in his flowing robes, worn with so much grace, formed a charming picture to the eye ; but his new reading of the play did not accord with the views of the critics. When, for example, he plunged hither and thither about the stage, until he had captured the fleeing Desdemona, and then, to make sure of her death, kneeled heavily upon the pillows he had piled upon her head ; and when, at the finish, he made a gesture as if to stab Iago, and then, as though suddenly changing his mind, turned the weapon upon himself, — he failed to find many ardent admirers of his interpretation of the scene. Macready wrote to Mrs. Pollock that the Frenchman's conception of Othello was shallow and melodramatic.

George Henry Lewes declared that not only was the conception unnatural, but that the execution was feeble ; while George Eliot, after seeing the performance, described it as lamentably bad, so deficient in the weight and passion necessary for deep tragedy as absolutely to degrade the representation.

In 1848 Gustavus V. Brooke made his London *début*, and on that occasion acted Othello better than he ever after interpreted the *rôle*. The stimulus of the first night aroused him to unusual vigor. The audience expressed unbounded enthusiasm, and

GUSTAVUS V. BROOKE AS OTHELLO (In Act III., Scene 3).

even Macready's young friend Westland Marston admitted that, with the exception of Salvini, he had never seen an actor so powerful in the great third act. Marston, watching keenly the performance, noticed also with admiration the discriminating expression Brooke gave to the single word "fool" in its triple repetition in the line of the fifth act, "O fool! fool! fool!" The first time it was pronounced in blended amazement and remorse; the second, with a slow, musing realization of his own wretched blindness to Iago's wiles; the third, with the mournful despair of a man who sees that the past is irrevocable.

Three years later, Dec. 15, 1851, Brooke bowed for the first time to an American audience at the Broadway Theatre, New York, and his character was Othello. At that time the Irish-born actor was in his thirty-third year, and with his fine figure and dignified bearing, combined with a sonorous voice and handsome face, could well depict the noble Moor. Fifteen years later, on board the ill-fated steamer *London*, while the waves swept over her deck, Brooke stood by the vessel, and, waving a courageous farewell to his comrades as they put off in their boat, remained with the ship till she sank in the depths of the Bay of Biscay.

In his boyhood days he had been a prodigy, — "The Hibernian Roscius;" but he had the wisdom to discard that title at the earliest opportunity. Many a story is told of his Othello, one of his best *rôles*. For example, when Forrest went to Manchester, England, the British players, knowing the pride that Brooke took in his own powerful voice, chaffed the sensitive actor immeasurably with the suggestion that the American player, who was noted for his tremendous lung-power, could utterly drown the voice of every one.

Brooke was put on his combative mettle. As Forrest in the character of Othello seized upon his Ancient in the great scene of the third act, and with magnificent force hurled his expletives against Iago, Brooke, utterly unmindful of the absurdity of his action, roared out in thunderous tones that completely drowned the strength of Forrest's voice, "O Grace! O Heaven, defend me!" Forrest was actually stupefied by the sudden explosion; it was the first time in his career that he had ever been over-matched in volume of tone. The audience was so astonished that it knew not whether to applaud or to hiss.

As brave as the hero he so often impersonated, Gustavus Brooke met his death in that stormy

January of 1866. Under the terrible strain of the situation the actor's sister, who accompanied him, had died on board, and the brother would not leave the ship.

Day after day he had labored incessantly with the crew at the pumps. At last, when the men made ready on the 6th of January to put off from the steamer, on whose deck remained only the captain and the solitary passenger, they cried, "Come with us, Mr. Brooke!" But he stood composedly, yet sadly, leaning against the half-door of the companionway, resting his chin in his hands, upon the top of the door, and made answer, "No, my good fellows; no. Good-by. Give my last farewell to the people of Melbourne." A few minutes later and the *London* had passed out of their sight.

At Brighton, weeks afterwards, a bottle was picked up bearing the following message : —

"11th January, on board the *London*. We are just going down. No chance of safety. Please give this to Avonia Jones, Surrey Theatre.

GUSTAVUS VAUGHAN BROOKE."

Accompanying this was another note addressed to Warden, Belfast Theatre, and reading : —

"Do what you can for poor Avonia."

Poor Avonia, the actress who had accompanied him on his last tour, and had become his wife, died a year afterwards in New York.

Now, to turn to those actors who are esteemed as absolutely American. I have spoken of the elder Booth's experience as Iago in London, and the impetuous force he gave the character of his Othello. Booth's son Edwin has said that when his father was going to act the part he would often wear a crescent pin on his breast all day, in order to keep himself imbued with his character, or would mumble over the words of the Koran; and on one occasion he even invited a travelling band of Arabic jugglers to visit his home in Baltimore on the day he was to act the Moor.

But his Iago became, as did the Ancient of his son in after years, a character of triumph. In that fifth act, when Othello is really the centre of the scene, Junius Brutus Booth could so picture in his face, with but a few lines of text to assist in calling attention, the terrible passions of the entrapped villain, as fairly to fascinate the eye of the spectators, and lead them to overwhelming applause. " The secret working of Iago's mind flashed in those powerful eyes," declared one who noticed this extraordinary effect, and sought to picture it; "the face reddened with suppressed rage, then turned livid with hate; and the bitter intensity with which he expressed the lines, —

'Demand me nothing; what you know, you know;
From this time forth I never will speak word,'

was marvellous. During the remainder of the scene his countenance revealed what the tongue disdained to speak, and retained its magnetic influence upon the beholders until the final exit."

Many a time Booth's indulgences in drink drove him to strange proceedings, yet apparently his power of acting never suffered thereby, although sometimes his engagements barely escaped cancellation.

At Providence, for example, one night just as the curtain was to rise on "Othello," our Iago was nowhere to be found. They sent to his hotel; he was not there.

"I'll find him," declared a gentleman in one of the boxes, who knew Booth's proclivities; and off he started for the low haunts of the town. There, sure enough, in Morris Deming's cheap sailor boarding-house they found the great actor in high glee drinking deep cups with mine host, — "a learned Theban, a sage philosopher," as Booth persisted in calling his associate at the table.

Dragged back to the theatre, the marvellous actor became sobered at once, and played superbly.

After another performance of " Othello " at Charleston, S.C., in 1837, Booth, indulging heavily in drink with his room-mate, Tom Flynn, became convinced that Flynn was Iago, and, seizing him by the throat, cried out the words of the text. " Villain, be sure thou prove my love a wanton," as he hurled him to the floor.

This was too much for Flynn, equally under the influence of liquor, and in self-defence the temporary Iago seized a fire-poker, brought it across Booth's face with a tremendous thud, and stopped the scene then and there. The result of the encounter was the broken nose which ever after marred the handsome face of the actor.

It was in the character of Othello that Forrest made his first appearance on that stage where he established his fame as a tragedian, — the Bowery. The night was Nov. 6, 1826: the Iago was Mr. Duff; the Desdemona, Mrs. Hughes. The frank, bright-faced youth, just passing his twentieth year, had finished his hard novitiate, and with a year's engagement at twenty-eight dollars a week felt happy and secure. But even better times were already at hand. With a characteristic oath his old manager had declared, on the night the youth played Othello at the Park Theatre at a benefit performance just before his appearance at the Bowery, "The boy has made a hit."

That, however, was nothing compared with the impression Forrest made in the same character a few days later at the famous New York home of tragedy. The audience fairly went wild over his acting. Gilfert, the manager, at once, after the night of "Othello," raised the actor's pay to forty dollars a week. To be sure, a little later the same shrewd Gilfert was loaning Forrest's services to other theatres for two hundred dollars a night, — pocketing the difference between the large sum and the stipulated salary of the player; but this reacted to Forrest's benefit, since, at the end of the season, he was in a position to demand, and secure, another contract in which the figures were placed at the sum Gilfert had been charging others, — two hundred dollars for each performance.

Just before the New York engagement Forrest had played second to Edmund Kean during an Albany performance, and into his Iago introduced business that astonished the English star. Previous to that day Iago had been pictured as a gloomy, sullen scoundrel whose villany was apparent to all.

Forrest gave him the light, airy dash and genuine
hypocrisy of the seemingly "honest Ancient." As
he repeated the lines, —

> " Look to your wife ; observe her well with Cassio ;
> Wear your eye thus, not jealous, — nor secure,"

he spoke all but the last two words in an off-hand,
easy way, but into that final suggestion, by dropping his high-pitched tones swiftly into a husky
whisper, he threw such a mass of evil suspicion
and fearful impression as to nerve even Kean to
responsive acting more magnificent than usual, and
to bring from the audience a tremendous storm
of applause.

"Where did you get that idea, my boy?" cried
Kean excitedly, as the two met in the green-room.

"It is my own conception," replied Forrest.

"It is great," declared the elder tragedian, "and
every actor from this day will have to speak the
lines as you spoke them."

As Othello, it is said that Forrest's utterance of
the lines, —

> "Silence that dreadful bell; it frights the isle
> From her propriety,"

was actually bell-like in the tone he gave it, and,
like all his utterances, was melodic without harsh-

ness. Moreover, the exaggerated force he gave to the first two words in the expression, "'*Twas I* that killed her" (the "I" being unduly prolonged, and accompanied by a stout thumping of the breast), was declared by John Foster Kirk to be a notable feature, not easily forgotten.

James Rees often stood in the wings when his friend played the Moor, and after the performance never failed to allude, with constantly increasing admiration, to two points. The first was the expression of great mental strife as the husband of Desdemona uttered the words, "Oh! now forever farewell the tranquil mind! farewell content! . . . Othello's occupation's gone." The actor's form lost its strength and vigor; the arms hung powerless by his side; his very reason, said Rees, seemed palsied, as if the spirit of life was drooping away with each word. The second point was the tragedian's rendering of the scene following the passage, " I had rather be a toad, and live upon the vapor of a dungeon." As the full conviction of Desdemona's guilt burst upon him, the actor became tremendously forcible, even terrific, in vocal expression and physical action.

Artemus Ward saw Forrest as the Moor. "He is a grate actor," declared the humorist. "I thot I saw Otheller before me all the time he was actin; and when the curtin fell I found my spectacles was still mistened with saltwater which had run from my eyes while poor Desdemony was a-dyin. Betsy Jane, Betsy Jane! let us pray that our domestic bliss may never be busted by a Iago. Edwin Forrest makes money actin out on the stage. He gits five hundred dollars a nite, and his board and washin. I wish I had such a Forrest in my garding!"

The lines of Othello were the last to pass the lips of Forrest before the public. On the 7th of December, 1872, at Tremont Temple, Boston, he appeared, as a reader, for the last time before an audience, giving selections from the tragedy. Five days later he was dead.

E. L. Davenport, who could dance the hornpipe and play Hamlet the same evening, made an admirable Othello. The Oriental scimitar hung at his side, while ponderous robes and surmounting turban formed his garb, — a dress never changed from the early scenes in Venice to the tragic chamber in Cyprus. But yet he played so strongly that careless costuming was forgotten in enjoyment of the grand force with which he drove on to the climax. It was not the passion-swayed Moor of

E. L. DAVENPORT AS OTHELLO (In Act 1., Scene 2).

Salvini, the Eastern love-poem of Edwin Booth, the honest, direct-dealing, but sadly tortured man of Barrett; but a modern American, full of fire and executive ability, to whom love and jealousy were merely episodes to be met and dealt with as an ordinary experience, and who, by some unwonted juggle, found himself called upon to marry a romantic belle of the Adriatic, conquer the Ottomites, restore a warlike isle to the ways of peace, and thus to meet and deal with unlooked for domestic difficulties. To him all was simply the decree of fate, to which he bowed with resignation, until the murder of Desdemona awoke him; then suicide was found to be the only relief.

It was some sixty years ago (1837) that Edward Loomis Davenport, as a member of the Tremont Theatre company of Boston, became a recognized stock actor. Previous to that date he had made his *début* at Providence, where he played a few small parts, and where, among other *rôles*, he was cast for William in "Black-eyed Susan," a promising performance of which led to the home engagement. From that time for exactly forty years Mr. Davenport was the most active figure in the dramatic annals of the American stage. Seven of the forty were spent in England, whither he accompanied

Anna Cora Mowatt as leading support. This visit won for him much fame but little wealth; a fate destined to follow him to 1877, when he died in Canton, Pa., after having toiled for twoscore years to find his accumulations represented by a mortgaged farm and a large but undesirable wardrobe. He played a number and a range of parts that were astonishing, and he played them well. Beginning with Parson Willdo, he closed with Daniel Druce, and, with the exception of King Lear, hesitated at nothing. Henry in "Speed the Plough ' one night, Othello the next; Sir Benjamin Backbite on Monday, Brutus on Tuesday; Rolando at 7.30, Bill Sykes at 9, — were actual experiences.

Of Rossi in Othello, the *Gazette de France* declared that in the senate scene he conquered as much by his cleverness as by his heart, and in illustration of this point thus compared the actor's interpretation of the scene with that of Salvini: "Salvini advances quietly, nobly; respecting the father's grief, but sure of the justice of his own claim, he pleads the cause of his love. He pleads it without moving a step, standing a short distance from the council. His hand, by an oratorical movement from time to time, barely emphasize his speech, which is imbued with the serenity of

a proud conscience. To his face, his eyes, his
lips, is intrusted the task of forcing conviction
upon the mind of his judges, or rather it is
these features which finish and complete the work
of his words. To attain such a dramatic result
with such a studied sobriety of means is a mar-
vel to which we have long been unaccustomed.
M. Rossi, who is nevertheless very fine, played
this scene in exactly the opposite manner. While
he argued, his gestures added the force of pantomime to his words; whilst he went on talking, he
walked to and fro: there was no lack of nobility
in his Othello, but there were also dexterity and
subtlety. The Moor, although commander-in-chief
and first soldier of the Republic of Venice, does
not lose sight of the fact that he stands before a
council of inflexible patricians, and that these patricians may easily refuse to admit the defence of
love by divine right. Thus Rossi's Othello deemed
it necessary at moments to summon to his aid a
smile, irony, familiarity, affected simplicity. Othello,
as enacted by Salvini, disdains these subtleties; he
does not even think of such fears, which he doubtless would consider unworthy of him."

McCullough, in the manly tenderness, simplicity,
and yet underlying vehemence of passion, was pro-

nounced well nigh perfect by studious critics who
could at the same time admit that there was something a little fantastic in the facial style this actor
used, and a blemish in the display of a wild beast's
head on the back of one of Othello's robes.

There were touches of fresh and aptly illustrative
business in the encounter of Othello and Iago in
the great scene of the third act. As was said by
his friend, Mr. Winter, " The gasping struggles of
Iago heightened the effect of the Moor's fury, and
the quickly suppressed impulse and yell of rage
with which he finally bounded away made an admirable effect of nature." McCullough's final scene
was likened to a solemn act of sacrifice, a deed of
justice rather than of barbaric murder, impressing
awe instead of horror upon the audience.

And now let us glance at a group of three actors,
of whom the centre figure is Edwin Booth. With
Tommaso Salvini and with Lawrence Barrett, Mr.
Booth in different seasons alternated the leading
rôles of the tragedy. His own Iago was absolutely
fascinating in its suggestiveness of satanic wickedness, and in its airy shrewdness of deception. The
keen, subtle plotting of the Ancient, as developed
by the American leader, was full of cunning and
of intellectual power. It was an inward, spiritual

TOMMASO SALVINI AS OTHELLO.

interpretation as compared with the outward, animal interpretation of Othello by the great Italian actor.

Salvini's Othello thrusts aside the nobler inclinations of the soul for the vigorous inclinations of the barbaric senses, and dropping the poetic side of this brave warrior, this hero who could win the tender love of Desdemona and the affection of Cassio, places more prominent the magnificent but brutal side of the soldier, whose anger is fearful and whose vengeance is terrible. For this *rôle* nature has admirably adapted Signor Salvini, with his grand physique and robust voice. In the scene wherein Othello parts the two combatants, Cassio and Montano, all of the vital energy of the Moor is brought out; there is less of pain and of grief at the fall of his favorite lieutenant than of terrible anger at the disgraceful proceedings. Othello's face flames with passion, and his eyes flash ominously from one rioter to the other. Finally, as he degrades Cassio, there is seen nothing of profound regret, but all of stern anger.

In the grand scene of the third act, Salvini's Othello, with visage distorted by rage, and with seeming unconsciousness of what he is doing, forces Iago to his knees, and then hurls him to the ground,

and tramples upon the prostrate form, only suddenly
to stop his wrath with the impulse of a quieting
thought, stand a while sadly motionless, and then,
reaching forth his hand, gently assist his Ancient
to rise. Again, in contrast, comes that fearful burst
of the final act, when like a tiger he rushes down
upon the tender Desdemona, then strides away, then
returns with rolling eyes and panting breast to bear
her away to death. And last of all, his own death,
— it is butchery! Drawing the terrible scimitar
swiftly across his throat, and slashing horribly, he
dies — not like a soldier of Venice, but like an
insane barbarian.

The powerful actor would always carry an audience with him by the very force of his colossal
physique, — and one night he literally carried a
brother actor by the same force. It was at Bologna,
when Salvini was acting Othello for the first time
in that city. The Iago, Signor Piccinini, a man of
great size and strength, persisted at rehearsal in
placing himself on the wrong side of the stage in
the notable scene of the third act. Quietly and
politely Salvini requested his subordinate to take
the other side at the regular performance, and
Piccinini sullenly consented.

" I don't see that it makes any difference," declared the supporting actor in a grumbling tone, "but I suppose I can do it if you want it."

"Suppose!" exclaimed Salvini. "Sir, there is no suppose in the matter. You will be there!"

But that night the still surly Iago deliberately placed himself upon the wrong side.

Instantly Salvini stopped in his part. Swiftly turning, he bounded over to the six-foot Iago, and seizing the giant around the waist, bore him, struggling in the air, across the stage to the desired spot, with the audible exclamation, "Now, sir, stay there!"

And he did stay there, while the audience, astonished, amused, and really delighted at the exhibition of strength, loudly applauded.

From that night on Piccinini and Salvini were the best of friends.

Of Salvini's necessity for working himself up to the crucial point, an interesting story was once narrated by Jules Clarétie. A party of friends one night asked the actor to recite the last monologue of Othello. Acquiescing, he rose, and in magnificent voice began. But before he had completed a half-dozen lines Salvini suddenly stopped, and with a gesture of despair exclaimed, "No, it is impossible! I am not in the situation. I am not

prepared for this supreme anguish. In order to
render the frantic despair of Othello, I need to have
passed through all his tortures; I need to have
played the whole part. But to enter thus the soul
of the character, without having gradually penetrated into it, I cannot — it is impossible!'' All
this was said without any affectation, but with the
air of a man who reveals the secret of his power.

Booth's Othello was a warm, passionate, and yet
noble husband and soldier. In scenes of oratorical display, as in the tale before the Duke, there
were not the equal eloquence and rich grandeur of
speech that marked, for example, Lawrence Barrett's portrayal; but in moments of impressiveness,
such as the declaration of faith in Desdemona, and
the dismissal of Cassio, Booth showed exceeding
power.

Mr. Barrett's Othello was a dignified but not
overawing Moor, — a man who attracted the sympathy by reason of his manifestations of noble nature. The hot fire of jealousy was shown consuming
the victim, and arousing pity by its causing pain.
His Othello was full of sighs, — sharp-turned sighs
of joy, long-drawn sighs of anger, staccato sighs of
mental anguish. His Moor appeared so wronged as
to temper the effect of all his acts of cruelty, and

make him as great a martyr, to the spectators, as was Desdemona. Barrett's Iago was real and plausible, thoroughly " honest " in appearance both to the audience and to Othello : yet it lacked the fascination of the subtle creation ; it never gleamed like the serpent's eye, brilliant and deadly.

Few Americans will forget the shock that ran through the country on the 4th of April, 1889, when it was announced in the press that on the previous night at the theatre in Rochester, N. Y., Edwin Booth had been suddenly stricken with paralysis, while struggling through the second act of " Othello." Mr. Barrett, coming before the curtain, said to the silent audience, " We fear that this is the beginning of the end. The world has probably heard for the last time the greatest actor who speaks the English language. The play cannot go on."

Fortunately the fears of Mr. Barrett were not realized, for Mr. Booth after a few days' rest returned to the stage.

The neatest and clearest description, in one paragraph, of Booth's Iago that I have ever seen was that given by William Winter when he spoke of the characterization being marked by " lithe, clear, rapier-like elasticity, both physical and mental, and

by a cool, sardonic, veiled, involuntary, cruel humor,
which was made to play like a lambent flame of
hell over the whole structure of the work."

When Mr. Booth visited England, in 1880, and
met with such ill-success at the poorly equipped
Princess's Theatre, — a house devoted to melodrama,
and utterly unsuitable for the appearance of America's most refined and polished actor, — he was invited to appear with Henry Irving at the latter's
grandly furnished Lyceum Theatre. There, on May
2, 1881, "Othello" was produced, with Booth in
the title *rôle*, and Irving as Iago; the next week
the characters were reversed. The talented Ellen
Terry, in her snow-white robes, so symbolic of the
purity of the heroine, made a lovely, pathetic Desdemona.

But even there and then the English critics refused to give full honor to the American star. One
or two were rough-handed enough to assert that
Booth's "make-up suggested at times an Indian
juggler, while about the head he seemed a low-caste
Bengali," and that "he had a tendency at times to
gobble like a turkey;" but they all had to admit
that his jealousy scenes with Iago and with Desdemona were of highest artistic order.

Irving's tall, dark — but not black — Othello, in

EDWIN BOOTH AS IAGO (In Act II., Scene 3).

long flowing robe and little white turban, was romantic in coloring and tender in character; but yet the critics who oppose his delineation have declared that Desdemona had no reason for loving or sympathizing with such a "jerky, fidgety, and undignified Othello," while his light-toned Iago was declared by many as more stormy than shrewd.

When Irving thus appeared with Booth, it was his very first impersonation of Iago. Undoubtedly it was clear-cut and picturesque; certainly it was gay in its banter. By a curious coincidence, in this first appearance in union with Booth, the English actor chanced upon a method of interpretation in the street scene that was exactly the same which the American had originated and presented for the first time in the history of the tragedy. The London critics, having never seen this act so played, called it a novelty. After Cassio is attacked by Roderigo, and after the latter is slain, the wounded lieutenant lies in the dark, silent street alone with the treacherous Ancient. Bending over the wounded man, Iago looks to see his condition, and at that moment is suddenly struck with the thought how easily he can rid himself of the man, and no one be the wiser. He raises his sword to strike — but just at that moment the voices and hurrying feet of people are

heard, and the treacherous villain is perforce obliged
to drop his weapon and assume a different mien.

Wilson Barrett naturally gave to his Othello a
score of novelties. His swarthy hero, with fierce
peaked beard and bristling mustache, roused to
jealous madness by Iago's intimations, hurled the
Ancient across the chamber, and with eyes glaring
as if demented, hacked fiercely with his scimitar at
the portrait of Desdemona. In the death scene he
grasped his wife in his arms, threw her bodily upon
the bed, and behind the curtains smothered her to
death. Then for his own destruction he drove a
short sword into his breast. The curtain fell with
Barrett leaning against the bed, and holding to his
dark throat the white hand of Desdemona.

"The African Tragedian," Ira Aldridge, whose
coal-black face was often seen in the character of
Othello, won fame in two continents. Born in
Maryland in 1804, he turned to the stage, making
his *début* in New York as Rolla, and then playing,
in an extensive *répertoire*, Shylock and Othello, as
well as Zanga, Mungo, Hassan, and Gambria, in
England and Russia, Prussia, Austria, Switzerland,
Turkey, and other countries, winning medal after
medal from European potentates, and gaining a commendatory letter even from Edmund Kean.

His tragic acting was always marked by a solemn intensity; but occasionally he would burst forth into a show of fierce passion, made more effective by the very darkness of his face. Nor was he averse to comic parts, and his broad grin and shining eyes were often utilized for the lighter *rôles*. He was originally intended for the church.

A few women have attempted Iago on the English stage in years gone by: while in America Charlotte Crampton, Mrs. D. W. Waller, and Marie Prescott have essayed the *rôle*.

OCCASIONALLY in these modern days we find a Le Beau in " As You Like It " who delights to disobey the injunction of his dramatic author by forcing a joke into the wrestling scene, crying to the Duke when he inquires the condition of Charles, "He *says* he cannot speak, my lord;" but a "bull" of better merit was unconsciously illustrated years ago in a provincial theatre while "Lear" was being performed.

The regular impersonator of Gloucester had been suddenly taken ill, and a substitute was therefore hurriedly secured. Our temporary player succeeded in committing to memory all the words of his part up to the scene where he has his eyes put out, but from there on the sightless Earl had to beg the permission of the audience to read his lines!

The country player, however, need not have felt the situation with any keenness, since in caring little for the audience he had a good example in his

67

great predecessor, Garrick, if the gossip of the old
actors is correct. Tom King used to say that the
night the famous Roscius drowned the audience with
tears at his pathetic portrayal in the great fourth
act of " Lear," and even while the enthusiastic pittites were leaping on their benches to cheer his
acting, the self-possessed player thrust his tongue
into his cheek, as he turned to King with the words,
"Hang me, Tom! it will do; it will do." And yet
Garrick could throw such wonderful power into
his mimic life, that Jack Bannister, hardened actor
though he was, standing in the wings, was absolutely thrilled by the utterance of the words, " O
fool, I shall go mad." " Why," cried Bannister,
" in Lear, Garrick's very stick acted!" The scene
with Cordelia and the physician was the most pathetic the brother player ever saw.

Sharp-tongued Kitty Clive, as we know, liked
to plague the great little actor with personal tor-
ments that only a hot-tempered woman could invent; but one night she too was carried away by
Garrick's Lear. Katherine had gone to the wings
on purpose to find some way for disconcerting the
player; but, listening to his words, she gradually
found herself absorbed in his acting, and finally
was so overwhelmed by his marvellous power that,

with uncontrollable tears in her eyes, and with spiteful anger in her heart at her own subjection, she flounced away to the green-room, muttering, "Hang that man! I verily believe he could act a gridiron!"

A strange-looking Lear would the great Davy seem if he could step upon our stage to-day. Imagine the ancient King of Britain clothed in a long-cut court dress of the eighteenth century, with lace cravat, ruffled wrists, and gold-braid adornments; while silk stockings and buckled shoes help complete the attire. In fact, Garrick might just as well have worn his Lear costume in a comedy. The author of "The Actor" hits this point as he thus describes the famous man's Lear (for Fondlewife is the aged uxorious husband in the comedy of "The Old Bachelor"): "When we see the little old white-haired man enter, with spindleshanks, a tottering gait, and great shoes upon the little feet, we fancy a Gomez or a Fondlewife; but when he speaks we find him every inch a king."

Feeble though he was in movement, with slow and languid steps, Garrick yet retained absolutely the air of royalty. It seemed as if misery was painted in every line of his face; and the pathetic, sorrowful way in which he fixed his eyes slowly and with difficulty upon each person before addressing him, told, with the expression of the face, the sad significance of the old King's misery even before a word was uttered. Garrick wore no beard in Lear, nor did Kemble after him. In fact, Macready was the first player to give the King a beard.

Those were exciting nights when Garrick depicted the brain-wrecked monarch; since the impetuous actor sought rivalry again, as he had in Romeo, with handsome, dashing Spranger Barry, the delight of the ladies on and off the stage. As for David at that time, "off the stage," said his enemy Murphy, "he was a mean, sneaking little fellow. But on the stage,"—and here, according to report, Murphy threw up his hands and eyes as he cried in ecstasy, "Oh, my great God!" Friend and foe were compelled thus to acknowledge the histrionic power of the stage-drawn wine-merchant.

It was this same Murphy who, in the wings, tried his utmost to disconcert Garrick while the latter was acting Lear, by talking in no indistinct tone with old Sam Johnson. Garrick, rightfully annoyed at this, exclaimed as he made his exit, "You two talk so loud you destroy my feelings!" upon which, irate Johnson, with contemptuous and contemptible reference to the actor's calling, responded, "Punch has no feelings."

For the rival Lears the public made these versified epigrams: —

> " The town has found out different ways
>   To praise its different Lears ;
> To Barry it gives loud huzzas,
>   To Garrick — only tears."

> " A king — Ay, every inch a king,
>   Such Barry doth appear ;
> But Garrick's quite another thing ;
>   He's every inch King Lear."

Tall and majestic, Barry won the eye in opposition to little Garrick, as a verse of the day, in harsh contrast, indicated : —

> " When kingly Barry acts, the boxes ring
> With echoing praise, ' Ay, every inch a king!'
> When Garrick dwindling whines, the assenting house
> Re-whispers aptly back, ' A mouse! a mouse!' "

But Barry, even with his silver voice, could not equal the passion and variety of Garrick's tones, nor could his great dignity in the *rôle* have such effect as the slow-moving, feeble, affecting Lear of the natural-born actor, his rival. The latter, too, excelled in emotional strength. When Garrick delivered the curse, cried Davies, the audience seemed to shrink from it as from a flash of lightning. Not even the unlucky tumbling off of his crown of straw could provoke a smile from the audience when

Garrick met with the accident, though such a ludicrous misfortune with a lesser actor would have ruined the scene.

One night when Garrick, throwing away his mantle and kneeling in his own impressive way, repeated the curse, while he clasped his hands and solemnly raised his eyes to heaven, the front row in the audience swiftly and spontaneously stood up to see him clearly. The second row, unwilling to lose the slightest portion of the scene, followed the movement, and then, as if by tacit understanding that no remonstrance should break the continuity of the acting, the whole pit silently rose to witness the grand, overpowering imprecation.

An odd trick shrewd Davy employed to cap his triumph over Barry. Being of small size, and therefore easily transportable, he would fall into a stage sleep in the character, and in that condition be borne gracefully from the stage, giving a scene impossible for his rival, "because he knew that Barry, on account of his size, could not be carried off the stage with the same ease that he could."

The veteran actor of the last century, O'Keefe, maintained that he liked Garrick best of all in Lear. No heart, he said, could fail to be touched by the pitiable climax of Garrick's cry, "I will do such things — what they are I know not," followed by the sudden recollection of his own lack of power. It was O'Keefe who declared, " The simplicity of his saying, ' Be these tears wet? — yes, faith!' putting his finger to the cheek of Cordelia, and then looking at his finger, was exquisite." And as Lear and Cordelia, Garrick and Mrs. Cibber are both said actually to have worked themselves up to the shedding of tears, showing that the actor who could glory over his effect upon the audience could occasionally, at least, himself be overcome by Shakespeare's genius. One cool old critic, however, not only thought this was bathos, but also commented on the anachronism of the handkerchief so frequently used by Garrick in the act.

Frankly, it must have been hard work for Garrick to keep the illusion in his mind on that night when gay Peg Woffington enjoyed, and probably returned, an unexpected salutation from an ardent play-goer. In the very midst of the scene wherein Lear, lying with his head in Cordelia's lap, recovers from his delirium, up to the stage leaps a gentleman from the audience, to clasp pretty Cordelia in his arms, and impress upon her lips a hearty kiss. And the spectators, as well as Peggy, seemed to enjoy the unexpected amendment to the drama.

The wits played in words on Garrick's well-known jealousy of Barry, by eulogizing the latter actor in the following double-turned lines:—

"Critics, attend! and judge the rival Lears,
  While each commands applause, and each your tears.
  Then own this truth — well he performs his part
  Who touches even Garrick to the heart."

The first time our hero played Lear was at Goodman's Fields on the night of March 18, 1742. It was his initial season on the stage, his *début* having been made in the same humble theatre on the 19th of the preceding October. The last time he played the *rôle* was on the 8th of June, 1776, the evening before his farewell to the stage. In fact, "Lear" was his final theatrical tragedy, since it was in comedy he chose to say, "Good-by forever." At that eventful performance of the play Miss Younge (afterwards Mrs. Pope) was the Cordelia; and Garrick, holding her hand tightly clasped in his as they walked to the green-room after the fall of the last curtain, exclaimed in sad reflection, "Ah, Bessie! this is the last time I shall ever be your father on the stage." So sad and solemn were his words, that the actress, moved by emotion, dropped on her knees at his feet, and raised her tearful eyes to his, to ask a father's blessing.

Mr. Garrick as King Lear.

DAVID GARRICK AS KING LEAR (In Act III., Scene I).

Until 1756 Garrick had played in Nahum Tate's adaptation of the tragedy; in that year he restored a part of the original Shakespearian version. Tate's "Lear" held prominence on the stage from 1681 down to Macready's day, no one daring before Macready to do away utterly with the contemptible interpolations of that poet laureate who, before he obtained the latter honor, had found in Shakespeare's "Lear" only "an obscure piece recommended to his notice by a friend," — a piece which on his examination proved a "heap of jewels unstrung and unpolished."

In the beginning of the Shakespearian tragedy, Dec. 26, 1606, when "Lear" was played by "His Majesty's servants," before the King at Whitehall, upon St. Stephen's night in the Christmas holidays, Richard Burbage, presumably, was the Lear; and possibly Joseph Taylor was the original Edgar, although Davies is the only one to suggest the latter impersonation. As for Burbage, the original of nearly a dozen of Shakespeare's heroes, his King is thus mentioned in an old elegy: —

> "Thy stature small, but every thought and mood
> Might thoroughly from thy face be understood.
> And his whole action he could change with ease
> From ancient Leare to youthful Pericles."

The great Betterton was probably the Lear after
the Restoration; but though much has been found
in the old-time records concerning his Othello, his
Hamlet, and his Macbeth, no description of his Lear
has been handed down.   Doubtless the tragedy enjoyed far less favor than other works, and its impersonators were thus less considered.   For nearly a
score of years after Betterton's probable appearance
in the title *rôle*, the play slept in the theatre's ar-
chives.   Then, indeed, when it was revived, in **1681**,
it was so altered that its author would have most
grievously condemned it could he have been present
on the opening night.   But Nahum Tate thought —
nay, knew — that his own work, in adaptation, made
the drama; for did he not set himself down on the
title-page of another play as " the author of the
tragedy called ' King Lear ' ! "

Such a wretched, mangled, inartistic mess of
master-work and apprentice jobbery!   The Fool was
taken bodily out of the play (perhaps, suggested
Campbell, because Tate " wished to have no other
fool than himself concerned with the tragedy "), and
never again returned until Macready, with fear and
trembling, restored the character.   Even Garrick,
who had thought of bringing back the Fool, and had
found Woodward ready to promise that in the act-

ing of the character he would conservatively " be very chaste in his coloring, and not counteract the agonies of Lear," lost his courage before the performance, and followed Tate closely in this and many other ways ; while John Kemble and Edmund Kean, though turning in part from Garrick's tracks, yet still feared the restoration of the banished court wit.

More yet did worthy Tate. In his wish "to rectify," as he said, " what was wanting in the regularity and probability of the tale," he wove in a love-thread between Edgar and Cordelia, and, to heighten the romantic effect, had Cordelia bravely rescued by her lover from two fierce ruffians who sought to earn their gold from Edmund by attacking the sweet daughter of the old King.

What the noble and dignified Elizabeth Barry, as the first Cordelia of this version, thought of the introduced love episode we know not; but from her customary solemn acting in the tragic *rôles* we may assume she took very unkindly to the innovation.

As for Betterton, he found himself condemned to mangle in many ways the lines he once had spoken so faithfully for his author. The great speech in the second act not being deemed sufficiently strong

by Tate, the new Lear was obliged to cry out at
the end : —

> " Blood! Fire! here — Leprosies and bluest plagues!
> Room, room for Hell to belch her horrors up,
> And drench the Circes in a stream of fire.
> Hark, how the Infernals echo to my rage
> Their whips and snakes!"

To prove unquestionably that he was the "hero"
of the play, Betterton, though supposed, as Lear, to
be near eighty years of age, and totally unarmed,
was made to cope so vigorously with four wicked
murderers as to win a victory over all of them in
bloody hand-to-hand conflict.

And then, having placed all the tragic scenes he
could invent in the middle of the play, Mr. Tate
proceeds to end all with a merry adjustment, the
entire last act being changed to give the good people of the play a happy settlement and prediction
of a glorious future, — Lear restored to the throne,
and Edgar and Cordelia married.

Thus it was that Mrs. Bracegirdle and the beautiful Mrs. Booth nightly ended their parts upon the
stage ; while the "inimitably expressive" Barton
Booth as Lear "rendered the character more amiable, or, to speak critically, less terrible, than Garrick." This says Davies. But Theophilus Cibber

has a stronger word for Booth's Lear. "Never," says the spendthrift actor-manager, "did pity or terror more vehemently possess an audience than by his judicial and powerful execution of that part."

That the well-born tragedian could delight in aged *rôles* was natural, since it was the curious chance of a gray-haired character that brought him into glory. He was cast for the title *rôle* in Addison's "Cato;" but the managers, failing to foresee the future of the play, feared so much that the young man would decline to impersonate a venerable character, that they took unmeasured pains to coax him into accepting it. Shrewd Barton, however, in a casual glance at the manuscript, saw the possibilities of the *rôle*, and, keeping his own secret, pretended to be indifferent to the part, while at the same time at home he zealously and confidently prepared himself for the opening night.

That night he fairly swept the house before him. Lord Bolingbroke not only collected a purse of one hundred guineas from his box-party to thrust into the actor's hand, but also started a movement to let the successful player into partnership in the management of the theatre. When jealous enemies sought to break down this friendship by keeping the actor busy with a part every night upon the stage, they simply fanned the fuel; for Booth immediately after each performance was whisked away in the carriage of some nobleman, to be entertained lavishly until the hour of the next performance. He acquired a share of the management. He married the pretty ballet-dancer, Miss Santlow, who became the Cordelia of his Lear. But at the age of forty-six the dissipations of his gay life compelled his retirement from the stage; and the subsequent bleeding, blistering, and dosing of a quack, with his prescriptions of two pounds of crude mercury, ended his life in 1733.

Two Lears appeared between Booth and Garrick, — Antony Boheme, the ex-sailor, who, with his exalted bearing, rich voice, and expressive features, made an admirable King; and Quin, who, excellent actor though he was, so neglected the rehearsals that in the ineffectual performance he nearly lost the favor of the public.

Then came the Garrick-Barry rivalry at Drury Lane and Covent Garden.

> "What man like Barry with such pains can err,
> In elocution, action, character?
> What man could give, if Barry were not here,
> Such well-applauded tenderness to Lear?
> Who else could speak so very, very fine,
> That sense may kindly end with every line?"

So sung the usually bitter Churchill in *The Ros-ciad.* (But though Barry conquered in the contest of Romeos, as Lear his opponent carried off the honors.) The tall, graceful, manly fellow, whose acting was studied by great Parliamentary leaders in order that they might from him learn how to stand and move and gesture with combined charm and stateliness, could present in Lear marked dignity and a venerable bearing, and could utter the terrible imprecation with impressive elocution; but he failed to give that variety of expression to the voice, and that awe-inspiring tone to the whole character, which the mobile-featured, emotional Garrick could present. Barry had an odd habit of pausing between his words that, carried to an extreme in Lear, proved wearisome in its artifice.

There was no question, however, regarding the effectiveness of Mrs. Barry's Cordelia. When she raised to heaven her large eyes, glistening with tears, said an old critic, and stood speechless, wringing her hands, it seemed as if she could claim "the aureole of a saint." "It is the grandest thing of the kind I have ever seen an actress do," the old play-goer cries in ecstasy; "my fancy still feeds on it, and the recollections of it will go with me to my grave."

Though Barry was a talented man he was also very modest. Oftentimes, at rehearsal, he would call aside the veteran stage carpenter, who in his day had seen so many giants of the stage act Shakespeare's *rôles*, and seriously consult with him on the most effective way to better the imper- sonation. John O'Keefe, the actor-dramatist, who praised this trait in Barry's character, liked to tell, also, to his friends of the stage about the perform- ance of "Lear" in which he temporarily assumed the duties of a "dresser," or actor's assistant. His friend Spranger asked him to exercise his reported skill in drawing, by making up Lear's face for that performance. So O'Keefe with camel's-hair pencil and India ink drew the wrinkles of care and age over the smooth cheeks and forehead of the player until, to his mind, the countenance was most ven- erable. No sooner had Barry entered the green- room, however, than the jolly fat Isaac Sparks, chief joker of the assembly, broke out, "Hallo, Barry! What's this? Oh, I see! You belong to the London Beefsteak Club, and so O'Keefe has made you peeping through a gridiron."

O'Keefe enjoyed as well the telling of Henry Mossop's experience in Lear. It was during a season when the actor was also a manager, and when the treasury was so low that "the ghost did not always walk." A wily actor, playing Kent, supported the afflicted Lear in his arms securely enough, to all appearances, beyond the footlights; but, as he gradually loosened and loosened his hold, he was whispering in Mossop's ear, "Give me your word, sir, that you'll pay me my arrears to-night before I go home, or I'll let you drop on the floor."

"Don't talk to me now, you villain," hoarsely returned Mossop, alarmed at the threat, but still more alarmed at the prospect of having his scene ruined. "Go on with the part; go on!"

"No," responded the determined Kent; "I'll drop you, sure, if you don't promise."

And poor Harry, caught in a trap, reluctantly had to yield his word.

One actor that night could enjoy beef and ale for supper; he was paid in full.

"Powell's King Lear ought not to be forgotten," says Davies; "it was a fair promise of something great in future." We must, therefore, in passing give a glance at this brilliant young actor, who, but for his untimely death, might have risen to the highest ranks. The version of the play in which he appeared at Covent Garden in 1768, when Garrick was in Italy, was prepared especially for him

by George Colman. Some of the original Shakespearian text was restored, and Tate's love scenes
between Edgar and Cordelia were banished. But
the happy ending of the play was retained, while
the Fool was still suppressed, though reluctantly.
"After the most serious consideration," said Colman, "I was convinced that such a character in
a tragedy would not be endured on the modern
stage."

Tate's miserable adaptation returned with the
Kembles; and John Kemble, "very great in the
curse," made King Lear a notable character in
his list. You remember what Mrs. Spranger Barry
said of the two successive styles of acting, — the
Garrick school, "all rapidity and passion, while the
Kemble school was so full of paw and pause that
at first the performers, thinking their new com-
petitors had either lost their cues or forgotten their
parts, used frequently to prompt them." Yet even
Garrick's admirers regarded Kemble's Lear as grand
when, six weeks after his marriage to Mrs. Brereton
(the widow of the actor who, his friends said, had
gone mad for love of Kemble's sister, Mrs. Siddons), he played the mad King of the play to the
Cordelia of that sister, at her benefit in January,
1788. The actress herself did not regard the *rôle*

of the pious daughter with much favor, since it was a secondary character of the play, in her mind; and she never made a deep impression in her interpretation.

Sometimes the spectators laughed when Kemble's Lear put on the crown of straw and the flowers, the wits even declaring he reminded them of the sugar king on a Twelfth-Night cake; but yet even the light-minded could not forget the magnificent force he had put into that terrible curse : —

"Hear, Nature, hear; dear goddess, hear!"

That benefit performance of 1788 electrified London, and gave the actor his first impulse into favor. As time went on Kemble gradually toned down his too hale and vigorous Lear, till it showed more decrepitude and more solemn dignity. His brother Charles played " Poor Tom " admirably, — in fact, some said he was always at his best on the stage when mad or drunk, — and later on he played the same character to the Lear of Junius Brutus Booth and the Edmund of W. C. Macready. This latter performance was at Covent Garden, in 1820, when the elder Booth and Edmund Kean were pronounced rivals.

For some time Lear had been banished from the

stage by royal command, as the affliction of the central figure bore too close a resemblance to the malady of England's monarch to prove agreeable.) But the death of George III., on the 29th of January, 1820, removed the restriction ; and on the subsequent 13th of April the play was produced. The Covent Garden manager hurried the date in order to take the edge from the announced revival by Kean at Drury Lane. At first he sought Macready for the leading *rôle;* but that conscientious man would not head such a move against a brother actor, though he was willing to accept a secondary part.

Mr. Booth received censure and praise. The friendliest words said, " His execution of this character was transcendently beautiful." The scene in which he is turned out to bide the pelting of the pitiless storm was declared by the same writer as one of terrific grandeur; while his recitation of the passage, —

> "Blow, winds, and crack your cheeks! rage! blow!
> You cataracts and hurricanoes, spout
> Till you have drench'd our steeples!"

was said to be sublime. But others cried, " Rant and bluster ! " The pit certainly applauded to the echo.

What could have been the thoughts of jealous

Sally Booth, the Cordelia of that evening, when she heard the applause showered upon the Lear? Only five years before, when the dashing young actor was just beginning his career in London, Miss Booth, fearing lest some one might think she was a relation of the subordinate player, kindly suggested that he relieve her of the odium by adding an "e" to his name!

A pretty incident illustrative of Booth's kindness of heart was told the writer by an actress who often acted in "Lear" with him, Mrs. W. G. Jones. One night long ago she was cast for Regan. In those days books of the play were hard to find, so she borrowed one to study her part. Lack of time, however, left her very imperfect in the lines; and yet Booth, at rehearsal, instead of being angry, generously said to the overwrought lady, "Never mind, my dear; I will not stop for cues." After the play Mrs. Jones heard two men commenting on the fine acting of the Lear, and adding, "That stupid Regan nearly ruined the whole scene;" but not a word of reproach did the whole-souled Booth utter, though he knew, better than any one else, how much his scenes were injured. A warm tribute, too, Mrs. Jones paid to Booth's power in acting Lear; it was expressed in a single sentence: "He played so grandly that I really cried throughout it all."

The next August after Booth's appearance in op-position to Kean, five months before his marriage to Mary Anne Holmes, and eight months before his sailing for America, Booth played Edgar to Ed-mund Kean's Lear at Drury Lane. Hazlitt could not commend this Lear of Kean, pronouncing it "altogether inferior" to the same actor's Othello. "He failed, either from insurmountable difficulties, or from his own sense of the magnitude of the un-dertaking," said the critic. His contrasts appeared to be too marked, the Lear acting at the first too violently, tearing the curse to tatters, so that it be-came a piece of downright rant, and then at the last becoming too tame. The poet Campbell went so far as to say that Kean so lowered the tone of the character at times, that it seemed like an an-cient whining beggar on the scene.

And yet the brilliant genius had many a time studied the part from midnight till noonday, stand-ing before the mirror that he might note the effect of his facial expression, and had even visited the asylums to learn the forms of insanity.

Alas for the actor! Three years after the per-formance I have mentioned, the audience actually

laughed at him — at him, the greatest player of
his era! He had declared that when Londoners
saw him, as Lear, over the dead body of Cordelia,
they would go mad with him, so powerful would
be his acting. But pretty Mrs. West, his Cordelia,
proved too heavy a load for the little actor to carry;
and so comical were his struggles with the weight
as to start the spectators into a roar of laughter
that did not cease until the curtain fell. That
was in 1823, when the management of Drury Lane
had, for the nonce, restored the original fifth act
of Shakespeare to Tate's version.

This humorous effect on the spectators was somewhat different from that produced by another rival
of Kean, the refined, gentlemanly player Charles
Mayne Young, upon the impressionable Mrs. Piozzi.
In her own words it is recorded under date of
April 27, 1819, in her "Autobiography and Letters:" "Dr. Gibbes is hurried to death, the people
are so ill. He saw me half in hysterics at Young's
giving Lear, and he came the next morning to feel
my pulse, kind creature."

But now the Fool returns, and with him comes
all the beauty of the play; for Macready, having
the absolute management of Covent Garden Theatre,
burned Tate at the stake, and restored the exiled

Master. Yet Macready feared the result. On the afternoon of Jan. 4, 1838, he superintended the first rehearsal of the tragedy, and that night wrote in his diary, " My opinion of the introduction of the Fool is that, like many such terrible contrasts in poetry and painting, in acting representation it will fail of effect ; it will either weary and annoy, or distract the spectator. I have no hope of it, and think at the last we shall be obliged to dispense with it."

At that time the revived character had been cast to the low comedian of the company, one Meadows, who did not at all meet the ideal of the manager. Macready in his mind's eye saw in the Fool a fragile, hectic, beautiful-faced boy. Happily he described his mental picture to stage-manager Bartley on the day after the rehearsal, and the latter quick-witted friend suggested at once that a woman could best fill a part of that kind.

" The very thing ! " cried Macready, delighted at the idea; " and Miss Horton is the person."

It was a happy thought.

Miss Horton (who afterwards was known as Mrs. Germon Reed) made a pronounced hit.

Macready's Lear ranked with Macbeth at the head of all his Shakespearian *rôles*. The gradual growth of the insanity was delicately sketched, while the tremendous violence of the first acts, and the touching tenderness of the last act, were beautifully contrasted. In his " Reminiscences," the actor-manager has given us his own conception of the character; —

"Most actors," he says, " Garrick, Kemble, and Kean among others, seemed to have based their conceptions of the character on the infirmity usually associated with 'fourscore and upwards,' and have represented the feebleness instead of the vigor of old age. But Lear's was in truth a 'lusty winter;' his language never betrays imbecility of mind or body. He confers his kingdom, indeed, on 'younger strengths,' but there is still sufficient invigorating him to allow him to ride, to hunt, to run wildly through the fury of the storm, to slay the ruffian who murdered his Cordelia, and to bear about her dead body in his arms. There is, moreover, a heartiness, and even jollity, in his blither movements no way akin to the helplessness of senility. Indeed, the towering range of thought with which his mind dilates, identifying the heavens themselves with his griefs, and the power of conceiving such vast imaginings, would seem incompatible with a tottering, trembling frame, and

betoken rather one of 'mighty bone and bold em-
prise,' in the outward bearing of the grand old
man."

Westland Marston, whose first play, "The Patrician's Daughter," was brought out by Macready,
praised the latter warmly in Lear, and as an instance of a fine touch of nature described the way
in which the actor's voice broke as his Lear re-
pudiated the once idolized Cordelia, and then, as
firmness quickly returned, hardened into inflexi-
bility. A writer in the *Cornhill Magazine* saw Lear
in a different light. This narrator said of Macready,
"He made the most horrible faces when his passions were aroused, insomuch that I was once nearly
put out of the theatre for bursting out laughing in
'King Lear,' when the mad king shrieked out,
'Look! look! a mouse!' And he made such a
tremendous face, and rolled his eyes in such a supernatural manner at so small an animal, in his
imagination, that if it had been at the end of the
world I could not have kept my countenance."

The revivals of Samuel Phelps at Sadler's Wells,
and of Charles Kean at the Princess's, were scholarly and elaborate. But Phelps, like Charles Dillon, though he touched the heart with his sad
picture of the suffering of the afflicted king, did

not inspire awe or veneration. At Kean's theatre
there was such ostentatious display of archæology,
that a pointed joke was passed around hinting at
a pedantic spirit in the manager. 'T was said that
at rehearsal, when Edmund was giving to Edgar
his key, Kean, watching the proceeding critically,
suddenly called out, "Here, sir, here! Make more
of that key, sir! Good heavens! you give it to
him as if it was a common room-door key. Let
the audience see it, sir; make 'em feel it, sir; impress upon 'em that it is a *key of the period*, sir."

Behind the gray, heavily lined face and the tangled, grizzly locks of Lear, at the London Lyceum
in the latter part of 1892, few play-goers could at
first discover the familiar and strongly characteristic features of Henry Irving, so admirably had he
drawn the king in his physical appearance. On
the mental side he gave scrupulous attention to
the delicate details of the character, picturing Lear,
as M. Taine has described him in the seemingly
paradoxical term, "violent and weak," from the
beginning to the end, raging in lack of self-control
and in semi-insanity even before his mind completely gave away. It was a natural, human Lear,
but not one that the public accepted as unreservedly
desirable. Ellen Terry was Cordelia.

In America the story of "King Lear" begins
on the 14th of January, 1754, when Hallam's company of players was closing its first season in New
York. Malone and Rigby were two friendly rivals; and, as a compromise, the former acted Lear
and Shylock, while the latter acted Romeo, in the
first delineations of those characters in America.
Succeeding Malone came Harman, the son-in-law
of Charlotte Charke, that wild-mannered, strange-
acting daughter of old Colley Cibber; and then
came Lewis Hallam. With the latter's advent to
the title *rôle*, his mother, Mrs. Douglass, retired
from the part of Cordelia, yielding to the younger
actress, Miss Cheer, who in turn gave over the
part to Mrs. Hallam, Jr.

The Baltimore Company, in 1782, saw Mr. Heard
as Lear, and Mrs. Bartholomew as Cordelia, while
Mr. Shakespeare acted Edmund. Six years later
Hallam and his company were evading the law in
Philadelphia, where a legislative statute forbade a
theatre, by "moralizing" on the "Crime of Filial
Ingratitude;" in other words, acting "King Lear."
When Boston first saw the tragedy, April 27, 1796,
Lear was acted by Mr. Chambers, and Cordelia by
Mrs. Snelling Powell.

The nineteenth century now opened, and with

its advance came, as Lear, the square-faceu, hook-nosed, wide-mouthed, brandy-loving George Frederick Cooke, of whom Lord Byron wrote, referring to his "Biography," "Two things are rather marvellous: first, that a man should live so long drunk, and next, that he should have found a sober biographer."

His King was a creditable performance, but not great. The staccato method of pronunciation he adopted, and the rumbling tones, militated against complete success. Yet it is said he was strong in the scene where he says, "No, Regan, thou shalt never have my curse," and when he cries, "Who put my man i' the stocks?" Thomas A. Cooper, in 1824, was declared unsuccessful, since a minor actor in the *rôle* of Edgar carried away the applause from the Lear of the night.

The acting of the elder Booth has been described; but, in connection with the American stage, mention may be made of that benefit performance of June 23, 1830, when Mrs. Trollope, as recorded in her "Domestic Manners of the Americans," saw Booth in the title *rôle*, and found the whole performance very bad. The Cordelia that night was Mrs. Mary Anne Duff, a Cordelia also to Edwin Forrest's King.

"Play Lear!" cried Forrest some years later,
when a friend remarked that he had never seen
the actor play Lear better than he had that night.
"Play Lear! What do you mean, sir? I do not
play Lear! I play Hamlet, Richard, Shylock, Virginius, if you please; but by God, sir, *I am Lear!*"

And the critical world could re-echo the phrase.
Forrest was, indeed, a Lear to be remembered. As
the years passed by, his impersonation of the character steadily increased in power, until at the end,
when Lear formed his last Shakespearian *rôle*, the
player was regarded as unsurpassable.

Sad was the final act. A new star, Edwin Booth,
had arisen in the theatrical sky, and the people's
favorite of earlier years found himself gradually
declining. When he played in New York for the
last time, in February, 1871, there was something
genuinely pathetic in his choice of Lear. He never
played the part better; but with a poor company
in support, with wretched scenery to surround his
acting, and a thin house in an unpopular theatre
to greet him, each auditor could but think of him
as the actual King Lear of the American stage.
"He gave to his children, the public, all he had,"
said one writer at the time, "and now they have
deserted him. They have crowned a new king, be-

EDWIN FORREST AS KING LEAR (In Act IV., Scene 6).

fore whom they bow, and the 'old man eloquent' is cheered by few voices. He bowed his head slightly in response to the acclamation of those scantily filled seats. But throughout the play there was an added dignity of sorrow which showed that the neglect of the public had wounded him. He knew his fate."

The poet Longfellow greatly admired Forrest's Lear, pronouncing it a noble performance. His portrayal of madness was true to nature, often pain-fully so, while his delivery of the great imprecation of the first act ever drew thunders of applause. What though at times he would "roar and bellow," and tear "a passion to tatters," his friends pointed out that he possessed the great power of making the spectator feel that the acting was real, not mimic life, and even caused shudders and tears by his performance.

On the night of March 30, 1872, at the Globe Theatre in Boston, Forrest acted Lear for the last time. The next day, Sunday, he caught cold; on Monday and Tuesday he labored through the part of Richelieu, and with pneumonia threatening him, yet bade the managers post the announcement for Virginius the following evening. In vain the strug-gle. Disease held its arms around him, and though he lived on until the 12th of the following December, and even gathered strength enough for a few readings (the final one in Boston, Dec. 7, 1872); yet he never more was to appear as the hero among the declaiming actors of the stage. When, on that fateful day in December, the servant opened the door of the chamber, he saw his master, with folded arms, in the embrace of death. The very last summons had come painlessly and with little warning.

"Mr. Forrest's countenance, as made up for Lear, is inflexible, stern, and forbidding," declared the comedian Hackett, thirty years ago, adding, "He has, too, a favorite grim scowl; his eyebrows are made so shaggy and willowy, they hide the eyes too much; and his beard, though long and picturesque, covers some useful and important muscles of the face, making it rigid, and incapable of depicting effectively the alternate lights and shades of benevolence and irascibility as they fluctuate in Lear's agitated mind. Nor do I fancy Mr. Forrest's tread of the stage, with his toes inclined somewhat inward, like that of an Indian, for the reason that it renders Lear's personal carriage undignified." Others might differ from Hackett, but the sharp outline picture is worth repeating.

Leigh Hunt regarded Forrest's Lear as the best he had ever seen. Dunlap maintained that Forrest's energy, pathos, and fidelity to the character, surpassed even the "wonderful efforts" of George Frederick Cooke — and he had seen both play the part. As regards this point of fidelity to the character, it may be remarked that Forrest united from first to last the physical infirmity of the old King with his nervous irritability. The study of insanity had been made by the actor a personal hobby, fed by visits to the insane asylums of Europe and America; and into his impersonation he brought many of the peculiarities which he had noted in real life. At the beginning of Lear's madness the twitching of the fingers, the pressing together of the hands, and the other little signs that constant observers of Forrest noted as particularly his own, added to the utterance of the words in holding the audience spellbound in almost painful suspense.

At New Orleans one night, just as Forrest had finished the fearful curse, a spectator was heard to groan aloud. Those around him turned quickly, only to see the man's face set as if in a rigid death-grip, the mouth open and the eyes fixed, while the hands were clinched tightly together. A neighbor seized the entranced stranger by the shoulder, and

with a sudden shake started the blood flowing
again through his veins. With a gasp the man
looked around, as if dazed, and then in a trembling
voice whispered, "Is he gone?" They told him
the scene was over. "A moment more." he responded, "and I should have been a dead man.
I know it. That terrible acting overcame me."

That Forrest himself could continue his acting
without diminution of interest, whatever unexpected
incident happened, or whatever wrought-up emotion
overwhelmed him, was illustrated one night in the
early fifties while he was playing at the Broadway
Theatre in New York. The last scene of the second
act was on, when Forrest, lost in the frenzy of the
part, tore from his head the white wig of Lear, and
in maddened excitement hurled it across the stage.
There he stood before the crowded house, a wrinkled
old man with long hoary beard — and glossy black
locks upon his head. Yet he neither hesitated in
his acting nor weakened in his intensity. With
harrowing sorrow he poured forth the awful denun-
ciation of the king and father. while the spectators, so far from laughing, never even smiled, but
remained closely rapt in the anguish of the scene.

The real Shakespearian "Lear" had not come to
the American stage until Macready, who had re-

vived the original in London, brought it here. On the night of Sept.. 27, 1844, at the last appearance of the English actor on the Park Theatre stage, New York, the hitherto banished character of the Fool was restored (Mrs. J. B. Booth, Jr., *née* DeBar, acting the character), while Cordelia (Charlotte Cushman) no longer struggled with the abducting ruffians, or listened to the words of love from Edgar (Mr. Dyott).

To Macready's Lear at the Astor Place Opera House, in the beginning of that stormy season (1848–1849) which culminated with the Forrest-Macready riot during a "Macbeth" performance, there appeared as the Fool the lady whose life continues even to the present generation, Mrs. Clara Fisher-Maeder. The Cordelia was Miss C. Wemyss, while Goneril was now bestowed upon Mrs. George Jones, the actress who a few months before had been playing Cordelia to the elder Booth's Lear.

The younger Booth (Edwin) first essayed the character in the fifties, when, as a youth of twenty odd summers, he was trying to fill his emptied purse by a benefit performance at San Francisco, preliminary to a return to the East. There can, perhaps, be no more interesting description of his interpretation of the character than that written a quarter of a century later by Walter H. Pollock when commenting upon Booth's performance in London.

"From first to last," he wrote, in the *Saturday Review*, "the character, with its senility, its slowly and surely increasing madness, its overwhelming bursts of passion, its moving tenderness and feebleness, and, underlying and seen through all these, that authority to which Kent makes marked reference, was seized and presented with extraordinary force. So complete are the interest and the illusion, that it is only when the play is over that the fine art which enters the storm of passion is apparent, and that such delicate inventive touches as the suggestion to Lear's wandering wits of the troop of horse shod with felt are remembered. The character is, of course, the more difficult because it begins at such high pressure in the very first scene, that any coming tardy off after that scene has been successfully played would be unhappily accented. Nothing could well be finer than Mr. Booth's rage and disappointment with Cordelia and the half-insane curse which follows them; and throughout the scene his senile yet royal bearing, and that grace and happiness of gesture to which we have on other occasions referred, were marked."

A Lear of different physical mould was John

McCullough. Like Forrest, he possessed a magnificent figure and a royal bearing, while, unlike Forrest, he could "discriminate between the agony of a man while going mad, and the careless, volatile, fantastic condition — afflicting to witness, but no longer agonizing to the lunatic himself — of a man who has actually lapsed into madness." Both in the delicacy of forlorn mournfulness, and in the torrent-like out-pouring of impetuous invective, McCullough could satisfy the critical listener. It was said of him that gentleness never accomplished more than in this actor's pathetic utterance of "I gave you all," and "I'll go with you," while the subsequent rallying of the broken spirit and the terrific outburst, "I'll not weep," had an appalling effect.

James R. Anderson, Lawrence Barrett, and a few other players have acted Lear; but we will pass them by to notice, in brief, the two Italian actors, Rossi and Salvini, whose interpretations of the mad monarch have won merited praises.

Ernesto Rossi's magnificent Lear has been termed the best of his interpretations by reason of great subtlety in the contrasting of the old King's peculiarities, — his child-like credulity with his unreasonable obstinacy, his desire for affectionate regard

with his terrible fierceness, and his forgiving nature with his revengefulness. His impersonation of
Lear, says a foreign critic, is "the most powerful
and pathetic interpretation of that onerous part
which has yet been put forward by any tragedian
— no matter of what nationality — since Macready's
retirement from the stage."

Tommaso Salvini is a pictorial interpreter of
Shakespeare. Thus Othello easily proves his best
Shakespearian part. Lear was artistically ineffective. He could look the King, but yet he was
not regal in his acting. His rich voice could nobly
give the words, but the psychological charm of the
interpretation was lacking. Of his theatrical mech-
anism in the *rôle*, William Winter has given us this
picture. Salvini, he says, "put the King behind
a table in the first scene, — which had the effect
of preparation for a lecture, — and it pleased him
to speak the storm speech away back at the upper
entrance, with his body almost concealed behind
painted crags. Salvini was particularly out of the
character in the curse scene, and in the frantic part-
ing from the two daughters, because there the quality of the man behind the action seemed especially
common."

SHYLOCK.

(IN EARLY DAYS.)

— · —

IT is a gala night at Lincoln's Inn Fields, and
every eye is intent upon the stage. The gay ladies
in vizards have even turned their flirting glances
for a time away from the young gallants in the
neighboring seats, while the serious critics of London town are forgetful of the notable people
around them in their contemplation of the scene
in front.

Most interesting of all is the adapter of the play,
George Granville, the young man of four and
thirty years, whose horoscope, as yet closed to his
vision, will in less than a decade show him among
the peers of the realm. As Lord Lansdowne, his
title will associate him with his grandfather's famous exploits, since brave Sir Beville Granville
fell fighting for the king at the battle of Lansdowne.

But the prologue is on. Let us listen. Shakespeare's Ghost is speaking, and thus addressing the

Ghost of Dryden (to whose son the profits of the play are generously given by Granville) : —

> " These scenes in their rough native dress were mine,
> But now improved with nobler lustre shine;
> The first rude sketches Shakespeare's pencil drew,
> But all the shining master strokes are new.
> This play, ye critics, shall your fury stand,
> Adorned and rescued by a faultless hand."

Mr. Granville may well blush at these complimentary words; but he need not hide his head from the audience, for the prologue is not his own, — it is supplied by a friend, one Bevil Higgons. Fortunate it is, since the adapter of the play has enough to answer for in the roughly transformed scenes. Gobbo, Launcelot, and Tubal are omitted from the cast, — and the loss of Tubal, as can easily be surmised, weakens greatly the picturing of Shylock's mingled grief and anger, — while Bassanio is given lines from brother characters, and is even made heroically to offer his whole body as sacrifice in place of Antonio's pound of flesh, and, that failing, to draw his sword for a battle then and there in his friend's defence.

Thus Bassanio cries (in Granville's words) : —

> " Stand off ! I have a word in his behalf,
> Since even more than in his Avarice,

In Cruelty this Jew's insatiable ;
Here stand I for my friend. Body for Body,
To endure the Torture. But one pound of flesh
Is due from him. Take every piece of mine,
And tear it off with Pincers. Whatever way
Invention may contrive to torture man,
Practise on me ; let but my Friend go safe.
Thy cruelty is limited on him ;
Unbounded let it loose on me. Say, Jew,
Here's Interest upon Interest in Flesh ;
Will that content you ? "

Notice that the great Betterton is playing Bassanio; perhaps some of the alteration is due to the
demands of this leading actor. It is a noble cast
in support. There is Booth, splendid actor, as
Gratiano; Verbruggen as Antonio; the coquettish
Mrs. Bracegirdle, with dark-brown hair and spark-
ling eyes, as Portia ; and Mrs. Porter as Jessica.

But stay. Shylock enters. Can we believe our
eyes? Is this little, lively, red-wigged fellow to
perform the part?

Why, this is Dogget ! Thomas Dogget, whose
songs and dances, and whose dialect acting, have so
often made audiences roar with laughter. Already
the smile goes round the play-house. Yes, and the
actor assists the smiling. He glides peculiarly
along; he casts odd glances hither and thither,
rolling his eyes and twisting his mouth in a ludi-

crous manner. He does not, to be sure, attempt burlesque or cheap guying; but every movement, expression, and turn of the voice is calculated to provoke a laugh, and proves successful.

Too true. Shylock is acted by the comedian of the troupe, and is acted strictly as a comic character. The great play of Shakespeare, which had completely disappeared from the stage after its author's death, had now for the first time returned, in 1701, and returned not only with its name changed to "The Jew of Venice," with its lines altered to suit the ideas of improvement of George Granville, but even with Shylock entirely transformed.

The die was cast. For a generation this mangled version of a masterpiece held the stage. As for our first known Shylock, Thomas Dogget, he is to-day best marked in fame through the really generous bequest in his will. On the river Thames, he said, every year on the 1st of August there shall be held a race open to the watermen of London; and to the winner shall be given "an orange-colored livery with a badge representing Liberty." The color of the livery and the date (celebrating the accession of George I. to the throne) indicate the strong political proclivities of the Whig actor. To this day his race is held.

When next Dogget acted Shylock, Booth had
risen to the part of Bassanio. The successors of
the famous little comedian himself were Benjamin
Griffin and Tony Aston. The former was a min-
ister's son, who had been designed for the trade of
glazier, but who preferred to run away and become
a wandering actor, and who ultimately won a good
place as comedian in Drury Lane, as well as some
note as a playwright. Aston was an odd fellow,
who liked, above all else in the world, to stroll
through country towns with his wife and son, giving a medley of scenes, and who, from his early
education as an attorney, could successfully defend
himself against threatened punishment for apparently infringing on the laws by his performances.

Away with the comedians, however; for at last
the tragic Shylock is to return.

The scene now is Drury Lane; the time Feb. 14,
1741; the actor Charles Macklin. Strange to say,
this Macklin had himself won his greatest praise
as a comedian; but now, in spite of protests from
manager and brother actors, rough, coarse, independent Macklin is determined to act Shylock in a
serious way, — and every one who knows his quarrelsome, self-reliant character understands that he
will have his way or die.

That the sturdy Irishman should aim to interpret his author correctly is not a matter of surprise, since we know how tenaciously he clung to
the rights of the play-maker. "What 's that?" he
cried in surly anger to Lee Lewes, when the latter
attempted to insert a supposed witticism into the
lines of his character in Macklin's "Love à la
Mode:" "what 's that you 're saying?"

"Oh," replied Lewes, in his off-hand manner,
"it 's merely a little of my nonsense."

"Humph!" grunted the playwright, "I 'd have
you understand, Mr. Lewes, that I regard *my* nonsense as better than *yours*, so you will stick to that,
if you please, sir."

When the revived Shylock strode upon the stage,
only a few months before David Garrick made his
début, and by his magnificent acting inaugurated in
England a new love for Shakespeare, Macklin was
forty-one years of age, and yet had acted only minor
parts in the plays of the master author. In "The
Merchant of Venice" he saw his opportunity, and
shrewdly led on Manager Fleetwood to announce
the production. For a time he kept his own de-
sign to himself, merely walking through the rehearsals, and showing no sign of a desire to change
the accepted Granvillian character. But in some

way his scheme leaked out, and the bumble-bees buzzed around him.

His good friends earnestly besought him not to essay so hazardous an innovation; his enemies chuckled at expected disaster, and hypocritically urged him on. Fleetwood all but withdrew his consent. Quin, cast for Antonio, swore that the new Shylock would be hissed; while the Portia and Nerissa of the cast, romping Kitty Clive and Mrs. Pritchard, agreed with the other actors that "the hot-headed, conceited Irishman, who has got some little reputation in a few parts, would bring himself and the theatre into disgrace." But Macklin, stubborn fellow always, never wavered a hair.

The night of the 14th came. The house was filled with the best people of the town, while in the very front rows of the pit sat the sober-faced critics with pencils and wits sharpened for a lively tilt. It was a momentous occasion for the actor; but though his heart beat faster than usual (as he afterwards confessed), yet he kept a bold front outside, and with an assumed confidence advanced to the stage.

A long, loose black gown hung from his shoulders; upon his face appeared a peaked beard; while his head was surmounted by the red hat which the actor, after patient research, had decided was always worn by the Jews in Italy.

During the first scenes Macklin made little extra effort, knowing that they were not strong enough to carry him to victory, and if overacted might bring instantaneous defeat.

His judgment was good. The critics saw that the keynote of the character was well taken, and with a wise nod to their neighbors were heard to whisper, "Very well; very well, indeed," "The man knows what he is about."

Macklin caught the remarks, and gathered renewed courage.

At last came the great third act, for which he had reserved himself. Seriously, earnestly, piteously, tempestuously, he poured out the words of mingled grief at Jessica's flight, and joy over the losses of Antonio.

Now his blood was on fire. They should learn he was right. They should see he could act. Those jealous fellows at the wings should understand the greatness of his skill, and the critical men and women in the audience should be thrilled by the very power of his emotion. And they were.

Applause with hand and foot shook the candles almost from their sockets, and rattled the windows in the old house; in fact, Macklin was obliged several times to stop the torrent of his acting in order to give the auditors chance to vent their enraptured feelings.

Fleetwood, overjoyed at having such a tremendous attraction thus unexpectedly placed near his treasury, grasped the actor by the hand as he came from the stage, exclaiming, "Macklin, you were right!"

After the trial scene, wherein a greater triumph was awarded Shylock, the green-room was suddenly crowded with critics and with noblemen rushing in to offer their honest compliments.

"I confess it," declared Macklin in his later years, "that was one of the most flattering and intoxicating situations of my life. No money, no title, could purchase what I felt. And let no man tell me after this what fame will not inspire a man to do, and how far the attainment of it will not remunerate his greatest labors. By heaven, sir! though I was not worth fifty pounds in the world at that time, yet, let me tell you, I was Charles the Great for that night."

"There was forcible and terrifying ferocity in his Shylock's malevolence," declared Francis Gentleman (*The Dramatic Censor*). "He possessed by nature

certain physical advantages which qualified him to
embody Shylock," said John Bernard in his "Re-
trospections," "and which, combined with his peculiar genius, constituted a performance which was
never imitated in his own day, and cannot be described in this." "If the Almighty writes a legible
hand," swore Quin, after the play, "that man's Shylock must be a villain;" while Pope's couplet will
ever be repeated: —

> "This is the Jew
> That Shakespeare drew."

But of all the descriptions of Macklin's acting,
that by Lichtenberg is the best. Referring to a
performance of Shylock when Macklin was well
along in years, the German writer says, "Picture
to yourself a somewhat portly man, with a yellow-
ish, coarse face, a nose by no means deficient in
length, breadth, or thickness, and a mouth in the cut-
ting of which nature's knife seems to have slipped
as far as the ear, on one side at least, as it appeared
to me. His dress is black and long; his trousers
likewise long and wide; his three-cornered hat is
red — I presume after the fashion of Italian Jews.

"The first words he speaks on coming on the
stage are slow and full of import: 'Three thousand
ducats.' The two *th*'s and the two *s*'s, especially

CHARLES MACKLIN AS SHYLOCK (In Act IV., Scene I).

the last after the *t*, Macklin mouths with such unc-
tion, that one would think he were at once testing
the ducats and all that could be purchased with
them. This at starting at once accredits him with
the audience in a way which nothing afterwards
can damage. Three such words, so spoken in that
situation, mark the whole character. In the scene
where for the first time he misses his daughter, he
appears without his hat, with his hair standing on
end, in some places at least a finger's length above
the crown, as if the wind from the gallows had
blown it up. Both hands are firmly clinched, and
all his movements are abrupt and conclusive. To
see such emotion in a grasping, fraudulent character, generally cool and self-possessed, is fearful."

On the 10th of January, 1788, when Macklin was
eighty-nine, he appeared as Shylock, after an absence of several years from the stage. With old-
time spirit he went through the first act, but in
the second began to stumble over the lines, and
soon was entirely confused. Before a word could
be said, however, by friend or enemy before or behind the footlights, the manly old actor advanced
to the front, and in solemn and touching accents
said, "Ladies and gentlemen, within these very
few hours I have been seized with a terror of mind

I never in my life felt before ; it has totally de-
stroyed my corporeal as well as mental faculties.
I must, therefore, request your patience this night,
—a request which an old man may hope is not unreasonable. Should it be granted, you may depend
that this will be the last night, unless my health
shall be entirely re-established, of my ever appearing before you in so ridiculous a situation.''

The audience applauded encouragingly ; and the
veteran player, nerved by this sudden expression
of good will, again took up his text, and with the
assistance of the prompter struggled through the
play.

Macklin lived to be ninety-seven years of age.
Eight years before his death he made his final appearance upon the stage, playing, on the 7th of
May, 1789, for his own benefit (and he needed
money badly), the character of the Jew. The old
man's mind had been failing for a year or more,
so that the management provided an understudy
in case Macklin broke down in his part. This was
wise.

"When our Shylock had dressed himself for the
stage, which he did with his usual accuracy," said
William Cooke, his friend and biographer, " he
went into the green-room, but with such a lack-

lustre looking eye as plainly indicated his inability
to perform; and, coming up to the late Mrs. Pope,
said, 'My dear, are you to play to-night?'—'To
be sure I am, sir! Why, don't you see I am dressed
for Portia?'—'Ah! very true; I had forgot. But
who is to play Shylock?' The imbecile tone of
his voice, and the inanity of the look with which
the last question was asked, caused a melancholy
sensation in all who heard it. At last Mrs. Pope,
rousing herself, said, 'Why, you to be sure; are
you not dressed for the part?' He then seemed
to recollect himself, and, putting his hand to his
head, exclaimed, 'God help me! my memory, I am
afraid, has left me.' He, however, after this went
on the stage, and delivered two or three speeches of
Shylock in a manner that evidently proved he did
not understand what he was repeating. After a
while he recovered himself a little, and seemed to
make an effort to rouse himself, but in vain: nature
could assist him no further; and after pausing some
time, as if considering what to do, he then came
forward and informed the audience that he now
found he was unable to proceed in the part, and
hoped they would accept Mr. Ryder as his substitute, who was already prepared to finish it.
The audience accepted his apology with a mixed

applause of indulgence and commiseration, and he
retired from the stage forever."

Thirteen years after Macklin first drew the proper
Shylock, Sheridan essayed the *rôle* with moderate
success at Covent Garden. His associate was Peg
Woffington, the best of Portias by reason of her
elegance in deportment, her spirit and archness;
in Macklin's second season of the Jew she had
played Nerissa to Kitty Clive's mimicking Portia.

Next, several comedians undertook the *rôle* of Shylock; but none dared turn it back so far into humor
as had the men of earlier days. Shuter, the Launcelot Gobbo of the Sheridan performance; King, the
original Sir Peter Teazle (and the Shylock on Dec.
29, 1775, to the Portia of Mrs. Siddons when that
accomplished lady made her first appearance on the
stage); and Yates, who, the *Dramatic Censor* wished,
"might never mutilate a line of blank verse again,"
— were all Shylocks of a wrong hue.

Henderson and Palmer were of different stamp.
The former, making his London *début* in Shylock
in 1777, achieved marked success, though his costuming was so shabby as to lead one man to sur-
mise that it had been borrowed from a pawnbroker.

" There 's good spirit in your performance," said
old Macklin, a spectator at the production.

"Thank you," responded the "Bath Roscius." "But I'm sorry to say I never had the advantage of seeing your Shylock."

"Sir," responded the gruff veteran, bridling up, "you need not tell me that. I knew you had not; for if you had, you would have played it differently."

And yet Henderson was a great actor, — great in Hamlet and great in Falstaff. It is said that he was the first to change the reading of the line, "Signor Antonio, many a time and oft on the Rialto," from a common proverbial expression to an implication that Antonio had baited him not only often, but even "on the Rialto," where merchants most do congregate. This he did by emphasizing the last two words of the line.

That Henderson had good enjoyment in humor was apparent by the way he would, in public, mimic one of the theatrical managers who sought to teach him, the actor, how to interpret Shylock. "Yes," this know-it-all manager would say, with the wisdom of a Dogberry, "this Shylock, though he is a Jew — he's a Jew that walks the Rialto at Venice, and talks to the magnificos, and you must not by any means act such a Jew as if he was one of the Jews that sell old clothes and slippers and oranges and sealing-wax up and down Pall Mall." And Henderson would solemnly assure him he would not.

Over Palmer's Shylock, Macklin was severe. "He played the character in one style," declared the old fellow. "It was all same, same, same; no variation. He did not hit the part nor the part hit him!"

Then there were Ryder and Harley; but when even John Kemble, who first played the part in 1784 to the Portia of his sister, Miss E. Kemble, could not win great fame in the *rôle*, what can we expect from these others? While Black Jack was acting the *rôle* in England, the play-lovers across the water, in the United States of America, were recalling the few performances of "The Merchant of Venice" they had seen in the thirty odd years of their stage's existence.

With our theatrical history the "Merchant of Venice" has an interesting connection, from its being the first play produced by that band of actors, Hallam's Company, which was to inaugurate a regular stage in this community in place of the spasmodic performances previously given.

The picture is an odd one to eyes accustomed only to the glamour of the modern superbly equipped theatre. The scene is laid in the capital of Virginia; but the date is Sept. 5, 1752, and the Williamsburg of that day is a far different place from what it was to become a century and four decades later. A scattered village of perhaps some two hundred buildings, it has a thousand souls to make up the population; but out of these numbers scarcely a dozen mansion-houses are to be counted, and only a few hundred white people.

On this brisk fall evening excitement has risen to fever-heat through the gossip that has spread far and near regarding the English play-actors just over on the *Charming Sally;* and while the people slowly file out of the country store before the early hour of closing, — for the proprietor, book-keeper, clerk, and boy (all represented in one person), could not have been tempted, by any number of pennies, to keep open his establishment, and lose the pleasure of that night's theatrical performance, — old-fashioned family barouches, farm-carts, mule-wagons, and gigs, dash or rumble up the road from every outlying district, bringing gayly decorated women and store-clothed men, all whipping their nags to the theatre.

A theatre only by courtesy. It stands on the outskirts of the town, so near the woods that the actors can amuse themselves by shooting pigeons from the windows, and it consists merely of a rough warehouse, altered rudely to suit the needs of comedians. But this night a jovial audience gathers in its pit, watches with amusement the antics of the negroes in the gallery, and gazes with something of awe at the country gentry in the stalls, who, following the custom of old England, dare venture upon the stage between the acts, and chatter with the ladies and gentlemen of the troupe. To be sure, it is a gala day for Williamsburg!

Nor are the actors less impressed with the occasion. True, they had hardly expected to come from the busy streets of London, where the gay throngs of fashionable people were even then wisely discussing the merits of David Garrick, and praising the vivacity of Peg Woffington, into a wilderness, where the theatre is practically unknown; but had supposed that a town which could boast a capital and a "palace" for the governor, would show some reflection of the cultivated city they had left behind. Yet, in spite of this disappointment, they recognize the fact that there are sturdy planters of intelligence before them, and an enthusiastic crowd of youths, who, with eyes and ears wide open, will swallow the sights and sounds of the night as phenomena never to be forgotten.

So, after Mr. Pelham, the solitary musician of the theatre, has supplied the want of an orchestra by drumming out a classical overture upon his harpsichord, and Mr. Rigby, later the Bassanio of the cast, has read the prologue, written especially for the occasion by Mr. Singleton, the Gratiano of a half hour later, Mr. Clarkson, Mr. Wynell, and Mr. Herbert, clothed respectively in the characters of Antonio, Salarino, and Salanio, walk upon the stage, and the play begins.

The company is small, and there must be some doubling of parts. Hence, Mr. Hallam himself plays both Launcelot and Tubal. His wife is Portia. His daughter is Jessica. Master Lewis Hallam, who later on is to become the leading actor of his time, but who was then, like his sister, making a first appearance on the stage, is cast for the servant of Portia; and though he has but one line to speak, he loses his tongue completely when the time comes, stands shivering with stage-fright before the audience for a few moments, and then rushes in tears from the stage. Much better would he feel if he could see, as we see, that fourteen years after this inauspicious *début* he would be acting with success the chief character, the Jew of Venice, at the first Philadelphia performance of the play.

Mr. Malone, the first Shylock and Lear of the American stage, is transformed into Mr. Pugsby in John Esten Cooke's "Virginia Comedians;" but inasmuch as Mr. Cooke also transforms Mrs. Hallam into her own daughter, and makes numerous absolute errors in facts, it is safe to assume that the novelist is also unattached to truth when he allows the manager to say after the performance that "Shylock was too drunk" to play his part well.

The Philadelphia playhouse, a few years after Hallam's Shylock, saw another Jew, whose record, though interesting, is not enviable. He was a clever performer, even if Hallam, his rival, ironically classed him only as a "splendid amateur actor;" and he could excel particularly in Irish characters. In fact, General Washington held John Henry as an admirable impersonator, and delighted particularly in seeing him act Patrick in the "Poor Soldier." When Henry first came over to this country from England, he did not hesitate to allow his name to be advertised, at his wife's benefit, as a performer of the Harlequin who would "run up a perpendicular scene twenty feet high." How he did it is not recorded in contemporaneous journals.

The tall, majestic, handsome actor was born in Dublin, and had made his *début* at Drury Lane in 1762. Five years later he was in America. His first wife, the eldest of a family of four girls, was lost at sea when the vessel on which she was voyaging from Jamaica was burned. Then followed the peculiar and far from honorable circumstances which stained this player's life. Mrs. Henry left a sister Ann, who afterwards, as Mrs. John Hogg, became a great favorite with the old Park Theatre audiences in New York. With Ann as wife Henry lived for a time, but finally deserted her to marry the youngest sister of the family, pretty little Maria Storer. She was a perfect fairy in person, according to the story of those who acted with her; but her character is not enhanced by this willingness to accept the man who, the widower of one of her sisters, could thus desert another sister. If you would see her picture, read these words by the veteran player, William B. Wood, as given in his " Personal Recollections of the Stage." " She usually came full dressed to the theatre in the old family coach; and the fashion of monstrous hoops worn at that day made it necessary for Mr. Henry to slide her out sideways, take her in his arms, and carry her like an infant to the stage entrance. The carriage was a curious and rather crazy-looking affair; and lest the gout, which rendered it indispensable to him, might not be generally known as an excuse for such a luxury, he decorated the panels with two crutches crossed — the motto, ‘ This, or These.’ ”

Poets of the last century wrote verses in Maria Storer's honor :—

> “ Enchanting maid!
> Whose easy nature every grace affords,
> And charms without the empty pomp of words.”

Wood declares she was a “ prodigious favorite.” Dunlap accounts her the best singer America had ever known before the final decade of the last century. But the slight, blue-eyed Ariel (for that was her ideal part) could be irritable and tempestuous, could refuse to act if she did not like the character allotted her, or had failed to win all the applause she thought she deserved, and, chief of all, could accept John Henry.

Her retribution was sufficient. A few months after Henry died, his widow, poverty-stricken and demented, passed away in miserable death in a house back of the theatre where she had met with so many triumphs.

Nor was Henry himself less capricious and quarrelsome. In fact, he was very often involved in personal encounters; and on one occasion, at least, the stalwart fellow received a severe and probably well-merited drubbing from his associate Hallam, an active fellow, though much smaller. Gradually Henry grew unpopular ; the chief *rôles* one by one slipped away from him, and the newspapers even allowed him to be insulted in their columns by letters railing at his incapacity. At last, worried on every side, he was driven to sell, for ten thousand dollars, his interest in the old American Company, and retired to die of quick consumption shortly afterwards, at the age of forty-seven.

Another Shylock of those early days, Mr. Chalmers, though an actor of experience on the English stage, seems to have been a vain and selfish man personally. The idolized Cooper, Mr. Fennell, Mr. Hipworth, and Giles Leonard Barrett, with one or two minor players, kept Shylock on the stage until the days of Kean and Booth. With the last two a new era opens.

SHYLOCK.

BEFORE the curtain rises on Edmund Kean and
Junius Brutus Booth struggling for supremacy,
there should be mention of the notable Shylock,
who led one of the greatest casts the play ever
saw, — I mean George Frederick Cooke.

With the impressive Mrs. Siddons as Portia, her
brothers, sturdy John Kemble as Antonio, and airy
Charles Kemble as Bassanio, and those princes of
comedy, Munden and Emery, as Launcelot and Old
Gobbo, Cooke found a support that could put him
to his mettle. That was in 1803, three years after
his first appearance in the character in London.
"I can conceive nothing so perfectly the Jew that
Shakespeare drew as the voice, face, manner, and
expression of Mr. Cooke," said the veteran Dunlap. "Mr. Macklin may have been better; but it
is almost thirty years since I saw Mr. Macklin,
and my memory is not of such tenacious stuff as

to enable me to make a comparison between him and Mr. Cooke."

With his long, hooked nose, his lofty forehead, and his dark, fiery eyes, the actor possessed a physiognomy that was strongly marked, even if not as elegant or classically striking as Kemble's. At the age of forty-four he first came to London, being engaged for a paltry six pounds a week at Covent Garden. His initial part was Richard III.; his second, Shylock. In the first character his triumph was complete; in the second, he won equal favor, particularly after his magnificent playing in the third act. Indeed, the savage exultation of his laugh in that scene was said actually to be frightfully impressive. Constantly he kept the "lodged hate" of the Israelite in view. When Portia asked that the bond might be torn, Shylock, in his reply, "When it is *paid* according to the tenor," showed not only a touch of fear lest she should tear it, but also a malignant delight in the realization of the penalty due.

And the man who could act this close, mean, and revengeful character was in private life one of the most open and reckless handlers of money the world ever knew. The day a certain man refused to fight the actor because Cooke was rich, and would there-

JUNIUS BRUTUS BOOTH.

fore hold the favor of friends in any contest, the
careless player pulled from his pocket a big roll of
bills, and thrust the entire amount into the fire,
exclaiming, "Look ye, sir! that was all I possessed
in the world, three hundred and fifty pounds. Now
I am a beggar, sir. Will you fight me now?"

Proud he was, too, when in his drink. Charles
Lamb tells the story of our Shylock's experience
with the architect of a theatre. At a dinner given
to Cooke and to Brandon, the theatre box-keeper,
by the man of plans and specifications, the player,
as usual, drank all the liquor in sight, until he was
beastly drunk. Then, having been politely shown
the door by his host, who had tired of the tipsy
fellow's noisy eccentricities, Cooke suddenly turned,
and, seizing his entertainer by both ears, exclaimed,
"To think that I, George Frederick Cooke, have
degraded myself by dining with bricklayers, to meet
box-keepers!" tripped him on his head, and left
him sprawling on the floor.

In equally energetic way did he attack with
words a Liverpool audience which had dared to
hiss him for being drunk on the stage. "What!"
he cried savagely from behind the footlights, as he
suddenly faced the condemning crowd, "do you hiss
me — me, George Frederick Cooke! you contemp-

tible money-getters! You shall never again have
the honor of hissing me! Farewell! *I* banish
you. Why," — and here he drew himself up to
his full height as he hurled his final taunt, —
"there is not a brick in your dirty town but what
is cemented by the blood of a negro!"

Another time, when playing Shylock, Cooke was
again hissed for the same reason; he was too intox-
icated to act. Two nights later, though advertised
for Richard III., he failed to appear at all at the
theatre. On the next night, when he did come on
sober, the auditors marked his appearance with a
storm of hissing. Instantly the fiery actor stopped
his impersonation, and, turning to a brother player,
exclaimed in anger, "On Monday I was drunk, but
appeared, and they did n't like that; on Wednes-
day I was drunk, so I did n't appear, and they
did n't like that. What the devil would they
have?"

But let us pass now from Cooke to Kean, with
one word to mention Charles Young's Shylock.

Our most striking glimpse of Kean shows a fiery
little man trudging through the snow on a blus-
tering January night in the year 1814. Over his
shoulders hangs a big coachman's coat, — "the man
with the cape," the taunting stage doorkeeper had

called him, — while in the pocket of that coat lie
an old pair of silk stockings, a pair of shoes, and
a collar, the scanty wardrobe the poor play-actor
could bring to piece out the theatrical costume of
the night.

He was on the edge of glorious success or terrible failure. Which was it to be?

Brought up as a waif in hard adversity, knowing with certainty neither father nor mother, tossed
about the world as a little declaimer, a strolling
actor, and possibly an acrobat, the poverty-stricken
husband and father had struggled through a hard
winter, — Heaven alone knows how, — until this
opening chance at great Drury Lane was proffered
him. The offer came simply because the managers
had nothing else to try. In all their company they
had no tragedian who could draw an audience;
Raymond, Henry Siddons, Rae, Pope, were fairly
good actors, no more. For one hundred and thirty-
nine nights the plays had been staged at an unin-
terrupted loss; bankruptcy was threatening.

And this young man from the provinces would
come for eight pounds a week. Why not try him?

They offered Richard to the newcomer for his
first night's *rôle*. Though controversy might ruin
his every chance, the actor had the courage to say

"No" to such a suggestion. For him to appear
as the crook-backed monarch, bringing his small
physique into contrast with the majestic Kemble,
would mean an unfair competition at the very be-
gining of the tourney.

"Shylock or nothing!" he cried determinedly;
and no pressure could move him from that ground.
Strange to say, the management yielded. "The
Merchant of Venice" was announced for the 26th
of January.

They gave the *débutant* just one rehearsal for this
momentous performance, and that on the morning
preceding the evening of the play. Sneers and
gibes met him on every side; but he cared naught
for the malignant-tongued professionals of the metropolis. His eyes were on the future. "If I
succeed to-night," he cried to his wife at home,
after the rehearsal, "if I succeed, I shall go mad."

For the first time in months he dined on meat,
a luxury that he felt then to be a necessity, with
the fearful strain of the coming night before him.

The hours flew by. The theatre doors opened,
and a small number of men and women straggled
in. When the curtain rose the house was not
half full. An old story for Drury Lane this had
been; but that night was to change all.

The utterance of the words, " Three thousand ducats, well ! " gained an approving nod from a capable critic in the front row. The strength of the phrase, " I *will* be assured I may," drew a round of applause. Steadily through the scene the favorable impression grew, until at the end of the first act even his supercilious associates who had gathered at the wings to scoff over his innovations (as witnessed by them earlier in rehearsal) admitted that the young man of seven and twenty had obtained a foothold.

They tried to congratulate him. The sensitive fellow shrank from the shallow praise, and lurked about the shadow of the stage until the curtain again rang up.

Once more he was on the scene. The applause grew stronger, the good impression deeper. People looked at one another with significant smiles and raising of eyebrows, while they settled down into unexpected preparation for an evening of real entertainment. Now Jessica's flight was divulged to the Jew — and the spectators no more even thought with pleasure on themselves and what they saw. They were lost to realization of their own existence. In the terrible whirlwind of passion upon the stage, the tempest of mingled anger and grief of Shylock,

they forgot for the nonce that they were simply
spectators, but lived with the bereaved father before
them.

Ah, what a triumph! The house fairly quivered
with excitement as the scene ended. A rain of
applause stormed the falling curtain. But with
the trial scene, full of novelties as well as power
in acting, the player was carried to still greater
heights; and none was found, on or off the stage,
to say that the success that night of Edmund Kean
was not phenomenal.

Stage-manager Raymond — he who had sworn
that the young player's innovations would never
do — now came to flatter and to fawn, and later,
as we saw in the story of Othello, received a taste
of Kean's resentment for such sycophancy.

Oxberry declared that it was beyond his com-
prehension how so small an audience could "kick
up so big a row."

But Kean waited for little of this. Half crazed
with excitement and joy, he rushed to his miserable
home, lifted from the rickety bed his little boy,
and, holding him in air, while he threw one arm
around his wife, cried in exultation, " Mary, you
shall ride in your carriage yet! And Charles —
Charles shall go to Eton!"

What hope beamed in Mary Chambers Kean's eyes! In his poverty she had gladly married the struggling actor, and for six years had suffered every possible trouble and sorrow in his company. Never had a word of complaint passed her lips. Alas, the future! Riches were to pour into the family coffers; but with them came trouble of a different character, even to estrangement. And yet to the last she remained faithful and devoted to her recreant husband, and when life was ebbing away hastened to his side to comfort the pain of the last sad hours.

But in this opening month of the year 1814 all is happiness. Richard follows Shylock; Hamlet and Othello next. For seventy nights the plays go on, and the managers place their profits at twenty thousand pounds. After the third performance Kean's pay is raised to twenty pounds a week, and gifts of one hundred pounds and five hundred pounds are made. In vain some of the meanest actors continue their sneers at the newcomer.

"Humph! I allow he 's an excellent Harlequin," snarls one.

" Yes," responds good-natured Jack Bannister, "that he is; for he 's jumped over all our heads."

But thirteen years later! The scene is different.

In the interval Kean has visited America, has earned
in all two hundred thousand pounds, has met with
disgrace through his unfaithfulness to his wife, has
been hissed in both continents for his ungentlemanly conduct, and now returns to Drury Lane,
again on a January night, to play Shylock.

"I shall not soon forget the scene," said Dr.
Doran, describing the night; "a rush so fearful, an
audience so packed, and a reconciliation so complete, acting so faultless, and a dramatic enjoyment
so exquisite, I never experienced. Nothing was
heeded — indeed, the scenes were passed over —
until Shylock was to appear, and I have heard no
such shout since as that which greeted him. Fire,
strength, beauty, every quality of the actor, seemed
to have acquired fresh life. It was all deceptive,
however. The actor was all but extinguished after
this convulsive, but seemingly natural, effect. He
lay in bed at the Hummum's Hotel all day, amusing himself melancholily with his Indian gew-gaws,
and trying to find a healthy tonic in cognac."

The magnetism of his name lasted, however, a
few years longer; then came that sad performance
of "Othello" on the 25th of March, 1833, when
the curtain dropped forever on the stage-career of
Edmund Kean.

Two years before his retirement Talfourd saw his
Shylock, and in one pithy sentence portrayed the
impressiveness of the impersonation: "His look
is that of a man who asserts his claim to suffer
as one of a race of sufferers; and when he turns
his sorrowful face in silence to the frothy coxcomb who rails at him, we feel the immeasurable
superiority of one who finds, in the very excess
of his misery, his kindred with a tribe oppressed
for ages, to the insect boaster of the day."

The actors at old Drury had soon been won over
to recognition of the genius among them; that is
to say, all but Comedian Dowton. They subscribed
for a silver cup to present Kean. "No," declared
the jealous player of humorous *rôles*, when asked
to contribute; "you may 'cup' Mr. Kean if you
like, but you shall not bleed me." Curiously
enough, this excellent Sir Anthony Absolute, Sir
Peter Teazle, and Sir John Falstaff, also tried
Shylock's *rôle;* but the audience saw little except
comedy in his impersonation, and even laughed
heartily at the innovation, devised by Dowton, of
Shylock dropping fainting into the arms of a party
of Jews in court when he was bidden to become a
Christian.

There seemed, about this time, to be another

craze among the comedians to capture the character. The ingenious and skilful actor of elderly
gentlemen, William Farren, made several essays at
the part; but that the audience never was held
intensely enraptured is illustrated by one incident
at Birmingham. Farren was at that time tall and
lean; and when, in the most serious tones of Shylock, he cried, —

> "The pound of flesh that I demand is mine;
> 'T is dearly bought, and I will have it,"

a gallery god shouted forth, "Let him have the
pound of flesh; let old Skinny have it! He needs
it bad enough!"

The next day the town was covered with plac-
ards (pasted broadcast through the humor of Bunn,
the well-known manager). They read: —

> "A reward will be given for the apprehension of a tall,
> thin, lanky-looking man, who last night committed a most
> barbarous murder upon a rich old Jew of the name of
> Shylock. The murderer is supposed to have escaped from
> Birmingham in one of the early Liverpool coaches."

The tragedians returned with Macready; but yet,
at the outset, that capable player was not satisfied with his own impersonation. "It was an utter
failure," he wrote in his diary on Sept. 30, 1839.

" I felt it. and suffered very much from it." Some
four seasons later, however, he admitted that he
performed the character "very fairly," and even
enjoyed the interpretation so well that he could
add, immediately on the next line in his diary,
the invigorating record that at supper he "took
a gin mint julep by way of experiment," and found
it "the most deliciously cunning compound that
ever I tasted. Nectar could not stand before it;
Jupiter would have hobnobbed in it." Surely
the "Merchant" that night must have gone off
remarkably well to lead the usually self-lashing,
unhappy diarist to write in so genial a vein.

With Samuel Phelps, the Jew was the first character to be portrayed on the London stage. The
young man came up from the provinces to startle
Macready somewhat with fear of a rival, and appearing on Aug. 28, 1837, at the Haymarket Theatre,
under Webster's management (to the Portia of Miss
Huddart, afterwards Mrs. Warner), was pronounced
by the *Morning Chronicle* of the next day, "Correct
and judicious, but not remarkable or striking."
The critics declared that he fell far short of Kean,
particularly in comparison with the latter's power
of throwing something of sublimity into Shylock's
character.

But Kean it was who, while acting Shylock, had first noted and praised the ability of the young player. That was in 1831, in a small town in the north of England.

" Who is that Tubal ? " queried the great actor, after his famous scene in the " Merchant of Venice."

"It's Samuel Phelps, sir," was the reply of the stage-manager.

" Send him to me."

Tremblingly the actor obeyed, supposing he was to be taken to task for some bad error.

" Phelps! " exclaimed the famous Kean, clapping him on the shoulder the moment he entered the dressing-room, " you have played Tubal very, very well. Persevere, and you will make a name."

Well did he remember the injunction! His later fame as a Shakespearian reviver who dared to bring out all but six of the thirty-seven plays of the Bard is alone glory enough, aside from the reputation he won as a sterling actor.

Meanwhile, the baby whom a half-crazed father's hands had lifted from the cradle, to predict a career at Eton as his future hope, had enjoyed that privilege, and had stood on the threshold of three professions, -- the army by his own desire, the navy by the desire of his father, the church by the desire of his mother. All these predilections, however, were thrown to the wind after the elder Kean's dissipations had squandered his fortune and estranged his family. In October, 1827, Charles appeared upon the stage.

Acquiring later the control of the Princess's Theatre in London, the younger Kean there brought out with magnificent, and then entirely novel, splendor "The Merchant of Venice." The scenery gave accurate views of Venice; the stage showed stately processions and busy throngs, a vivacious carnival and masquerade, besides gorgeous pictures of Belmont and the Hall of the Senators. But Kean himself as Shylock was pronounced only passable.

"Too much youthful vivacity and grace of movement for an old money-lending Jew," was Herman Vezin's comment as he viewed his fellow-actor with a professional eye; while Punch acknowledged the actor-manager's deep research into antiquarian lore by dryly remarking that Kean (who never could pronounce "m" otherwise than by the sound of "b") had evidently proved Shylock a vegetarian, since he read the lines thus : —

> " You take by house when you do take the prop
> That doth sustain by house, you take by life
> When you do take the *beans* whereby I live."

A mispronunciation this, which reminds one of the slip of the tongue made by Charles Kemble in Shylock, when he tried to say, "Shall I lay perjury upon my soul?" and instead so tangled his tongue as to exclaim, "Shall I lay surgery upon my poll?"

With Charles Kean as Shylock in the grand representation of 1858, appeared Mrs. Kean as Portia. The Launcelot Gobbo was Harley. On the night of August 20 this last-mentioned veteran comedian, then seventy-two years of age, had amused the audience by his customary buoyant acting, and with lively step rushed across the stage bridge to make his exit. Scarcely had he reached the wings, while the laughter of the audience still rang in his ears, when he fell to the floor, stricken with paralysis. Friends rushed to give assistance. The actor tried to speak, but could not utter words coherently. In a few hours he was past all consciousness, though still breathing. On the afternoon of August 22, suddenly waking from his lethargy, he murmured, in the words of Nick Bottom in the "Midsummer Night's Dream," "I have an exposition of sleep come over me," closed his eyes, and passed away.

Come we now to the last of the great English Shylocks, Henry Irving. His conscientious revival

HENRY IRVING AS SHYLOCK.

of the comedy gave the entire play to the stage,
rather than the customary version ending with the
discomfiture of Shylock in the trial scene, and
with the splendid stage dressing presented a feast
for the eye.

Mr. Irving's Shylock is a "gentlemanly Jew."
On the night of his first appearance in the character, at the London Lyceum, Nov. 1, 1879, the
spectators looked with astonishment at the new
portrayal before them. The commonplace Hebrew
money-lender, dirty in costume and in appearance,
had disappeared, giving way to a refined, well-
dressed dealer in money. As the trial scene opened,
there approached no crouching, bloodthirsty miser,
scowling and greedy, but a distrustful, adroit, and
dignified pleader; while Shylock's baffled departure
from the scene, with tottering movement and bewildered look, combined with a single glance of
scorn cast at the insulting Gratiano, made a strong
contrast to the "old school" bombastic methods,
and formed an artistic picture.

Twice, at least, Irving on a Shylock night has
had to meet a diplomatic emergency, and twice
has he met it well. The first time was in Edinburgh, when the students of the University, in
boyish fashion, made themselves obnoxious with

talking and laughter, mixed with applause and
cat-calls. They drowned the words of the actors.
Suddenly the curtain fell in the midst of the scene.
Every one was instantly on tip-toe of curiosity to
see what would happen. Instead of an angry manager appearing on the scene, Mr. Irving, cool and
smiling, came to the front, said he noticed that
there seemed to be some misunderstanding on the
part of certain members of the audience, and that
since the first scenes, as a result of the misunderstanding, had not been heard at all, he proposed
beginning the play all over again. This unexpected, good-natured dealing carried the hearts of
the auditors, and the play, begun again, went on
happily to the end.

On the other occasion, when the hundredth performance of the " Merchant of Venice " at the Lyceum was celebrated by a dinner on the stage, given
after the performance by Mr. Irving to his friends,
Lord Houghton proposed the host's health in a
speech that was either very sarcastic or very ill-
judged. Formerly, he said, Shylock had been performed as a ferocious monster, but under Irving's
treatment he became " a gentleman of the Jewish
persuasion, in voice very like a Rothschild, afflicted
with a stupid servant and a wilful and pernicious

daughter, to be eventually foiled by a very charming woman." Furthermore, the gentleman said he
supposed if Mr. Irving undertook the character of
Iago, he would, on the same principles, make him
a very honest man who was devoted to watching
over Othello's wife. To reply courteously to such
a speech must, indeed, have been a hard task to
the actor; but he lost neither his temper nor his
wit, turning aside the awkward statement of Lord
Houghton with courteous yet pertinent remarks.

The actor who may well serve as the link con-
necting the stage across the water with the stage
of this land is Junius Brutus Booth. His early
experiences were in competition with Kean in London; his later life was as a leader, with few com-
petitors, in America. As for his Shylock, in that
he could take genuine interest; for he was as well
versed in the Koran as in the Bible, could sympa-
thize with the Jews deeply, since he honestly regarded them as an oppressed race, and could, by
his knowledge of the tongue, even repeat the lines
of the character, when he chose, in the Hebrew
dialect.

His Jew was gloomy but grand, the embodiment
of merciless fate. Yet, says a critic of former days,
speaking of the elder Booth's impersonation, "Shy-

lock's more special personality, — if we may so express it, — his hatred of Antonio, not simply 'for
he is a Christian,' but because he has hindered him
in his usurious practices, was not merged and lost
in his representation of the character. Booth kept
the two distinct, skilfully using the former in order to throw out in darker background the shad-
owy presence of the latter. Finally, in keeping
with this rendering of the part is the exit of Shylock from the machinery of the piece on the termi-
nation of the fourth act. The lighter and more
graceful work of the play goes on; but Shylock
withdraws, and with him this grand, gloomy, cruel
past which he represents, while the light-hearted,
forgiving, and forgiven children of the day bring
all their wishes to happy consummation."

Edwin Booth would tell the story of his father
passing hour after hour in learned discussion in
the vernacular with a scholarly Israelite of Baltimore, contending on Hebrew history, and particularly maintaining that he himself was of Hebraic
connection, since the Welsh, from whom he was
descended, were of Jewish origin.

Once the peculiar eccentricity of Junius Brutus
Booth broke out during a production of "The Merchant." It was in Philadelphia in 1851. The actor

was seen about the green-room very early that evening, but when the curtain was to be rung up he
was nowhere in sight. What should be done?
Had he run away, — after the manner of some of
his odd doings, — or had he fallen through a trap?

The question was hastily discussed; and, as the
audience was getting impatient, it was decided best
to start the play, and trust to finding Shylock
before the time of his entrance. Meanwhile, the
theatre was searched, and messengers were hurried
to the hotels and the neighboring bar-rooms. No
Shylock to be found.

The time had almost come for the Jew's appearance, and Mr. Frederick, the stage-manager, in despair made ready to go upon the stage and inform
the audience of Mr. Booth's "unprincipled conduct," when suddenly a door in a little dark scene-
closet opened, and Booth, calm and stolid, quietly
walked out, gently pushed aside the stage-manager,
and, proceeding upon the scene, delivered his lines
in magnificent manner. Whether, as his daughter
always maintained, Booth had been nervous over
his appearance that night, and had retired to this
queer spot in order to be absolutely undisturbed,
or whether it was the freak of a great mind to
madness closely allied, no one can tell.

It was about a year after this that an interesting production of the " Merchant of Venice " occurred in New York. On the 6th of September, 1852, at Castle Garden, a centennial performance was given " in commemoration of the introduction of the drama in America, at Williamsburg, Va., in 1752." Charles W. Couldock acted Shylock : Mr. Burton, Launcelot; and Mrs. Vickery, Portia. With the Shakespearian comedy was given also the same Garrick farce, " Lethe," played by the Hallam Company a hundred years before.

James W. Wallack was a notable Shylock, and in that *rôle* had the distinction of acting at his own New York theatre thirty-three successive nights, beginning Dec. 9, 1858, thus assisting in the longest run up to that date ever enjoyed by a Shakespearian play. His Portia during the run was the talented Mrs. Hoey : Bassanio was Lester Wallack. The close of the run, Jan. 9, 1859, marked the last performance of the Jew that Wallack ever gave, while it preceded by only four months his retirement from the stage. The latter event occurred on the 14th of May, when the veteran actor played Benedick in " Much Ado about Nothing."

Edwin Forrest for a time acted Shylock, but soon dropped it from his *répertoire*. George Vandenhoff, Gustavus V. Brooke, who, like Kean, made the character an exalted avenger of his race ; E. L. Davenport, less impetuous than Kean, but with impersonation more highly colored than Young ; Lawrence Barrett and Bogumil Dawison, have appeared with success as Shylock: but none of these equalled Edwin Booth in that character.

It was as Shylock that Mr. Booth made his first London appearance, in the autumn of 1861, at the Haymarket Theatre, and under very unfavorable circumstances. The celebrated Buckstone was the manager, and the preparation for that event reflects but slight credit upon British kindness or courtesy in management or criticism. No pains seem to have been taken to secure even a respectable introduction of Mr. Booth to London audiences.

The American himself, justly annoyed at his poor surroundings, acted with indifference, while the English supporting company, with some few exceptions, were supercilious and offensive to the visitor. In fact, Mr. Booth's sister asserted that on that fateful night every one on the stage, in the expectation of a storm of hisses for Shylock, was more nervous and frightened than the untried actor himself. His Shylock was coldly received.

His later success as Richelieu, during this same engagement, brought a tardy tribute from actors, press, and public.

Mr. Booth made an elaborate American presentation of the "Merchant of Venice" at the Winter Garden Theatre, New York, on Jan. 28, 1867, and the play ran seven weeks. The Winter Garden was then under Mr. Booth's sole management. In later years another notable revival of the play brought Lawrence Barrett as Bassanio, and Mr. Booth as the Jew, before the public as united stars.

One interesting if not remarkably pleasant experience Mr. Barrett and Mr. Booth had with the "Merchant of Venice" at the very beginning of their combined career in the fall of 1887. They had contracted to open with the tragedy a new opera-house at Kansas City, and therefore were promptly on hand on the desired night. But what a sight met their eyes! The management, in spite of all efforts, had not been able to keep the contractors up to the agreed time; and as a result the theatre was entirely destitute of roof, and was rough and cluttered from top to bottom. But the tickets had been sold, the actors were there, and the managers desired the performance to go on. One scene had to answer for the entire

LAWRENCE BARRETT.

play; fortunately that scenery was boxed in, so
that it partly protected them from the cold. The
spectators wore their hats and coats, and the actors
willingly sought refuge inside their ulsters when-
ever they could escape from behind the footlights.
One bit of realism was probably never before carried out in any modern theatre; for the night scene
the actual moon lighted up the stage.

Mr. Booth's Shylock reached its height in the
trial scene, in the contrast of the hard, rapacious
Jew in his seeming triumph (illustrated by Mr.
Booth through the glittering eye and crouching form
that marked his advance with the knife upon Antonio) with the opposite phase of portrayal, the
broken, wrecked old man who staggers away from
the room defeated on every point. But in the
quieter parts of the play Mr. Booth was equally
great, though less noted by the careless observer,
and in instances such as that wherein he ponder-
ingly intrusted the keys to Jessica, displayed fully
the thoroughness and finish of his impersonation.

If ever there was a character that came hard to
Booth it must have been Shylock, judging by the
actor's letters to Mr. Furness, when he was assisting that eminent Shakespearian scholar with
practical suggestions. "Shylock haunts me like a

nightmare," he wrote one day. "I can't mount the animal — for such I consider Shylock to be. I made an effort to get at him through G. F. Cooke's notes on his own acting of the part, and was surprised to see how he was influenced by tradition. He acknowledged having followed Macklin in much that he was praised for in this part."

A few months later, in a humorous vein, Booth wrote to the same correspondent about the character, which he had once called so "earthy" that he could feel no inspiration in the atmosphere of the play. "My dear Furness — Hold on! The Jew came to me last evening just as I was leaving Pittsburg, and stayed with me all night on the sleeping-car, whence sleep was banished; and I think I've got him by the beard or nose, I know not which, but I'll hang on to him for a while, and see what he'll do for me. I'll have his pound of flesh if I can get it off his old bones."

When Lawrence Barrett played Shylock he gave a justification — the Jew's own justification — of the brutality of the coveted penalty. He acted the part with dignity, while at the same time he filled it with intensity. As for his appearance in the *rôle*, no better portrait can be given than that of a playgoer of 1886, who pictured the imper-

sonator as "tall, moving with slow strength across
the boards in front of the scene that does duty for
the Rialto, standing in a quietude almost statu-
esque in its pose, robed in his black Jewish gaber-
dine, bordered with red, and marked with a red
cross on the elbow, a black and yellow cap on his
gray, bent head, his richly jewelled hands betray-
ing the nervous eagerness of his nature as they
clutch and twine upon his long knotted staff, with
a withdrawn look of his strong-featured face, and
a reserved intelligence dwelling in his eyes."

Richard Mansfield has essayed Shylock, as well
as Richard III.; but as yet the chief fame of this
actor rests with his vivid character sketches in
" The Parisian Romance " and " Dr. Jekyll and Mr.
Hyde."

CORIOLANUS.

ONE night Edwin Booth and his father were sitting before the bright open fire, enjoying the play of "Coriolanus." The elder Booth was reading the book; the younger, then a mere lad, was listening with undisguised pleasure. On went the glorious recitation until the little clock on the mantel had struck the small hours of the morning. No sooner were the last words of the text reached, than Junius Brutus Booth launched forth into a noble tribute to the marvellous acting of his former rival, Edmund Kean, giving to his eager son, for the first and only time in his life, reminiscences of the struggling days in England.

"Father," cried Edwin, as the elder player finally ceased his grand description of the acting of Coriolanus, "why don't you take that character?"

"I?" replied the veteran. "Nonsense! 'T would seem absurd for one of my inches to utter such boastful speeches. I cannot look Coriolanus."

This, then, was the reason the elder Booth, hero of so many of Shakespeare's plays, never attempted the *rôle* of the haughty Roman. And yet, as Edwin Booth has declared, his low stature militated not in Brutus, when from the very force of his curse of Tarquin, the patriot seemed to tower ten feet high, while his pathos in the part moved even the stage supernumeraries, who played the mob, to genuine tears and sobs.

In America, Booth would have found few comparisons possible. In fact, up to the beginning of the present century but two impersonators of Coriolanus are known to have appeared. The first was John P. Moreton, of the Philadelphia Company.

Moreton's real name was Pollard; but financial troubles in India, where he appears to have indiscreetly loaned funds from the bank of Calcutta, in which he was employed, drove him back to England in disgrace, and presumably led him to cancel his real name when the actor's profession was opened before his eyes. He was an American by birth, it is said, his father having served in the British army in the colonies. Moreton's progress was rapid here; for quickly he rose even to the character of Hamlet, and before many years could demand thirty dollars a night for his special performances.

In the cast of that Philadelphia production of "Coriolanus," on June 3, 1796, the Volumnia was the amiable Mrs. Whitlock, the youngest sister of the great Mrs. Siddons of the English stage.

As the last year of the eighteenth century was turning its meridian, a second Caius Marcius strode upon the mimic field of battle. This was Cooper, the wealthy but prodigal Thomas Abthorpe Cooper, who by his performance at the Park Theatre, on the 3d of June, 1799, may stand recorded in history as the first Coriolanus of the New York stage.

A young actor then, just passing his twenty-third summer, and with a stage experience of less than seven years, Cooper yet could show the strength that was in him in a far different manner from that fateful day in 1792, when, making his *début* in the character of Malcolm in "Macbeth," he broke down so completely that Stephen Kemble, the manager, bade him take his salary and leave the theatre. But the plucky youth would not leave the stage. In 1796 he came to America, and here became a leader, playing in triumph through the chief cities, and earning a fortune of two hundred thousand dollars. His money, however, disappeared under his extravagant living and reckless improvidence.

As illustrative of the latter characteristic a story may be told.

One day while talking with a friend on Broadway, New York, the tragedian noticed a load of hay approaching. "I will bet you the value of my benefit to-night," exclaimed Cooper, on the spur of the moment, "that I will pull the longest wisp of hay out of that load."

"Done," cried his jovial friend. "I'll bet a like amount."

They pulled, and Cooper lost. "Oh," he exclaimed, in the most careless manner conceivable, "there's two hours of acting lost." But those two hours meant the receipt of twelve hundred dollars.

That he must have made a noble Coriolanus may be surmised when we read the poetic description of his personality, as written by Samuel Woodworth : —

> "For when in life's bright noon the stage he trod,
>   In majesty and grace a demi-god,
>   With form, and mien, and attitude, and air,
>   Which modern kings might envy in despair ;
>   When his stern brow and awe-inspiring eye
>   Bore sign of an imperial majesty ;

THOMAS ABTHORPE COOPER.

> Then — in the zenith of his glory — then
> He moved, a model for the first of men.
> The drama was his empire : and his throne
> No rival dared dispute — he reigned alone ! "

And yet this man of noble mien and majestic look could play odd tricks of ungentlemanly eccentricity. Joe Cowell, the comedian, was sitting on the sofa in the green-room one night, waiting for the tragedy to end so that he might go on in the farce. The mirror being directly over Cowell, when Cooper came forward to adjust his toga, the brother player moved aside his head to give the great actor a chance to use the looking-glass, but did not move his person. Thereupon the dignified stage Roman, in the most undignified manner, put his own head a few inches in front of Cowell's face, and stared contemptuously at him.

Cowell was more than his match. He returned the stare, and at the same time emphatically uttered the one contemptuous word, " Booh ! "

There was a roar of laughter in the green-room ; and Cooper, astonished at the temerity of the clown, left the place. A few days later, however, he practically apologized to Cowell, and thereafter accepted him as an intimate associate.

One of the strangest whims of this famous actor

was disclosed in later conversation with his new-
made friend. Cooper was boasting that his children never cried. He stopped that habit, he said,
in the following unique way : " When my children
were young, and began to cry, I always dashed a
glass of water in their faces, and that so astonished them that they would leave off ; and if they
began again I'd dash another, and keep on increasing the dose until they were entirely cured."

To one of those same children came the distinction of being the daughter-in-law of a President.
Miss Priscilla Cooper, born of the tragedian's second wife (the daughter of the famous wit, Major
James Fairlee, and grand-daughter of Chief Justice
Robert Yates), married Robert Tyler, a son of
President Tyler, and for a time, while the President was a widower, presided at the White House.
It was through her influence, moreover, that her
father in his later years, after his fortune had been
dissipated, secured a government appointment at
the Arsenal near Philadelphia, and later another
appointment in the New York Custom House.

A pretty story is told of their first appearance
together ; for Miss Priscilla had taken to the
stage in her girlhood, in order to assist her im-
poverished father. It was in 1834, on the occa-

sion of her first appearance, and of her father's benefit in New York. As Cooper, in the *rôle* of Virginius, bade them send to him his daughter Virginia, and the girl came tripping in, exclaiming, in the appropriate words of the text, "Well, father, what's your will?" the whole audience burst into a prolonged round of cheers and applause, so cordial and so enthusiastic as to move both the father and daughter to tears. Fifteen years later Cooper died in the arms of Priscilla.

Blessed with a splendid voice in tone and compass, with wonderfully expressive eyes and a fine figure, with the power to make "his form in anger that of a demon, his smile in affability that of an angel," Cooper yet lacked the judgment in understanding and interpreting Shakespeare necessary to place him in the front rank of all the impersonators of the Bard's characters.

With Cooper, in that first New York production of "Coriolanus," there appeared as Volumnia an actress of towering stature and tragic skill, Mrs. Giles Leonard Barrett. In England, as Mrs. Rivers, she had been a pupil of Macklin, and one of the scores of Portias to his famous Shylock. Two years before this "Coriolanus" performance, she had made her American *début*, with her husband.

And now an actor of longer record on the English stage tempts the favor of Americans. He is John Vandenhoff, the father of George Vandenhoff. His Coriolanus, on the night of Sept. 11, 1837, at the National Theatre in New York, marking his *début* there, had as support Mrs. Flynn in the *rôle* of Volumnia, and Henry Wallack in the part of Tullus Aufidius.

Westland Marston had seen the actor in London, and there declared that as Coriolanus he displayed great dignity, a powerful and melodious voice, and a finished and impressive skill in acting, due to careful preparation. He was never great, however. Strange to say, this impersonator of the Roman hero was, in his own person, mortally afraid of a cat. He could not bear a feline near him. One day, in fact, at the house of a friend, when the innocent pet of the household chanced to enter the room with its customary friendly "meow," the tragedian gave forth a shriek that startled not only his friends, but drove the innocent kitten in a rush of terror out of the room.

Vandenhoff had been originally intended for the priesthood. He visited America twice before his retirement in 1858. Three years later (October, 1861) he died, at the age of seventy-one, follow-

ing, by one year, his daughter, the original Par-
thenia in "Ingomar."

A contemporary of Vandenhoff, James R. Anderson, made his first appearance as Coriolanus in
America at the Park Theatre, New York, April 14,
1845, with Miss Clara Ellis as Volumnia. Anderson was then twenty-six years of age, and in Macready's company in England had the honor of being
the Chevalier de Mauprat in the original production of Lord Lytton's "Richelieu." His several
visits to America made his name well known here;
but, like the elder Vandenhoff, he continued to the
end an English actor.

The American players are now in the green-room.
Let us marshal forth their Coriolanuses. First,
there steps forward a muscular, heroically moulded
figure, with strikingly robust face, a man who might
have stood as a model for Hercules in form, and
whose face could well depict the Roman. It is
Edwin Forrest, the idol for many years of the
theatre-going public.

Recall the story told of him in former years,
if you desire a good illustration of the physical
characteristics of the man. He was playing then a
Roman general, and, according to the directions of
the play-book, was to be attacked by six minions

of the enemy. At rehearsal Mr. Forrest was dis-
satisfied. The supernumeraries fought too tamely.
They did not make the scene sufficiently realistic.

With good round oaths he bade them fight,
fight, fight! and not dodge back and forward
as if engaging in a child's game. The supers at
first sulked over his hot words, and then they
formed a plot among themselves. At the performance that night it developed. They were going
to make a genuinely hot fight, a rough and tumble
that their traducer would remember. To his astonishment they leaped upon him in the fiercest manner, raining blow after blow against his head.

For just one instant Forrest fell back astounded.
Then, as he realized the situation, his breast ex-
panded in indignation, his brow grew dark in
cloudy rage, and with a half-suppressed oath he
leaped into the midst of the crowd, struck out
with his powerful arm now to the right, now to
the left, and in a trice had vanquished the enemy
completely, leaving one super sticking fast in the
bass-drum in the orchestra, whither he had been
knocked by a powerful blow, four of the rest dressing their wounds in the green-room, and the sixth,
terrified out of his senses, rushing from the theatre,
yelling "Fire" at the top of his voice.

The audience applauded to the echo. They had never seen Forrest "act so splendidly," they declared one to the other.

It must have been with somewhat of that same enthusiasm that the audience cheered the actor when he played Coriolanus at the notable engagement in the Broadway Theatre, New York, a number of years after his first appearance in the part. The interpretation was so admirable that the spectators lost sight of the actor, and saw only the heroic soldier. "The crowning triumph," declared one of those present that night, "came in the closing scenes of the third act, when the banishment of Coriolanus is announced by Brutus, amid the huzzas of the populace. The stage of the Broadway Theatre had even more than the usual gradual elevation as it receded from the footlights. In the position where Forrest stood he seemed to have acquired additional height, as with flashing eyes and dilated form he rushed towards the retreating rabble, and thundered out his concentrated scorn in the exclamation, 'I banish you!'"

When Forrest acted the title *rôle* of the tragedy at Niblo's Garden, in November, 1863, with Mme. Ponisi as Volumnia, the Cominius of the production was a young player destined some years later

to assume in his turn the chief character, — John
McCullough. The Irish-born lad, totally ignorant
of art and literature, and with not even the ability
to write, though he could read a little, had immi-
grated to America at the age of fifteen. Working
in a chairmaker's shop, he chanced to meet a
"stage-struck" fellow-workman; and being thus led
to an acquaintance with the theatre, eagerly and
devotedly studied for the stage. In 1857 he made
his *début*, and for twenty-seven years continued an
actor; then his mind gave way, and he was retired
to an insane asylum until death speedily ended his
misery.

In 1861 Forrest had become interested in the
youth, and before long had made him the leading
man in his company. Next came McCullough's
starring tour, when Virginius, Brutus, and Spar-
tacus, as well as Othello, Richard III., Lear, and
Coriolanus, won him fame and wealth. Kind, generous, and high-minded in his ambition, McCullough was regarded as a warm friend by hundreds,
while thousands pitied the sad ending of what had
seemed a rugged, sturdy life.

The best words that can be said of his Coriolanus are those of his warm friend and admirer,
William Winter. Mr. Winter pronounced McCul-

JOHN McCULLOUGH.

lough's impersonation equal to that of Forrest in physical majesty, while it was superior in intellectual haughtiness and in refinement. The actor's declamation was as fluent as his demeanor was massively graceful. He looked Coriolanus to the life. "The stormy utterance of revolted pride and furious disgust, in the denial of Volumnia's request," said Winter, "the tempestuous outburst, 'I will not do it!' made as wild, fiery, and fine a movement in tragic acting as could be imagined; but the climax was reached in the pathetic cry, 'The gods look down, and this unnatural scene they laugh at.'"

Meanwhile, England's great Coriolanus had long since passed away. There had been but one actor on the British stage to identify himself with the *rôle*, and that was John Philip Kemble, the most stately, dignified player of the last century. To be sure, his Coriolanus was not sufficiently barbaric to satisfy Leigh Hunt, since by the substitution of a polished patrician manner he failed to meet that critic's ideal of the rough soldier of primitive Rome; but yet its tremendous force and grandeur were irresistible.

It was strange Kemble could not break away entirely from the ruthless adapters of Shakespeare, and present this tragedy from the original version; but though he gave more of the master's lines than had his predecessor, Sheridan, yet still he could omit passages of such excellence as that beginning, "His nature is too noble for the world," and could adopt many phrases from Thomson.

It was in 1749, forty years before Kemble's Coriolanus, that Thomson's version had been brought out at Covent Garden, with gay Peg Woffington painting her pretty face into wrinkles, in order to portray faithfully the character of Volumnia.

The poor poet had died suddenly, before this last work of his had ever been performed; and so his friend, kind-hearted old Quin, the veteran actor, arranged to bring out the declamatory tragedy for the benefit of the author's destitute family, and, free of charge, to play the hero's *rôle*. Lord Lyttelton, too, was interested in Thomson's family; and so, to help the production, wrote an epilogue for Mrs. Woffington, in her own person, to speak, its lines running in this vein : —

> "If an Old Mother had such pow'rful charms
> To stop a stubborn Roman's conq'ring arms;
> If with my grave discourse and wrinkled face
> I thus could bring a hero to disgrace,
> How absolutely may I hope to reign
> Now I am turned to my own shape again."

JAMES QUIN AS CORIOLANUS (In Act V., Scene 3).

It may be unjust to have a bit of fun over generous Quin in Coriolanus; but as the audience laughed merrily one hundred and fifty years ago, we of to-day may be forgiven. The roar went up when Quin, who had acquired the affectation of pronouncing the "a" long in fasces, bade the soldiers lower their fāsces, and they literally obeyed, until their faces even touched their bows.

Quin's costume to-day would bring a smile. Topping his long flowing-haired wig was a cap with upright plumes at least two feet in height, while beneath his elaborately decorated tunic was a short, stiffened skirt, that stood out much the same as does a ballet-dancer's of to-day. Skin-tight breeches and buskins completed the attire.

Two adaptations had preceded Thomson's: that wretched affair of 1682, by Nahum Tate, brought out under the title "Ingratitude of a Commonwealth; or, The Fall of Caius Marcius Coriolanus;" and the failure of 1719 by John Dennis, the good critic and the bad playwright, brought out under the title of "The Invader of his Country; or, The Fatal Resentment," and acted for three nights only, with Booth as Coriolanus, and Mrs. Porter as Volumnia.

But never did a combination equal that of John

Kemble and his sister, Mrs. Siddons. The actress, indeed, won even higher praises than did the actor.

Charles Young, the experienced Shakespearian interpreter, sat in the audience on the 7th of February, 1789, and actually wept when the Siddons wept, and smiled when she smiled. He told of the scene afterwards. " Ah," said he, " in that triumphal entry of her son Coriolanus, her dumb show drew plaudits that shook the building. She came along marching and beating time to the music, rolling (if that be not too strong a term to describe her motion) from side to side, swelling with the triumph of her son. Such was the intoxication of joy which flashed from her eyes, and lit up her whole face, that the effect was irresistible. She seemed to me to reap all the glory of that procession to herself. I could not take my eyes from her. Coriolanus, banner, and pageant, — all went for nothing to me after she had walked to her place."

As for the noble Coriolanus, eight and twenty years later he was playing the *rôle* with all the strength and glory of his early years, with no abatement of spirit and energy, as Hazlitt said, and none of grace and dignity. This was his farewell of the stage.

It was a Monday night, the 23d of June, 1817, and the house was crowded. Applause showered upon him constantly. When, after the last act, he approached the footlights to make his formal address, a shout, as from one mighty voice, filled the theatre, "No,— no farewell."

But it had to be. Infirmities were pressing upon the actor, now in his sixtieth year; and, though he knew it not, he was then within a few years of his last scene upon earth.

The actors crowded around him in the green-room after the curtain fell, saw Talma's wreath of laurel presented to the great English player, and then, in their turn, begged for memorials. He gave to each a trinket of some sort, — something that he had worn upon that very stage, and, finally, to Mathews presented his sandals. "Yes," cried the comedian, "I have John Kemble's sandals. I never could tread in his shoes, but in these, at least, I can step."

It is said that even to the last the force of "Black Jack's" acting was such, that when Coriolanus in haughty pride dashed against the mob, the crowd involuntarily fell back, without the aid of assumed acting, driven by the very impetuousness of his mighty power.

Even upon John Howard Payne, whose " Home,
Sweet Home " was to make his name immortal, this
allusion of reality was forced. Payne was in London in 1817, and, writing to a friend in America,
thus described the Englishman in the tragedy : —

" I can never forget Kemble's Coriolanus; his *entrée* was
the most brilliant I ever witnessed. His person derived a
majesty from a scarlet robe which he managed with inim-
itable dignity. The Roman energy of his deportment, the
seraphic grace of his gesture, and the movements of his
perfect self-possession, displayed the great mind, daring to
command, and disdaining to solicit admiration. His form
derived an additional elevation of perhaps two inches from
his sandals. In every part of the house the audience rose,
waved their hats, and huzzaed ; and the cheering must have
lasted more than five minutes."

And yet this proud actor was not without his
enjoyment of humor. During one of his favorite
impersonations — it might possibly have been Coriolanus, for that was dear to him — a child in
the audience began to cry, and, uncontrolled by its
mother, kept up the bellowing for an annoying
length of time. At last Kemble could stand it
no longer. He came to the front, and with significant emphasis, but yet with a smile on his lips,
said, " Ladies and gentlemen, unless the play is
stopped the child cannot go on with comfort."

The play was not stopped, — but the child went out.

This humorous turn was akin to the witty manner in which the actor retorted to Shaw, the musical director who was attending to the rehearsal of " Cœur de Lion." " Mr. Kemble," cried the irritated leader, after the player with his bad singing voice had ineffectually attempted the song set down to his part, " you are murdering the time ! "

" That may be," promptly replied the actor ; " but it's better to murder time outright than to be forever beating it, as you are ! "

Even better was the quotation at the toll-gate, when, returning with a friend from dinner, he tossed a coin to the old toll-keeper, and, waving away his proffer of the amount to be returned, cried out to his friend in exactly the tone, as well as the words, of Rolla, " We seek no *change ;* and least of all such *change* as he would bring us."

And this was the sedate and precise chieftain of the solemn, declamatory school of the eighteenth century, " the noblest Roman of them all," as some one declared when praising his grand assumption of characters like Shakespeare's haughty Caius Marcius.

Born forty years before the first Coriolanus ap-

peared on the American stage, this English hero
of the tragedy had passed through a hard novitiate
before reaching the highest degree. The son of
an itinerant player, he was destined by his father
for the priesthood, and to that end was sent to
a Roman Catholic seminary. There he displayed
one admirable characteristic for theatrical work by
committing to memory fifteen hundred lines of
Homer. — learning this number in order to remove
by himself the entire task placed upon his class for
a general indiscretion. This remarkable memory
stood by him all through life; in fact, one night
he was willing to bet that after four days' study
he could repeat every line in any newspaper, ad-
vertisements and all, in regular order, and without
missing or misplacing a single word.

In 1776 he gained his desired foothold on the
stage, and seven years later, at the age of twenty-
six, made his London *début*, playing Hamlet. Although very ambitious and earnest, he yet progressed more slowly than his sister, the great Mrs.
Siddons, but finally won eminence both as actor
and as manager. In the latter *rôle* he lost his
theatre, Covent Garden, by the fire of Sept. 20,
1808; but while all others were dismayed and dis-
heartened, he boldly looked forward to a phœnix-

like rising. Through the generosity of the Duke of Northumberland it came; that nobleman, unsolicited, giving ten thousand pounds toward the new house.

The prices for playgoers were raised, on account of the expense; and, as a result, came the famous O. P. (or Old Price) riot, that lasted for sixty-six nights, and nearly resulted in the mobbing of Kemble's family.

As he now neared the end of his career, no actor could be found to challenge comparison, until, in 1814, Edmund Kean dashed upon the stage, and with his fiery enthusiasm overthrew all the idols of the stately Kemble school.

But hot-blooded Kean, as Coriolanus, could not present the requisite repose for the hero, and therefore never equalled Kemble there. Moreover, he lacked the physical size and the bearing. Yet Doran said none but a great actor could have played the scene of the candidateship and that of the death as Kean did; though in these very scenes it was admitted that he really deserted his own school, and followed the Kemble ideals.

Macready was but twenty-seven years of age when he attempted the character of the Roman, and yet in the *rôle* was well received. Barry Cornwall paid him a poetic tribute that declared: —

"And he shall wear his victor's crown, and stand
    Distinct amidst the genius of the land."

In later years, when Macready was his own manager, he gave to "Coriolanus" a magnificent revival. The senate scene saw nearly two hundred
white-robed Roman fathers on the stage, with the
Consul seated in state before the brazen wolf and
its human sucklings, and behind, the sacred altar
with its blazing fire. The "Siege of Rome" was
pictured by a small army of finely equipped soldiers,
with moving towers and battering-rams.

But to an ill-judging friend of Macready, who
attempted to prove the actor superior to Kemble,
by arguing that it was a mistake to suppose Coriolanus "an abstraction of Roman-nosed grandeur,"
James Smith replied in an epigram that grew popular in a day: —

"What scenes of grandeur does this play disclose,
    Where all is Roman — save the Roman's nose!"

Phelps was held to be "too impetuous and ex-
citable for Coriolanus;" and no one in England
since his day has achieved fame in the part. In
fact, the British stage, as well as the American,
awaits a worthy successor to the giant Coriolanuses
of old.

MACBETH.

THE young Pepys had been to the play, and, of course, had to put down in writing in his private diary the sights he saw at the theatre. Listen, then, to his critique on "Macbeth," as given at the Duke's play-house in London on the 21st of December, 1668.

"The King and Court there,"—thus the prelude reads, with the personal line to follow,—"and we sat just under them and my Lady Castlemaine, and close to a woman that comes into the pit, a kind of loose gossip that pretends to be like her, and is so, something. And my wife, by my troth, appeared as pretty as any of them." Pepys always had an eye for beauty, and, in his own frank way, wrote just what he thought. "The King and Duke of York minded me," he continues, with a touch of his own simple vanity, "and smiled upon me, at the handsome woman near me. But it vexed

179

me to see Moll Davis, in the box over the King's and my Lady Castlemaine, look down upon the King, and he up to her; and so did my Lady Castlemaine once, to see who it was; but when she saw Moll Davis she looked like fire, which troubled me." No uncommon thing, this, for our good friend Pepys to be troubled over the actions of those about him: he kept his eyes open to find out all manner of disturbances.

But what said he of the play, "Macbeth"? Not a word. The people in the pit and the boxes, particularly the latter, were the things of interest to worthy Pepys, and presumably also to his wife.

And this, we may take it, was the case with many other play-goers of that day. They went to the play-house for fondness of the fashion more than for love of Shakespeare. To be sure, Pepys has very calmly told us, in writing of "Macbeth" at a previous performance, that it was a "pretty good play," but his adjectives never ran any stronger.

What would the wide-eyed gossip have said could he have seen other more interesting sights in the auditorium when "Macbeth," in later years, lived and died behind the candles? One king, in 1668, was enough to distract Pepys's mind from the stage; what would he have done with four kings to watch? They were American kings, aboriginal chiefs, brought over to London, and entertained at the theatre by the actor Bowen, who shrewdly saw how great a card they would be, as spectators, on his benefit night of "Macbeth." In fact, they were so big a card that the gallery gods would not rest content at the noble red-men remaining quietly in their box, but raised such an uproar that there was nearly a riot, until the Indians were induced solemnly to march down and gravely seat themselves in four chairs on the stage, there to look upon the murder of Banquo, and the misery of Macbeth.

More exciting was the act played by the audience in the year 1721, when hot-tempered Quin and his associates were performing the play of ambition to the best of their ability. In those days it was easy for a play-goer to obtain admission behind the scenes; and, on the night in question, one drunken earl had the effrontery to stroll across the stage, from one wing to the other, while the players were carrying out their *rôles*. Naturally the manager, Rich, remonstrated. The reply was a stinging slap on the cheek.

"What!" cried the insulted play-man, "must I

stand this?" His action on the instant gave the
answer, for the cheek of the noble earl burned
with the sharpness of the returning blow.

With the insult both drew their swords. A half-
dozen gallants rushed to the side of the "gentleman," and, with weapons pointed at the daring
Rich, plunged forward to end his life. But Quin,
Walker, Ryan, and the other actors were there
too. They scented the coming battle, and, seizing
weapons, bore down upon the array of nobles before them.

Helter-skelter the gilt-laced, perfumed beaux fled
out to the street, and then, after the enemy had
retired, boldly burst into the unprotected front of
the house, and proceeded to cut and slash the furni-
ture and curtains of the auditorium. Undismayed,
the actors too resumed the battle, until, with the
aid of the city watch, they captured the rioters,
and forced them to trial. It was this scene that
led to the placing of a guard of soldiers thereafter
in the theatre, a custom which held in England
until the early part of the present century.

But all this was years after the first production
of the tragedy, when Richard Burbage, greatest
actor of his day, created the title *rôle*. Of his
acting we may judge by the elegy of 1618: —

"Tyrant Macbeth, with unwashed, bloody hand,
We vainly now may hope to understand."

After this Macbeth of 1606, no others appear
until Pepys's day. From the year 1672, for some
threescore years and ten, we lose sight of the
original Shakespearian version in the mangled adaptation of Sir William Davenant. The first Macbeth of the Davenant version was Betterton. At
Dorset Garden Theatre, managed by the widow of
Sir William, by Betterton and by Joseph Harris
(the Macduff of the cast) the tragedy was brought
out, with its blank verse turned, for the most part,
into the cheap rhymes then so much in favor with
the wits, and with a dance of furies and an oper-
atic accompaniment to give variety. The Lady
Macbeth was grandly performed by Mrs. Betterton, while, most curious of all, Banquo in life fell
to the lot of handsome, well-formed Smith, with
Banquo's Ghost acted by the homeliest man in
the troupe, the deformed impersonator of villains,
"round-shouldered, meagre-faced, spindle-shanked,
splay-footed Sandford," as Anthony Aston pictured
him, "the best villain in the world."

And here we may say that the two murderers
met with the disapproval of England's king, who,
being himself swarthy of complexion, took to heart

the constant making-up of stage villains with dark countenances. " Forsooth!" quoth His Majesty, " what is the meaning that we never see a rogue in a play, but, odsfish! they always clap on him a black periwig, when it is well known that one of the greatest rogues in England always wears a fair one?" — a delicate allusion to the Earl of Shaftesbury.

Of Betterton's Macbeth we know little, except that it was admirable. Of one of the performances of the tragedy in his time we have an interesting anecdote, noting the origin of a slang phrase that has lasted even to this day. In the pit that night sat John Dennis, the author of a tragedy to which, though Betterton had played the leading *rôle*, no praise could be awarded save for a piece of clap-trap, the invention of a new method of making stage thunder. In " Macbeth " Dennis heard his " thunder " repeated; and, rising in indignation, he cried out in a loud voice, " See how those rascals use me; they won't let my play run, but *they steal my thunder!*"

The fine-looking but mediocre-acting John Mills tried the leading *rôle;* and then there came to the front a long line of players, of whom a condensed criticism is best given in the somewhat harsh, but

yet aptly descriptive, verse of a satirist of their
day, — an anti-Macklinite during the Macklin controversy, which we shall note later. Thus the lines
run : —

> " Old Quin, ere fate suppressed his lab'ring breath,
> In studied accents grumbled out ' Macbeth.'
> Next Garrick came, whose utterance truth impressed,
> While every look the tyrant's guilt confessed.
> Then the cold Sheridan half froze the part,
> Yet what he lost by nature saved by art.
> Tall Barry now advanced toward Birnam Wood,
> Nor ill performed the scenes — he understood.
> Grave Mossop next to *Forres* shaped his march,
> His words were minute guns, his actions starch.
> Rough Holland, too, — but pass his errors o'er,
> Nor blame the actor when the man's no more.
> Then heavy Ross essayed the tragic frown,
> But beef and pudding kept all meaning down.
> Next careless Smith tried on the murderer's mask,
> While o'er his tongue light tripped the hurried task.
> Hard Macklin late guilt's feelings strove to speak,
> While sweats infernal drenched his iron cheek.
> Like Fielding's kings, his fancied triumph's past,
> And all he boasts is that he fails the last. "

Cast a look now upon the first of these rhyme-
imprisoned heroes, doughty old James Quin, who
first played Macbeth in 1719, and kept the *rôle* in
his *répertoire* for a generation. He is " cumber-
some," the critics of his day say, as they watch
Quin's Macbeth; his sole merit in tragedy consists

in his declamation and show of brutal pride.   A
sturdy-looking Macbeth he made, indeed, but a
Macbeth destitute of animation or variety in utterance.   Moreover, the expression of mental agitation,
of the remorse, despair, or frenzy of the ambition-
wrecked prince, was beyond his ability.

The actor himself knew so little of the real play,
that he was astonished, in later years, to learn from
Garrick that the lines he uttered were not from
the original of Shakespeare, but the polluted verse
of Davenant.

And what say the critics of Garrick's Macbeth,
as he dashes upon the scene in the full court-
dress of the time of George II., — scarlet coat,
gold-laced waistcoat, powdered wig, and all?   They
say naught against the costume, for to them any
idea of appropriateness in dressing is as foreign
as crinolines to an Eskimo.   They say much in
praise of the acting ; for earnest, natural Davy
is a splendid impersonator of the haunted Thane.
With Mrs. Pritchard for the lady, he so captivated
Davies by the acting of the murder scene, that
the latter declared he could not adequately describe the impression the two made.

" Garrick's distraction of mind and agonizing
horror," he exclaimed, " were finely contrasted by

Mr. Garrick as Macbeth

DAVID GARRICK AS MACBETH (In Act II., Scene 2).

Pritchard's seeming apathy, tranquillity, and confidence. The beginning of the scene after the murder was conducted in terrifying whispers. Their looks and actions supplied the place of words. You heard of what they spoke, but you learned more from the agitation of mind displayed in their action and deportment. The poet here gives an outline of the consummate actor: ' I have done the deed! ' 'Didst thou not hear a noise?' 'When?' 'Did you not speak?' The dark coloring given by the actor to these abrupt speeches makes the scene awful and tremendous to the auditors. The wonderful expression of heartfelt horror which Garrick felt when he showed his bloody hands, can only be conceived and described by those who saw him."

The night Mrs. Pritchard took her farewell of the stage, April 24, 1768, after thirty-eight years of service, she played Lady Macbeth; that evening again Garrick played Macbeth, and never after essayed the *rôle*. This was twenty-one years from the season they had first played the characters together.

A propos of his costume, they say that Garrick was terrified at the suggestion of a change to Highland dress. "You forget," he said in a stage-whisper to the friend who mentioned the idea,

"you forget that the Pretender was here only
thirty years ago, and, egad! I should be pelted
off the stage with orange-peel."

With the same timidity the actor refused to venture "Macbeth" just as it was written by Shakespeare ; but though he thrust aside completely the
Davenant version, yet he persisted in making alterations in the original text, to better, as he thought,
the scenes. Thus Macbeth needs must have a
long and harrowing dying speech, to give Davy
a chance to exhibit his ability in delineating convulsive death-agonies.

Conceive, however, the grand power of an actor
who could hold a private gathering of talented men
and women, of another nationality than his own,
absolutely entranced with his acting. In Paris,
where our Roscius was visiting temporarily, he
astounded the critics. Wearing ordinary dress, in
a parlor, he acted out the dagger scene of "Macbeth," following with his eyes the course of the
air-drawn dagger with such intensity of emotion as
to cause the whole assembly to burst into a prolonged cry of admiration at the end. This was
what Grimm said.

As for impulsive Clairon, the famous French actress, so carried away was she by the little man's

impersonation in a pathetic recital accompanying his show of Macbeth, that she threw both arms around his neck, and imprinted two rapid kisses in succession on either cheek. "Pardon," she said to Mrs. Garrick, "I really could not help it."

Is it not strange, then, to know that a player who, with no appropriate costume at all, could so wonderfully impersonate a character, could also at another time neglect his character so much as to omit his by-play in a minor scene, in order to button more neatly his Macbeth coat, — a bit of vanity that gave a secondary actor a splendid chance to shine, in contrast, by faithful attention to duty.

Turn the lights now upon a Macbeth around whose first impersonations hung threats and riots, — rough, honest old Macklin. Old, indeed, since when he originally assumed the *rôle* of the ambitious Thane the actor had passed, by three years, the age-stone of threescore and ten. He had made a contract with Covent Garden Theatre, and, to the astonishment of the manager, insisted on showing, as a novelty, his Macbeth and Richard III., instead of presenting his familiar and accepted Shylock. Smith was the recognized representative of the former *rôles* at this time, and hence there came a conflict; finally a compromise was effected by which they should alternate the parts. When old Macklin, however, advanced to the front dressed as Macbeth, there was hissing, an emphatic sign of that opposition which in the public print had already shown its head.

One would have thought, indeed, that the novel costuming introduced by Macklin might arouse a party-feeling; for Garrick, with his court-dress and his officer's uniform, had established the "proper" garb of the Thane, while Macklin deliberately appeared, instead, in a Highland kilt. "An old Scotch piper stumping along at the head of his army," one man called him. Later on, as we see in the antique print, he changed his costume.

But this was not the point of antagonism. Enemies might swear that, while the old fellow acted well enough in the witch scene and the interview with Lady Macbeth, and carried out well the scene with the murderers and the bits of passionate rage and of mental depression, yet in all else he failed, making a lamentable exhibition in the dagger scene and at the banquet. But it was chiefly on personal antagonism to the man that the anti-Macklinites built their opposition.

On the first night, Oct. 23, 1773, they hissed the

CHARLES MACKLIN AS MACBETH (In Act II., Scene 3).

hero. On the fourth night, after growing signs of disapproval, they fairly drove him from the stage with their insults. How they did crowd the play-house on those tumultuous evenings, the Macklin friends and the Macklin enemies! " One hour I was squeezed to death at the door in Bow Street," wrote George Stevens to Garrick ; "another spent I in the pit, among half the blackguards about town; and for the space of three and a half more I was imprisoned to hear the lines of Shakespeare elaborately pumped up from the bottom of a well as deep as that in Dover Castle."

Stevens's characterization of the acting was per-haps only less suggestive than that of Arthur Mur-phy, who called Macklin's interpretation a " black-letter copy of Macbeth ;" while Cooke, the actor's biographer, admitted that it was a lecture rather than a theatrical representation. The critics were intensely sarcastic. One paper said that it under-stood Mr. Macklin was contemplating the *rôles* of Ranger "when he has learned to dance," and then Master Stephen, Tony Lumpkin, the Schoolboy. "and to conclude his theatrical life with playing the Fool ;" while another affirmed, with detailed explanation. that Macklin had mistaken Shake-speare's instructions, since as early as the first

scene of the second act he murdered Macbeth
instead of Duncan.

It was a hot fight, and some thought jealous
Garrick was behind it all. But Macklin accused
only Reddish, the capable actor of villains, and
Sparks, the son of an actor, both of whom, he said,
hissed his performance on the first night, and so
started the trouble. Hireling roughs were enlisted
by the friends of the two men, were filled with
drink at a neighboring town, and were further
stirred to action by the promise that "after the
work should be completed, and this old unknown
villain of the name of Macklin should be driven
to hell," they should be treated to a supper at
Bedford Arms. Then they were led into the play-
house. "The Merchant of Venice" had been substituted for "Macbeth," to stop the clamor; but
Shylock was a victim just as good for the rabble
as the Thane. An apple struck him full in the
face, and then the fight began.

"At the command of the public Mr. Macklin
is discharged." So read the black letters on the
big board the managers held up before the crowd,
— for the noise was too great to allow a word to
be heard, — thus acknowledging defeat, after the
battle had fiercely raged for some time.

The sturdy old player, however, had the happy faculty of never knowing when he was beaten. Though temporarily exiled from the theatre, he could seek the courts; and there he secured the conviction of his enemies for conspiracy and riot. But just at this point the play-actor — perhaps from generosity, perhaps for effect — stepped to the front, and in a touching and impressive speech declared he would stay all proceedings provided the defendants paid the costs of the suit, and purchased one hundred pounds worth of tickets to the benefits of his daughter, his manager, and himself. They agreed.

" Mr. Macklin," said the judge, Lord Mansfield, " you have met with great applause to-day. You never acted better."

And yet some of the players only a short time before had complained that the aged Irishman was growing prolix and tedious. He had kept the rehearsal dragging so long, with his instructions to the younger men, and with his own slow speech, that witty Ned Shuter, the eccentric but bright comedian of the day, had blurted out in a stage-aside to a friend, " The case is very hard; for the time has been that when the brains were out the man would die, and there an end."

Whereat quick-eared Macklin, old but yet nimble with the brain, responded, with a sly hit at Shuter's proclivities, " Yes, Ned ; and the time was that when liquor was in, wit was out, but it is not so with thee."

And good-natured Shuter honestly rejoined, " Now — now thou art a man again ! "

Holland also, when he played Macbeth in York, during a summer season, had an experience with a sharp tongued subordinate.

" There's blood upon thy face," whispered the Thane to the foremost Murderer, in the banquet scene, and then nearly fell over backward as the underling shouted at the top of his lungs, and in a most tragic style, " 'T is Banquo's, then ! "

" My dear sir," said Holland sarcastically, the moment the scene was over, " there's no need of uttering that speech *quite* so loud ; it isn't supposed to be a war alarum, you know."

At once the Murderer drew himself up to his full height, and in a most dignified, overwhelming tone replied, " Hark ye, Master Holland, *I* have a benefit to take in this town as well as *you*."

What could Holland say to this?

Pathetic was the association of Macbeth with the

tragedian Powell. Lying on his death-bed, with no one near except Hannah More, — for Mrs. Powell had just left the room, — his pale cheek was suddenly observed to flush with flitting color; and then, with staring eyes, he thrust himself up in bed, threw out his hands, and cried with all the expression of his best days, "Is this a dagger which I see before me?" The next instant he gasped. "O God!" he cried, and was dead.

It was in the second act that Ireland said of Henderson, "I think the countenance of horror and remorse he assumed was equal to anything I have ever seen."

When Thomas Sheridan played Macbeth, he wore, like Garrick, a scarlet and gold English uniform, varying it after the Thane became king by adding a Spanish hat, turned up in front, and bedecked with glittering diamonds and flowing plumes. John O'Keefe, who saw the father of Richard Brinsley Sheridan in this costume, also tells us concisely how oddly Digges — West Digges — carried out the combat scene. First, he would invariably thrust his hands into the bosom of his waistcoat, and throw it entirely open, "to show he was not papered — a previous defence which was thought unfair and treacherous;" then, tapping the side of his hat with his open right hand, he would draw his sword, and fight to the death.

Vain, arrogant and unlucky Harry Mossop had a trick also in his Macbeth, but one of more mechanical mould. He would arouse thunders of applause by the tremendous force he threw into the scene with the shrinking messenger when, rising to the height of unreasoning anger, he actually broke his heavy truncheon in two over the envoy's head — and then would laugh in his sleeve at the game, after the curtain had fallen, as he calmly picked up the two parts of the trick-truncheon, and fitted them lightly together, just as they originally had been fitted. But Mossop had considerable power of expression; and had he been easier in bearing, and gifted with more variety of action, might have won more praise. He was a most rigid man at rehearsals, and because one unlucky wight, the Seyton of the cast, persisted in missing his cue, fined the fellow a crown for every slip.

All these Macbeths, however, were forgotten when the great Lady Macbeth of the age, Mrs. Siddons, came upon the scene. Her story has been told in "Shakespeare's Heroines on the Stage." In this volume let her brother, John Kemble, advance to the front. Not at first was he able to do this;

for by the traditional rights of those days the leading *rôle* belonged to " Gentleman" Smith, the airy, genteel actor, the original Charles Surface, who even in his seventieth year could show a youthful alertness to put the real youngsters to shame, winning from the audience a hearty round of applause, as with agile step and graceful bend he caught and raised the fallen fan of a Lady Teazle before the other gentlemen on the scene could reach her side. This was the light Macbeth who first accompanied in London the heavy Lady Macbeth of Mrs. Siddons; this was the actor to whom, after his secret marriage with the sister of Lord Sandwich, quick-witted Jack Bannister exclaimed, with punning wit and prophetic truth, " Well, I'm glad you've got a Sandwich from the family, but if ever you get a dinner from them, hang me ! "

John Philip Kemble on his benefit night had a single opportunity to play Macbeth, and later, as manager, could cast himself regularly for the *rôle*. Yet, on account of his weak voice, he never won a favor equal to Garrick in the part. " His Macbeth has been known to nod," said Charles Lamb, commenting on the liability of the actor's flagging occasionally in the intervals of tragic passion.

But, for all that, who of us would not have

liked to see the performance of April 21, 1794, when, at the opening of new Drury Lane Theatre, John Kemble played Macbeth, his sister acted Lady Macbeth, and the younger brother, nineteen years of age, Charles Kemble, then, to be sure, ungraceful and awkward, but later to become the most graceful and refined of actors, made his London *début* as Malcolm?

More notable, because more exciting, was the night of Sept. 18, 1809, when a furious audience, angered at the increase of prices in Kemble's theatre, hissed, hooted, and stormed the players, while the latter tried to utter the lines of "Macbeth." The soldiers in the house, five hundred in number, placed there in anticipation of trouble, had all they could do to quell the disturbance without bloodshed. This was the first of seventy nights of riots, wherein Kemble was called "fellow" and "vagrant" by the angry people, and wherein hireling pugilists were engaged to break the heads of the noisy rioters — and, instead, found their own heads broken.

That evening when majestic Kemble for the last time acted the Thane, one of his successors, William Macready, then a young man, was present in the audience. It was the benefit night of Charles Kemble; and the famous sister of the two actors,

Mrs. Siddons, had been induced to reappear, after her formal retirement, for the performance. Talma, the great French player, was in the audience, while the number of people around him was so great as to force the orchestra out of the building, in order to secure extra room. But artistically the production was a disappointment. Mrs. Siddons was merely the shadow of the past. Kemble for four long acts was correct, but tame. Then suddenly he seemed to wake to energy.

"The Queen, my lord, is dead!" said Seyton.

Macbeth, to the spectators' eyes, seemed struck to the heart. Gradually collecting himself, he sighed, "She should have died hereafter;" and then, as with the inspiration of despair he hurried out, distinctly and pathetically, the lines beginning, —

> "To-morrow, and to-morrow, and to-morrow,
> Creeps in this petty pace from day to day,"

rising to a climax of desperation that brought enthusiastic cheers from the house.

It is thus Macready describes the sudden burst that seemed to show Kemble all at once carried away by the glorious strength of the scene. "At the tidings of 'the wood of Birnam moving,'" con-

tinues Macready, "he staggered as if the shock
had struck the very seat of life, and in the be-
wilderment of fear and rage, could just ejaculate
the words, 'Liar and slave!' then lashing himself
into a state of frantic rage, ended the scene in perfect triumph. His shrinking from Macduff, when
the charm on which his life hung was broken by
the declaration that his antagonist was 'not of
woman born,' was a masterly stroke of art; his
subsequent defiance was most heroic; and at his
death Charles Kemble received him in his arms,
and laid him gently on the ground, his physical
powers being unequal to further effort."

Several alterations were made in the play by
Kemble, notably the changing of "a bell rings"
in the second act to "the striking of a clock
twice," his reason lying in Lady Macbeth's exclamation in the sleep-walking scene, "One, two;
why, then, 't is time to do it." Realizing, also, his
own deficiency in harmonious elocution, compared
with Garrick, he reduced the invocation to the
witches to two lines. As for the dagger scene, in
that Boaden thought Kemble too explosive and
too much in action. The actor-manager tried to
abolish the ghost of Banquo from the stage, and
also the dance of the witches over their broom-

sticks (an innovation that had been introduced years before); but the public had grown accustomed to the earlier rendering, and demanded the restoration of both features.

One night there was a lively little episode noted by Kemble during the spectacular caldron scene, in which the " spirits " (otherwise boys) found themselves mischievously tripped up and pushed over by one of their number, a reckless little firebrand. Kemble took the street imp in hand, scolded him vigorously for the confusion he had wrought, and sent him off in disgrace. Years later this same boy was to drive the elder actor from his pedestal; it was Edmund Kean.

Yet, as Macbeth, Kean did not eclipse his predecessor, perhaps in part because he carried that same mercurial disposition and nervous agility of his youth into the character. Particularly did he fall behind Kemble in lacking the thoughtful melancholy which the elder player exhibited in reading the soliloquy, " My way of life." It is true, however, that in the scene after the murder he won from Hazlitt these glowing words: " As a lesson of common humanity it was heartrending. The hesitation, the bewildered look, the coming to himself when he sees his hands bloody; the manner in which his voice clung to his throat and choked his utterance; his agony and tears; the force of nature overcome by passion — beggared description."

Mrs. Trench told her boys, after taking them to a performance of Kean in "Macbeth," that never had she seen remorse so finely pictured as by the little actor in·that same scene following the terrible crime.

Yet, on the whole, he failed to express the poetry of the character. The natural he could interpret: the supernatural demands of the *rôle* were not within his grasp.

Kean fought, it was said, more like a fencing-master of modern days than a mediæval Scottish chieftain; while in dress he was "too much docked and curtailed for the gravity of the character." That curtailed dress consisted of a tunic ending above the knees; covering the body was an armor-plated shirt with a scarf flung across the breast and hanging under the arm.

Kemble used to crown his Thane's noble head with a bunch of plumes, that rose and fell in a sweeping mass at every nod of the chieftain, until Sir Walter Scott, with his own hands, took away those plumes, and in their place stuck a single eagle feather.

Charles Mayne Young's Macbeth was strangely attired in a green and gold velvet jacket.

Most peculiar costuming of all was that sometimes given the witches in those performances of old. The singing hags of Garrick's day, for example, wore red stomachers and ruffs, with laced aprons hanging below, while on their hands were thick mittens, and on their heads were plaited caps. One of their number, pretty Mrs. Crouch, rouged her face to a beautiful pink and white, powdered her hair, and covered her body with "point lace and fine linen enough to enchant the spectator." In fact, up to the day of Kean the weird sisters, with their songs and dances and antic doings, had been really of the comic nature. "I 'll have none of this rubbish!" cried the fiery little actor; and away it went forever.

Meanwhile the American stage had been developing.

Far back, in 1759, on the twenty-sixth day of October, the newly erected theatre on "Society Hill," in the Quaker City, was filled with a fashionable audience gathered to see Douglas's American Company give the first performance in this country of the masterpiece. "Hamlet" had just received its initial performance at the same play-

house; and the original Dane, with the original
Thane, was one and the same person, — Lewis
Hallam, the destined leader of the American stage,
but at that time a young man acting with his
mother, Mrs. Douglas (cast as Lady Macbeth),
with his stepfather, Mr. Douglas (cast as Macduff), and with others of the same family, Adam
and Nancy Hallam (cast respectively as Donal-
bain and Fleance). Mr. and Mrs. Harman played
Duncan and Hecate, so that it was, indeed, a family
party.

The three witches in the production were impersonated by Messrs. Allyn, Harman, and Tomlinson, the latter two doubling their characters, as
Tomlinson also played Seyton. At the Southwark
Theatre, in the same city, eight years later, all
the three witches for the first time were given to
women, — to Mrs. Harman, Miss Wainwright, and
Mrs. Tomlinson. Probably the American stage
failed to see all the weird sisters again performed
by women until the time when Fanny Davenport
brought out " Macbeth " (with herself as the Lady,
and Tearle in the title *rôle*) at the Walnut Street
Theatre, Philadelphia. That was in 1881. The
three witches then were played by Miss Minnie
Monk, Miss Mary Shaw, and Miss May Daven-

port (Mrs. William Seymour), a sister of the star. Miss Davenport adopted a novel appearance for the witches, dressing them in flowing gray " transparencies," made to give a cloudy effect, and having their faces pale, but yet displaying the natural loveliness of the young actresses, while their outstretched arms, bare to the skin, were plump and neat.

Hallam was never disturbed in the title *rôle* of " Macbeth " until after the Revolution. In 1783, at New York, the nervous but yet creditable tragedian Mr. Heard carried the part to the Lady Macbeth of Mrs. Ryan.

In the year 1794 Hodgkinson, then dominating the American Company, essayed the chief *rôle*, and won commendation. Soldierly must have been his appearance, with his broad shoulders and his six feet ten of height; but his round face, with its flat nose and unequal-sized eyes, could not have made an attractive appearance, while the slight inclination to bow-legged ungracefulness hampered him still more. The breeches and buckled shoes which he persisted in wearing off the stage did not set off to advantage his clumsy legs, nor did the powdered curls on either side of the head, and the dangling cue behind, mark him for fashion's glass, when all the rest of the world around him were wearing short, cropped hair.

His was the first Macbeth that Boston saw (Dec. 21, 1795). At that time Hodgkinson was only thirty years of age, but had won a splendid reputation. The son of an English tavern-keeper, John Meadowcraft — for that was his real name — had started out to make his fortune with but a crown in his pocket and a fiddle under his arm. His musical abilities won him a place in the Bristol Theatre, and before long he was a real actor, and acquiring fame. In 1792, induced by Henry. Hodgkinson, visited America, and here remained, as actor and manager, until his death, in 1805.

Graceful and elegant James Fennell, who in his early stage days in England had on one occasion at least played the Thane to the Lady Macbeth of Mrs. Pope, was an American Macbeth in those days, just after the great war. Another impersonator of the character was the comedian Chalmers.

But greater than these was the Macbeth of 1796, the capable tragedian Thomas Abthorpe Cooper, then, on the 9th of December, at Philadelphia, making his first appearance in America. Here he became domesticated; and though at first, on account of Fennell's popularity, success came slowly,

— in fact, in order to draw an audience to his
first benefit, he deemed it necessary to have an
elephant as an additional card on the stage, — he
later rose to eminence, and gained a fortune, which
he rapidly threw away. His first attempt in England had also been in "Macbeth," though in a
secondary character; and there likewise he failed
to receive especial favor. Indeed, Stephen Kemble,
the great (physically great) Kemble, as manager,
discharged Cooper after the performance, declaring
that a man who could break down in the *rôle* of
Malcolm had not the slightest requisite for an
actor. But the determined youth persevered, and
in America soon was esteemed as a star, with but
one rival, Hodgkinson. With Cooke and Kean he
could also tempt comparison in all but a few characters.

Washington Irving, in 1815, declared that he
never saw in England Cooper's equal as Macbeth;
yet the English people, twelve years later, received
the tragedian so ungraciously in that character, that
he would not venture a second appearance. Perhaps his talents had been dimmed then; for a
performance of 1803 had been commended by the
London Mirror of that date as one meriting dis-
tinguished notice. The dagger scene, said the

critic, and the scene subsequent to the murder, were performed in most masterly style, and proved the best achievement of the actor. But Irving went further. "I shall never forget Cooper's acting in 'Macbeth' last spring," he wrote on the 28th of December, 1815, "when he was stimulated to exertion by the presence of a number of British officers. I have seen nothing to equal it in England. Cooper requires excitement to arouse him from a monotonous, commonplace manner he is apt to fall into, in consequence of acting so often before indifferent houses."

In the year 1820 Joseph T. Buckingham, declaring that Macbeth was Cooper's *chef d'œuvre*, pronounced his dagger scene as one of the sublimest efforts of histrionic genius; and of the last part of the play, after Macbeth has "supped full with horrors," exclaimed, "The moral reflections are given with such exquisite beauty and feeling, that we almost forget the crimes of the murderer, and pity the wretched victim writhing with the tortures of his own conscience!"

As a manager, Cooper's great stroke was inducing the erratic but talented George Frederick Cooke to visit this country. Here we saw the gifted, dissipated actor winning theatrical applause in Macbeth, and obtaining moral condemnation in his own person. His introduction to the weird tragedy was a curious one. At the age of sixteen the printer's apprentice — for such he was at the time — became head and front of an amateur company of boys who gave performances in a deserted barn in the town of Berwick. At that juncture a real dramatic company visited the place, and young Cooke determined he must see the play. He had no money, but he had resources of another kind. Slipping through the stage-door before the keepers were posted, he made his way to a dark corner behind the scenes, and safely stowed his body within a large barrel. Inside he found also two twenty-four pound cannon-balls: but they did not disturb his peace of mind; he used them to uphold his cramped knees.

The orchestral music began; and, before the lad knew what was happening, the property man threw a piece of carpet over the open head of the barrel, tied it with a stout rope, and then, just as the curtain rose, gave the barrel a lusty push, and rolled it backward and forward over the floor.

Cooke was inside the "stage thunder." The cannon-balls were intended to make the noise of the storm that opened the play of "Macbeth."

With yells of fear and pain the boy kicked and pounded as the iron globes beat around him. By his exertions he unknowingly steered the barrel full upon the stage; and there, to the astonishment of the audience, George Frederick suddenly burst forth through the carpet head, and, with a howl and a roll, bumped into the three witches, scattering them over the stage. He had made his *début*.

Properly, George Frederick Cooke belongs to the British stage; but inasmuch as he was the first noted English actor to cross the Atlantic, he may for this chapter have his place just following the manager who brought him here. It is said that Cooper, after having his offer of twenty-five pounds a week declined by Cooke, contrived to get him drunk in a Liverpool den, and then smuggle him aboard a ship bound for the United States. This was in 1810, when his drunken freaks had culminated in the disfavor of his formerly applauding audiences. In America he remained until his death, in September, 1812.

When sober his success was enormous. But escapade after escapade followed as soon as the first glow of earnest ambition had worn away. Odd, is it not, that this dissipated *roué* could know his Bible so well that, when asked at a private party what was the most beautiful passage he had ever read (the questioner thinking at the time only of the drama), the quick reply came, "St. Paul's Defence at the Tribunal of King Agrippa"? And then Cooke, calling for a Bible, read the passage with most exquisite feeling and expression. He was neither tall nor graceful, strong nor symmetrical, and had but a weak voice; yet he was a great actor.

It must be admitted that Macbeth never counted among his best parts. Leigh Hunt said of it, that while the character ought, at least, to be a majestic villain, with Cooke Macbeth exhibited nothing but a desperate craftiness; and Dr. John W. Francis declared that he had "seen a better Macbeth," since "the transitions of Cooke were scarcely immediate enough for the timid, hesitating, wavering monarch." Undoubtedly Cooper was the better Macbeth to whom Dr. Francis referred.

Probably John Taylor best described our player when he declared that his acting "was strong, but coarse. He had not the advantage of much education, but had a shrewd, penetrating mind, was well acquainted with human nature, and was powerful in those characters for which his talents were adapted; and they were chiefly of the villanous."

But the witches chant to a Macbeth whose performances were noted in both England and America,
— one who, unfortunately, in addition formed a link
in a controversy and disaster of sad international
concern. Macready's Macbeth, then, may open the
second chapter on the play.

MACBETH.

MACREADY merited the laughing ridicule of
Prince Pückler-Muskau, the German traveller,
when, after Lady Macbeth had bidden him put his
nightgown on, he threw over his armor a gaudy
flowered chintz dressing-gown of the fashion of
the actor's own day; but he deserved also the
warm praise of the prince for his acting in the
murder scene, the banquet scene, and the last
act.

Moreover, the French play-goers found the Englishman's Macbeth full of fire and intelligence
when, in this season of 1827–1828, he visited Paris
with other sons of Britain, to give those performances of Shakespeare that inspired Alexandre Du-
mas and Hector Berlioz to their greatest efforts.
" His play of expression," said the critic of the
Journal des Débats, speaking of Macready's acting,
" redeemed the irregularity of his features, while

his voice, in its lower register, possessed tones which penetrated to the very soul."

It was only a few weeks before this that Stephen Price, the grouty London manager with whom Macready had so many conflicts, made his curt answer to the actor.

" The bill is very long to-night," said Macready to the chief of Drury Lane; " why not cut out the music in 'Macbeth'?"

" I can't do that — the public would n't like it," gruffly responded the manager; " but I 'll cut out the part of Macbeth, if you like."

As a fact, Alfred Bunn says that Macready proved so poor a drawing card in this engagement, that after twenty-four performances Price actually gave him his salary of twenty pounds a night for sixteen nights, and released him from further contract. But Bunn was not on the best terms with Macready. During a later season of the haughty player under the pugnacious manager at Drury Lane, though Macready was paid thirty pounds a week, he yet found much to displease him; and when, at last, he was cast in a three-act version of "Richard III.," forming part of a triple-play performance, there was mutiny.

" Tetchy and unhappy," Macready says of him-

WM. C. MACREADY.

self, he revenged this insult by entering the manager's private room, knocking him down, closing
one eye completely, and spattering the august
body of Drury Lane's leader with blood, lamp-oil,
and ink. Bunn returned the blows, and there was
danger of a more direful conflict had not friends in-
terposed. "Great Fight. B——nn and M——y,"
said the newspapers the next day in big type.

"It makes me sick to think of it," wrote the
super-sensitive Macready in his diary. But the
public rather enjoyed the blow to Bunn, and
made Macready its hero. When for the first time
after the fight he appeared at Covent Garden,
playing Macbeth, the pit rose to the player, waved
handkerchiefs and hats, and cheered most heartily.

Bunn never challenged the gentleman whom he
had politely called "a very magnificent three-
tailed bashaw," though every one thought he
would; but instead he sued for assault. His opponent allowed judgment to go by default, and the
much-battered manager pocketed his one hundred
and fifty pounds. It is doubtful if the actor paid
this sum with much good grace; for his reputation, so far as money matters were concerned, was
not characterized by brother actors as "generous."
In fact, the bright old lady whose life has ex-

tended into the present generation, Mrs. Keeley, curtly remarked on the day, half a century and more ago, when Macready, absent from rehearsal, was said by the prompter to be suffering from heart disease, " What ? What's that you say ? Macready suffering from heart disease ? Nonsense ! You might as well make me think Walter Lacy could suffer from brain-fever."

But yet that heart must have beaten faster and more warmly on the night of June 14, 1843, when his Macbeth planned and plotted for the crown of Scotland. It was his last appearance as a manager; and, as he himself tells us in his diary, the whole house literally rose to him. " When wearied with shouting, they changed the applause to a stamping of feet, which sounded like thunder; it was grand and awful ! I never saw such a scene ! " Never did he play Macbeth so well, and at the end he retired " with the same mad acclaim."

A little later came the American tour, with its resulting riot. It had been charged that Macready induced his friends to cry down Edwin Forrest when the American was acting in England ; and that Forrest had hissed the Englishman for his fantastic handkerchief-waving before the play scene in "Hamlet." Thus hostilities were opened. On the 20th of November, 1848, at Philadelphia, Macready attempted Macbeth, and, while acting the tragic *rôle*, was suddenly interrupted by a flying egg and a copper cent hurled at his head. This peculiar contribution was exceeded in Cincinnati, where half the carcass of a sheep was flung over the footlights to the feet of the player. Hot words followed in the newspapers, and feelings of resentment burned on both sides.

The real tragedy came in New York in the spring of 1849. Forrest opened with Macbeth at the Broadway Theatre on Monday, the 7th of May; the same night Macready opened with the same character at the Astor Place Opera House.

The onslaught on the Englishman began early in the evening. Words first flew against him: "Down with the English hog!" "Three groans for the codfish aristocracy!" Then more substantial symbols of disapproval flew at his head, — more copper cents, "four or five eggs, a great many apples, nearly, if not quite, a peck of potatoes, pieces of wood, and a bottle of assafœtida," as Macready himself statistically enumerates in his diary. These little suggestive bits of feeling he passed by unnoticed; but when a couple of chairs crashed down from the gallery to the stage, Macbeth thought best to retire in good order, and let the curtain fall.

Another performance was essayed on Thursday night. Unlucky attempt! Disorder was feared, and the police were therefore stationed in the house. Only seven ladies were present. The rowdies started their cat-calling and hissing, but at the end of the first act were summarily swept out of the house by the blue-coated guardians.

It seems, however, that the rioters outside were more numerous and more noisy than those within, and before long they made themselves evident by a storm of cobble-stones through the windows. But the play kept on. The chandelier was shattered, the waterpipes were burst. Still the play kept on. Even to the end the players acted, and then Macready retired to the dressing-room to change his clothes. As he did so, the roar of musketry resounded in the street, followed by the sharp commands of the officers and the yells of the crowd. The militia were on the scene. Unable to cope with the crowd, the police had summoned the aid of the soldiery, and one hundred and seventy armed men stood facing a mob of ten or fifteen thousand.

How the stones flew! It was dark as Egypt, and the rioters were then in ugly spirit. Driven to the wall, and with wounded men about him, General Hall could stand it no longer, but bade his soldiers fire. Three volleys and a charge cleared the street, yet not until the dead lay upon the pavements.

As for Macready, in disguise he escaped from the theatre, and in the early morning sped away to Boston. Ten days later he was on board the steamer bound for England. A round of farewell visits through Great Britain, and then in February, 1851, he retired.

His farewell character, on the 26th of the second month, was Macbeth. Samuel Phelps closed his own theatre in order to act Macduff under his old leader; Mrs. Warner was the Lady Macbeth. "What a sight that was!" cried George Henry Lewes. "How glorious, triumphant, affecting, to see every one starting up, waving hats and handkerchiefs, stamping, shouting, yelling their friendship at the great actor who now made his appearance on that stage where he was never more to re-appear! There was a crescendo of excitement, enough to have overpowered the nerves of the most self-possessed; and when, after an energetic

fight, — which showed that the actor's powers bore
him gallantly up to the last, — he fell, pierced by
Macduff's sword, this death, typical of the actor's
death, this last look, this last act of the actor,
struck every bosom with a sharp and sudden blow,
loosening a tempest of tumultuous feeling, such as
made applause an ovation. Some little time was
suffered to elapse, wherein we recovered from the
excitement, and were ready again to burst forth
as Macready the man, dressed in his plain black,
came forward to bid 'Farewell, a long farewell, to
all his greatness.' As he stood there, calm but
sad, waiting till the thunderous reverberations of
applause should be hushed, there was one little
thing which brought the tears into my eyes; viz.,
the crape hat-band and black studs, that seemed
to me more mournful and more touching than all
this vast display of sympathy.'' Macready's eldest daughter, "Nina," had died Feb. 24, 1850, aged
twenty.

For two and twenty years the actor survived
this last appearance, passing away the 27th of
April, 1873. To him Macbeth had always been
the favorite character, and the public placed that
rôle and Lear at the head of his list. Leigh
Hunt complained of a lack of kingliness in the

murder scene; Lewes said, " He stole into the
sleeping chamber of Duncan like a man going
to purloin a purse, not like a warrior going to
snatch a crown ; " Westland Marston spoke of the
" crouching form and stealthy, felon-like step of
the self-abased murderer," though he thought this
change from the " erect, martial figure " of the
first act made visible the moral of the play; but
in all the other scenes Macready won high commendation.

After the murder, when Macbeth realizes his
situation, the acting was grand. With face turned
from his wife as she dragged him from the stage,
and with arms outstretched as if to grasp the past
that had gone from him, he presented a picture of
fearful agony that stirred most deeply the emotion
of the spectators. Again, there was a very effective stage contrast in his majestic order to Seyton,
" Give me mine armor," compared with his collo-
quial query, " How does your patient, doctor ? "
while the physical energy and grandeur of his
closing scenes made Marston cry, " He has turned
upon Fate, and stands at bay ! " Lady Pollock was
struck with " his singular power of looking at
nothing," so that " when he spoke into the air we
could almost see the hags pass away like a wreath

of vapor. In the scene with Banquo's ghost he surpassed even his greatest predecessors, and there are no two opinions as to the magnificence of his playing in the last act."

Sometimes the critics complained of Macready's " too fitful, hurried, and familiar " delivery of Macbeth's lines; but this, undoubtedly, was due to his effort to make the blank verse sound natural and easy.

His prolongation of words was, I fear, sometimes ludicrous; evidently it so struck one of our sharp Yankee actors. The American was severely criticised by Macready for announcing the approach of Birnam Wood in this wise, " Within these three miles you may see it a-coming."

" Don't you-a know," cried the tragedian, " that coming begins with a *c*, not with *a* ? Speak it a-this way: ' Within these three-a miles you may-a see it a-a-a-coming.' "

" Mr. Macready," cried the little actor, " for my part I don't see any difference between my way of giving it and yours, except that I put one *a* before 'coming,' and you put half a dozen."

Edward Fitzgerald had a criticism of Macready's enunciation in one of his letters to Fanny Kemble. He had asked the descendant of the great Siddons how she emphasized the line: " After life's fitful fever he sleeps well ; " and she had replied that she laid the emphasis on *he*. Fitzgerald then rejoined: " Yes; so I thought . . . and yet I do not remember to have heard it so read. (I never heard you read the play.) I don't think Macready read it so. I liked his Macbeth, I must say ; only he would say, ' Amen st-u-u-u-ck in his throat,' which was not only a blunder, but a vulgar blunder, I think."

Another thing which undoubtedly nettled our players when Macready criticised them was the haughty manner the English star assumed toward the under-actors. He tried the same manner with Joseph Jefferson, the brilliant grandfather of our own " Rip Van Winkle," at a rehearsal of " Macbeth " in Philadelphia, during the season of 1826-1827. The comedian, who was cast for First Witch, was lame with gout, and had therefore been accorded the privilege of carrying a cane on the stage.

Macready, without inquiring the reason, or without a word of explanation, exclaimed in an arrogant, supercilious voice, "Tell that person to put down his cane."

Instantly Mr. Jefferson responded, " Tell Mr. Macready that I shall not act with him during this engagement," and immediately left the theatre.

Still more embarrassing to the English actor was
the naïve method of remembrance shown by the
First Murderer in a London performance. The
minor actor, at rehearsal, persisted in marching to
the centre of the stage, thereby putting the star out
of the focus of the audience. Explanations and
objurgations were useless; his dull head would not
hold the lesson ten minutes.

" Bring me a hammer and a brass-headed nail! "
finally shouted the tragedian, exasperated beyond
endurance. " There now," quoth he, when the
implements were brought, "drive the nail there.
And you, sirrah, see that your foot is on that
brass head every time before you attempt to
speak."

Again they started the rehearsal, and this time
all things went well.

But when the evening came, to the astonishment
of Macready, the First Murderer entered, and immediately, with dazed eye and head bowed low,
began wandering up and down the stage. The
audience laughed. Macready scowled. But still
the man walked on.

"In Heaven's name," growled the tragedian in a
hoarse voice, as he stalked to the First Murderer's
side, " what are you doing? "

"Sure," replied the innocent fellow, "ain't I looking for that blessed nail of yours!"

It is now time to glance at the performances of later days, — at the productions of Phelps, of Kean the younger, and of Irving. Not until the former began his reign at Sadler's Wells Theatre was there any attempt in "Macbeth" at accuracy of scenery and costume.

In the 1844 production of the play the Thane appeared dressed like an Anglo-Saxon warrior of barbaric days, with conical helmet, tunic, crude armor, and cross-garters. It was the opening performance at Sadler's Wells under the new *régime* (May 27). Mr. Phelps was beginning that splendid series of Shakespearian revivals by which he attracted the attention of all London, and made the little, dilapidated, almost unknown play-house the most fashionable and popular of the city. With earnest energy and straightforward effort Mr. Phelps interpreted the chief *rôle*, winning praise from the critics, and visibly affecting the audiences that at the beginning were composed of people little used to classic productions. The Athenæum thought that Phelps was better in the part than any other actor since Edmund Kean, declaring of his vigorous impersonation, "It is essentially distinct from, and stands in contrast with, Mr. Macready's, which, however fine and classical in conception, is but too obviously open to the Scotch sneer of presenting 'a very respectable gentleman in considerable difficulties,' so studied is it in all its parts, and subdued into commonplace by too much artifice."

But clearest of all is Professor Morley's description of Phelps's Macbeth: "A rude, impulsive soldier . . . turbulent of mind, restless, imaginative, quick of ambition, but with a religion strong in leaf, although fruitless and weak of root."

Phelps was true to Shakespeare. Instead of dropping the curtain on the death of Macbeth, he made his exit "fighting," permitting the scene of the bringing in of the head, and Macduff's greeting of Malcolm as King, to close the play.

In the first production by the Sadler's Wells manager, Mrs. Warner was the Lady Macbeth. Later on, when Helen Faucit (now Lady Martin) played the heroine, she found occasion to pick a flaw in Phelps's manner as a gentleman and actor. At a performance given in honor of the Princess Royal's marriage the two were acting in "Macbeth;" and the lady, being then practically retired from the stage, felt uncertain whether her voice, from lack of practice, could fill the theatre. She therefore suggested to Mr. Phelps, at rehearsal, that it would be necessary for her to keep as far front on the stage as possible, and he assented. But, on the night of the performance, at his very first entrance Macbeth stationed himself far in the rear of his Lady, so that the poor woman not only had to retreat behind the proscenium in order to picture the scene artistically, but also had to keep her back turned towards the audience, and thus destroy much of the effect of her impersonation. It was a trick for which Lady Martin never forgave the "inadequate successor" of Macready, as she styled Phelps.

And here it may be well to narrate an exciting experience Phelps and Macready once had in "Macbeth." It was at the Covent Garden Theatre, when the future manager of Sadler's Wells was leading man under the elder actor. On this particular occasion he was playing Macduff; and Macready, probably afflicted with his chronic dyspepsia or his chronic jealousy, suddenly grew angry in the fight scene, and, as Phelps said, "let fly at me, nearly giving me a crack on the head as he growled, 'D——n your eyes! take that!'

"For the moment I was flabbergasted," declared the younger man, telling the story afterwards; "but when he returned to the charge, I gave him a dose of his own physic. He returned the compliment. Then he went for me, and I went for him; and there we were growling at each other like a pair of wild beasts, until I finished him, amidst a furor of applause.

" The audience were quite carried away by the cunning of the scene, shouting themselves hoarse; roaring on the one side, ' Well done, Mac!' on the other, ' Let him have it, Phelps!' When the curtain fell I gave him my hand to get up. He was puffing and blowing like a grampus. As soon as he could recover his wind he commenced:—

"' Er-er-er, Mr. Phelps, what did you mean by making use of such extraordinary language to me?'

"' What did you mean, Mr. Macready, by making use of such extraordinary language to me?'

"' I, Sir?'

"' Yes, you, sir! You d——d my eyes!'

"' And you, sir, d——d my limbs!'

"' I could do no less than follow so good an example.'

" With this the absurdity of the thing struck us both, and we burst out laughing. Everybody said the combat was realistic, and I think it must have been. I know I had the greatest difficulty in preventing his slipping his sword into me; for, to tell you the truth, we were neither of us very graceful swordsmen, but what we lacked in elegance we made up for in earnestness. One thing is quite certain — we never got up steam to such an extent again."

Charles Kean, like Phelps, attempted to blend historical costuming with the drama, but, unlike the other actor, dressed his hero in the style of Alexander the First, with a hauberk of iron rings sewn on leather, and a red and blue tunic; the supporting characters wore clothes of mingled purple, red, violet, and blue. The "gods" had a great deal of fun over Kean's pedantry in filling his programs with long-spun descriptions of the historical dressing he gave "Macbeth;" and when one recalls that, on an amusement bill, were cited as authorities Diodorus, Siculus, Strabo, Pliny, Xiphilin, Snorre, Ducange, and the Eyrbiggia Saga, it is no wonder there were mental snickers.

Kean's Thane was exciting for the gallery in the combat scene. The despondent way in which he had retired to rest, or rather to unrest, brought praise from one little bit of pantomime, — his leaning against a pillar as he passed, as if utterly

heartsick with despair, — while his exhibition of
savage bravery, in a swashing, hewing fight, won
thundering applause. But the remainder of his
impersonation was weak and monotonous. His conception of the character was that of a man who
had lost all confidence in himself, and was sure of
nothing.

When Henry Irving introduced his Macbeth to
English audiences, he gave a novel interpretation.
They condemned the conception; but the actor never
faltered in his consistency, and years later repeated
the impersonation on the same lines. That first
performance was in September, 1875, when the
student-actor was seven and thirty years of age,
and with a London experience of only nine years.
Mrs. Bateman had taken the theatre formerly managed by her husband, and to the part of Lady Macbeth, Miss Kate Bateman (Mrs. Crowe) was cast.

Those who then saw the actor declared that in
some scenes he was effective; his terror in describing the voice that said, "Sleep no more! Macbeth
doth murder sleep!" was called the incarnation of
the despair of a mental and spiritual hell, the expression of a hollow, ghastly, hope-bereft experience of a blood-stained soul. But, on the other
hand, his deliberate pronunciation and prolonging

of syllables brought actual laughter into some of the more serious scenes.

On the 29th of December, 1888, Irving had the pleasure of repeating his impersonation in London, this time under his own management at the Lyceum Theatre, with Ellen Terry as Lady Macbeth. The scenic effects were superb; and in several scenes novelties were introduced, noticeably in the casting of the three weird sisters to women. Occasionally one of the witches had been an actress, but not for a century and more had all three been given over to women. At Manchester, England, in 1775, when Younger was Macbeth, and Mrs. Ward the Lady, the witches were three actresses of the stock company, two of whom were Elizabeth Farren, afterwards Countess of Derby, and her pretty sister Kitty. Henry Irving cast the characters to Miss Marriott, Miss Desborough, and Miss Julia Seaman — large, gaunt women with deep, heavy voices.

The Lyceum manager conceives Macbeth as a man who, while not absolutely seeking crime or wicked ways, is yet perfectly willing to meet them half-way, and to yield with facility. Making this complete inability to resist inducements to crime a central and continuous feature of the character,

Irving has opened the way for a criticism of mo-
notony in the acting, as it destroys the chance for
a mental conflict between the good and the bad in
Macbeth's nature.

When John Oxenford, the celebrated critic of
former days on the *London Times*, saw Irving's
first Macbeth, he described him as scared by the
witches; scared by the project of murder; scared
by the progress of its execution. "When thoroughly convinced that resistance is useless," said
Oxenford, "he can rush into the murder of Banquo; but when the ghost appears he is scared as
never man was scared before, and he wraps his
cloak over his face that he may not behold the
horrible spectre. He is only brave when there is
clearly nothing to be lost or won — namely, in the
final combat; that is to say, he can die game."

This cowardice of Irving's Macbeth is not, in
his conception of the character, intended as a physical, but as a moral, cowardice. In an address
delivered in both England and America, he distinctly stated that he did not want to be mistaken in regard to Macbeth's bravery; that there
could be no doubt, either historically or in Shakespeare's play, of the chieftain's physical courage.
It was solely in his moral qualities that he was

condemnable. Mr. Irving has no sympathy with the commonly accepted idea that Macbeth was led into wrong-doing by the influence of a wicked wife, but insists that from the beginning he was a most blood-thirsty villain. It is quite possible, he admits, that the ambitious Thane led his wife to believe that she was leading him, but that was only a part of his hypocritical nature. The pathetic picture of the murdered King and his attendants, smeared with blood, was all hypocrisy, says the English actor, enlarged upon because of the Thane's own imaginative, poetic nature. His beautiful similes and expressions of seeming tenderness, such as are exhibited in his words about his guest, the King, who is "here in double trust," and whose "virtues will plead like angels, trumpet tongued," are, in Irving's mind, so thoroughly ironic as to be almost grim humor.

From first to last the actor's conception of the character has been consistently carried out; but he has not won over to his thinking many students of the drama.

When Charles Dillon played the title *rôle* to Helen Faucit's Lady in 1858, he chose an opposite extreme of characterization; making a brave Scotchman, who, driven by Fate, commits a crime against which his moral nature revolts, but which when once committed is followed by successive crimes of physical boldness. An anecdote of Dillon will illustrate the unconscious growth of stage business. One night when apostrophizing Banquo's ghost, he was so carried away by frenzied enthusiasm that as he cried, — no, fairly yelled, — " Hence, hence ! horrible shadow, unreal mockery, hence ! " he tore his collar into bits, covering the floor with its pieces. The audience went wild over the realistic intensity; but Dillon, after the play, confessed to Westland Marston that the whole business of the tearing of the collar had been done unconsciously in the excitement of the scene. " However," said Dillon, " I 'll make it a part of my business after this." And he did.

A determined schemer was the Macbeth of Barry Sullivan, not instigated to crime by his wife, but simply assisted by the Lady. With Sullivan's strong hero, the spectator was obliged to believe either that Lady Macbeth did not fully know his darker moods, when she considered him " too full o' the milk of human kindness," or else that his nature was completely changed after meeting the witches.

James R. Anderson, Gustavus V. Brooke, and

the elder Vandenhoff (an elocutionary Macbeth) are also to be counted among the heroes of the play in the past. From the early Macbeths down to the last performers, there are a score whose names are worthy of record. Aside from rugged Forrest and vigorous Davenport, Edwin Booth and his associate Lawrence Barrett, and Rossi and Salvini, the visiting players, there were Wyzeman Marshall and Joseph Proctor, veterans of another generation, who to-day walk the streets of Boston still hale and hearty, the elder J. W. Wallack and the younger J. W. Wallack, Edwin Adams, J. B. Booth, Jr., and George Vandenhoff, the last of Charlotte Cushman's Macbeths.

Edwin Forrest was the first American actor of greatness to appear upon the English stage. His earliest appearance in Britain was on Oct. 17, 1836. Then they praised his Macbeth. Macready welcomed him, not then regarding him as a rival. But the English actor was ever jealous and suspicious; and when, seven years' later, he visited America for a second time, and found the people comparing him unfavorably with the robust Forrest, envy entered his heart. In 1845 it found its vent, or at least Forrest thought it did, in influencing England's writers against the American during the latter's second visit to the tight little isle. On the opening night Forrest was greeted with a hurricane of hisses, while the next day the former friendly papers attacked him so fiercely that he was obliged to cancel his engagement.

No one persisted in unjust persecution of the visitor more relentlessly than Macready's particular friend, Forster, the critic of the *London Examiner*. He even went to such an extreme as to write these outrageous words: "Our old friend Mr. Forrest afforded great amusement to the public by his performance of Macbeth on Friday evening at the Princess's. Indeed, our best comic actors do not often excite so great a quantity of mirth. The change from an inaudible murmur to a thunder of sound was enormous; but the grand feature was the combat, in which he stood scraping his sword against that of Macduff. We were at a loss to know what this gesture meant, till an enlightened critic in the gallery shouted out, 'That's right! sharpen it!'"

No more would our sturdy American call upon Macready; and, unfortunately for both, during an Edinburgh performance of Hamlet by the Englishman, Forrest in one of the boxes injudiciously hissed the handkerchief business in the play scene.

Then the storm burst. England and America tossed
the question of courtesy and discourtesy back and
forth and international feelings ran high.

In the fall of 1848 Macready again came to
America, and in the following May both actors
were playing in New York City. The sad result
was the Astor Place riot.

How the American audiences felt is best illustrated by the action of one during the engagement
of Forrest just before the riot. As his Macbeth
uttered the lines, " What rhubarb, senna, or what
purgative drug, will scour these English hence? "
the people in the house rose to their feet and cheered
and cheered again.

Probably the most interesting, certainly the most
notable, appearance of Forrest in " Macbeth " was
at the Broadway Theatre, New York, in February,
1853, when a magnificent revival of the tragedy
was prepared, with Mme. Ponisi as Lady Macbeth,
and with Duff, Conway, Davenport, Davidge, and
Barry in the support. For twenty nights the play
held the boards, thus achieving the longest run
up to that date of any Shakespearian play in this
country.

Yet Wemyss thought Forrest's Macbeth did not
even deserve the name; indeed, he declared that

the herculean player was not above mediocrity in any Shakespearian character except Othello, though admirably great in the characters written for him and for his physical requirements. Charles T. Congdon, too, refused to praise the "gladiatorial exhibitions," as he called them, of Edwin Forrest; and he particularly indorsed the laconic but not over-complimentary criticism which Fanny Kemble wrote in her diary after she saw the then young tragedian at the Bowery, " What a mountain of a man!" " He was born for single combat," says Congdon, and adds truthfully that the Macduff with whom he contended had a hard time of it.

Some of the minor players, too, had a hard time at rehearsal with the quick-tempered actor. They all feared him when in angry mood, for none knew to what extreme he would go. In fact, one intimate friend of Forrest once told the writer that there were really two Forrests, according to moods, — Forrest the gentleman and Forrest the blackguard.

One day in Washington, when "Macbeth" was under rehearsal, a certain performer who took the part of the Second Apparition became so frightened over the frowns of the star, that when he was called upon to utter " Macbeth ! Macbeth ! Macbeth ! " his trembling voice was almost inaudible.

With pointed sarcasm Forrest emphasized the third word in his responding phrase, making a new and personal reading, "Had I *three* ears I'd hear thee!"

More confused, the Apparition continued, "Be bloody bold, and resolute," laying the emphasis on the *bloody*, and letting it qualify *bold*.

Immediately Forrest rushed upon the young man. "You're a butcher, sir!" he cried in tumultuous anger; "a perfect butcher! Shakespeare doesn't want me to be 'bloody bold;' he wants me to be 'bloody, bold, and resolute.' Go down, sir; go down and do it again!"

In vain the scared fellow tried to catch the idea; his wits were gone. Finally Forrest insisted upon the First Apparition "doubling" *rôles* and giving the lines of both.

The same youth had also to act the Second Officer in the fifth act, and announce the coming of Malcolm's army. On the night of the performance, when Forrest rushed upon him, and, in the words of the text, cried, "The devil damn thee black, thou cream-faced loon; where gottest thou that goose look?" the youth managed to stammer out, "There are t-t-ten thousand"—

But as Forrest in his Macbeth rage grasped him

by the throat, crying, "Geese, villain," the half-
choked little man, instead of replying as he
should, "Soldiers, sir," weakly whispered in terror,
"Ye-e-e-s, Mr. Forrest."

Away he flew over the stage. The burly actor,
now boiling with real anger, had fairly hurled him
into the wings.

A little later Forrest saw the fellow behind the
scenes. With forced calmness the tragedian, gaz-
ing fixedly at the man, exclaimed, "Sir, you are
a butcher by trade, are you not?"

"I — I?" responded the Second Officer. "No,
sir: I'm an actor."

"An actor!" returned Forrest with withering
scorn. "You are not, sir. You are a butcher, sir.
Go back to your calling; kill sheep, kill oxen, kill
asses, if you like, but never more kill Shakespeare!"

A few months later another stupid player, act-
ing Seyton, instead of saying to Macbeth, "The
Queen, my Lord, is dead," confusedly announced,
"The King, my Lord, is dead."

Forrest could not resist the chance for joke.
"Is he?" he replied; "then what am *I* doing
here?" And the audience, in the humor of the
extempore scene, did not criticise, but laughed.

Now we come to a less tumultuous hero. Although not reckoned as a leading *rôle* in Edwin Booth's *répertoire*, in the sense that Hamlet and Iago were considered, Macbeth yet offered opportunities for that display of varying passion which the actor controlled to so large an extent. Boldness and fear were both pictured in capable manner. In the scene with the witches, when first the revelation of future greatness is laid before Macbeth, the changing of face mirrored the deep thoughts of the mind; and the eager query with which further knowledge of the unknown time to come was impetuously sought, gave with the word and look and action the key for interpreting the great ambition of the Thane of Glamis. The tragedian's acting there laid bare, like a flash, all the emotion which was to influence the aspiring soldier to deeds of crime and treachery.

But chief in Booth's representation was his conception of the night scene, when Macbeth pauses before he commits his terrible crime. This was the most excellent point in his performance, even exceeding in its artistic finish the ghost scene at the banquet table. The inward workings of the conscience seemed to be laid open to the sight of all as the Scot gazed stealthily around the bordering pillars, starting at every sound, and even quivering violently at nothing when the nervous mind conjured up a thought that made it seem as though some one was beside him. These are the more notable scenes in an impersonation that cannot rank among Mr. Booth's best parts.

Salvini used to say that Booth could not succeed in Macbeth because he was so dissimilar from the character. Macbeth was ambitious; Booth was not. Macbeth was barbarous and ferocious; Booth was agreeable, urbane, and courteous. Therefore the nature of the courtly, generous Booth rebelled against the portrayal of such a character. An interesting reasoning, surely, but hardly logical or true. For example, Booth by nature was not an Iago; yet by art he assuredly was.

When Charlotte Cushman acted to the Thane of Edwin Booth in Philadelphia, in 1860, she observed, "that judging from Mr. Booth's rehearsal of Macbeth, he had a refined and very intellectual conception of the character; she begged him to remember that Macbeth was the grandfather of all the Bowery villains." Booth, however, would not accept her ideas on this point.

Davenport was another of Cushman's Macbeths. It was at the Howard, in Boston, on one occasion, that the noted Bostonian, in support of Miss Cushman, dressed his ambitious Thane in a towering brass helmet, brown tunic, and tights, relieved by the great stand-by of all travelling New Englanders, a Highland shawl, and at the close of the performance came before the curtain to make a stirring war speech, urging enlistment, and a vigorous prosecution of the war. Mr. Davenport's efforts before the curtain were characteristic. He was known on such occasions audibly to greet acquaintances in the boxes, tell amusing incidents of travel, award praise to rivals, laughingly give such a conundrum as, " Why am I like a poor plaster? — Because I don't draw well," allude to some favorite of the company by his Christian name, and send away his hearers *en rapport* with the man instead of the artist.

As a star he was ever flitting, and his wanderings would have astonished even some modern combinations. The first of the month once found him playing a farewell in the Boston Theatre, as Benedick, to a crowded assembly of friends; and the last of the same month saw him encountering, with brave courage, the mortification of a life at the Metropolitan in San Francisco, where the curtain rose upon "standing room only" to the first

act of his Hamlet, and fell upon the closet scene
to empty benches. He once played Damon, in
Missouri, in conjunction with a strawberry festival,
and laughed heartily as he recalled the occasion ;
often, as Lawrence Barrett remarked, he "wasted
his fine talents in undignified versatility."

As for Salvini, impressive in the banquet scene
particularly, he naturally was forcible throughout
the play. He made the ambitious man no tool to
his Lady, but an equal associate in crime, selfish,
without conscience, and without remorse. With
his massive form, surmounted by a strong, heavily
bearded face, and with long tawny hair, matching
the beard in color and length, the Italian showed
a warrior who could well carry through any plan
of mighty ambition. When he cried out, "To-morrow, and to-morrow, and to-morrow," there was no
melancholy in the tone, but simply the fretting
worriment of overwhelming selfishness. As he uttered the lines in grief of his dead wife, "She
should have died hereafter," he threw himself into
a seat, and with his hands covered for the moment
his face in sudden thoughtfulness ; but the subsequent exclamation and expression were indicative
of personal trouble rather than saddened affliction.

When the foreign star first played the part in

TOMMASO SALVINI.

Boston, he introduced new "business" that seemed absurd from the inartistic way it was carried out. In other words, he attempted literally to picture the stage direction of the sixth scene of the fifth act of the original play, "Enter, with drums and colors, Malcolm, Old Seward, Macduff, etc., and their army with boughs." Inasmuch as Malcolm's army, in Salvini's production, consisted of only a dozen lank and slender-limbed soldiers, their appearance with large green boughs in front of their faces was scarcely imposing. The effect was even more ludicrous when, at the words of the play, "Now near enough: your heavy screens throw down, and show like those you are," they deliberately dropped their verdant screens in a mathematically straight line in front of the footlights, and then marched away behind the wings. To allow the next scene to go on, stage-hands had to enter and carry off the fragments of trees.

Not until Salvini was associated with Booth in the "Hamlet" and "Othello" performances did American play-goers see the tragedian surrounded by stage accessories that could assist, rather than hamper, the effect of his strong impersonations.

HAMLET.

THE Ghost of Hamlet's father stood on the stage of the royal Blackfriars play-house in London town, while around him were grouped John Hemings and William Sly, Joseph Taylor and Henry Condell, and all the other play-actors of that day.

"Speak the speech, I pray you," said the Ghost, "as I pronounced it to you, trippingly on the tongue; but if you mouth it, as many of our players do, I had as lief the town-crier spoke my lines."

These were surely the words of Hamlet. Why, then, was not Dick Burbage, the great Dick Burbage, "King Dick," as the actors called him, uttering the lines? There he stood, the original Hamlet of the world, the greatest Hamlet the stage ever saw for years and years, — perhaps, for aught we know, the greatest Hamlet who ever

247

trod the boards, — and he was listening with reverent attention while the young man of eight and
thirty, whose part was simply that of the Ghost,
not only repeated the lines as an illustration for
the chief actor, but also pointed their lesson with
significant meaning to all the players.

And well might Burbage listen carefully. Well
might they all follow with closest attention the
words of the speaker. For it was Shakespeare
himself uttering the lines of which he was the
author.

Perhaps, — who knows? — the poet turned his
bright eyes sharply upon Will Kempe as he reached
the words, " And let those that play your clowns
speak no more than is set down for them; for
there be of them that will themselves laugh, to
set on some quantity of barren spectators to laugh
too; though, in the meantime, some necessary question of the play be then to be considered: that 's
villanous, and shows a most pitiful ambition in
the fool that uses it."

For comical Kempe, the original First Gravedigger, witty and eccentric, was far too apt to "gag"
a play, much to the annoyance of the author; and
Shakespeare had him in mind when he wrote those
reproving lines.

So, too, the dramatist had well considered the natural characteristics of Burbage, when he revised his sketch of Hamlet; noting the leading player's short, stout form, he decided it was better to let Hamlet be "fat and scant of breath" to suit the actor. Strange, is it not, that no one knows, or can know, how Shakespeare acted the Ghost, or how Burbage acted the Prince! We simply know the tribute paid the latter after his death, when the poetic elegy said: —

> "He 's gone, and with him what a world are dead,
> Friends every one, and what a blank instead;
> Take him for all in all, he was a man
> Not to be matched, and no age ever can.
> No more young Hamlet, though but scant of breath,
> Shall cry 'Revenge' for his dear father's death.
> Oft have I seen him leap into the grave,
> Suiting the person which he seemed to have
> Of the mad lover with so true an eye
> That there I would have sworn he meant to die."

At the time of that first performance of "Hamlet," in 1602, Burbage was thirty-six years of age. Thoroughly sincere in his work, he would never, after assuming a part, allow himself to leave that character till the final act, not even returning to himself in the retiring-room, but still keeping his mind and action with his *rôle*. Moreover, when on the stage, he never ceased from action, or

rather expression, so that, even while others were
speaking, it was a delight for the spectators to
watch the looks and gesture of Burbage as he listened or acted out an aside scene. Some older
writers have claimed that Joseph Taylor was the
original Hamlet, but the claim is not by any means
substantiated; let the glory of being the original
Iago to Burbage's Othello prove sufficient for Taylor's fame.

A younger Hamlet follows, a mere youth of
twenty-six, but such a glorious Hamlet! To be
sure, he wore the dress of a courtier of the day
(and afterwards he added cocked hat and powdered
wig), but yet his acting was faithful to the part,
and magnificent in effect. If his scenes with Ophelia were the better, who can blame him; for was
not fair Mistress Saunderson his sweetheart, and
were they not destined soon to be married? His
low, gentle voice, his native dignity of bearing,
his entrancing gracefulness of movement, all these
were noted in every act. What care we, — or what
cared they, the audience at Lincoln's Inn Fields, on
that December night in 1661, — if the impersonation was not entirely original, but was learned from
Sir William Davenant's description of Taylor's acting as he had seen it?

Pepys was there; and Pepys, who, as a rule, saw little to please him in Shakespeare's works, was simply carried away by Betterton's acting, declaring he "did the Prince's part beyond imagination." And later on, after witnessing another performance, he affirmed enthusiastically, "I was mightily pleased with it, but above all with Betterton, the best part, I believe, that ever man acted."

Admiration without stint was poured by Colley Cibber upon the acting of the elder player. Sitting one night in the theatre, side by side with Addison, Colley had noted with regret the applause that showered down from an unthinking audience upon another Hamlet (Robert Wilks), who, on the first appearance of the Ghost, had literally thrown himself into a tumult of noisy expression with voice and action, "tearing a passion to very rags."

"I like it not," said the old fellow to the Tatler.

"Nor do I," returned the scholar. "I am surprised to think any player should put Hamlet into violent passion with the Ghost; it seems to me the appearance should astonish, not provoke, the Prince."

And then Cibber, finely expressing his criticism, responded, "Yes, Mr. Addison, in that beautiful speech the passion never rises beyond an almost breathless astonishment, or an impatience, limited by filial reverence, to inquire into the suspected wrongs that may have raised him from his peaceful tomb, and a desire to know what a spirit, so seemingly distressed, might wish or enjoin a sorrowful son to execute toward his future quiet in the grave. This was the light into which Betterton threw this scene, which he opened with a pause of mute amazement; then, rising slowly to a solemn, trembling voice, he made the Ghost equally terrible to the spectator as to himself. In the descriptive part of the natural emotions which the ghastly vision gave, the boldness of his expostulation was still governed by decency, manly, but not braving, his voice never rising into that seeming outrage or wild defiance of what he naturally revered."

And what think you this great actor, Betterton, received as salary? During all his long career in London, the highest pay ever awarded him was four pounds a week for his own services, plus one pound given as pension to his wife after her retirement. Yet when he died all England mourned; and, indeed, if we are to believe the poet of the day, the sorrow of his death drowned the signs of grief for Queen Anne's demise.

Only one man ever spoke ill of Betterton; that was the cross-grained, cynical old Anthony Aston.

When the famous actor, nearing his threescore
years and ten, was still playing in the tragedy,
Anthony thought he ought to " have resigned the
part of Hamlet to some young actor who might
have personated, though not have acted, it better."
And then follows the bill of particulars : " When
he threw himself at Ophelia's feet, he appeared a
little too grave for a young student lately come
from the University of Wittenberg;" "His rep-
artees seemed rather apothegms from a sage philosopher than the sporting flashes of young
Hamlet."

But Anthony went too far in his caricaturing;
for he saw fit to paint the favorite of the town as
ill-shaped, with large head, short, thick-set body,
stooping shoulders, and long arms. There were
pock-marks on his face, swore the ugly tempered
critic, his body was too fat, his feet too large, and
his voice was low and grumbling. And yet the
fellow had to admit that the same heavy voice
could be so turned by Betterton as to enforce uni-
versal attention, even from the leering fops and
flirting orange girls in the pit.

Regarding Wilks, whom Cibber severely criticised, Barton Booth, a Ghost of those days so slow
and solemn and noiseless as to inspire the audience

with genuine awe and terror, spoke his mind very freely one day at rehearsal.

"Bob," said he to Wilks, "I thought last night you wanted to play fisticuffs with me; you bullied that which you ought to have revered." And then he paid a glowing tribute to the other player, by adding, "When I acted the Ghost with Betterton, instead of my awing him, he terrified me."

"Yes," responded honest Wilks, with becoming modesty. "Mr. Betterton and you could always act as you pleased; I, for my part, can only do as well as I can."

Indeed, on one occasion Betterton's Hamlet, with its intensity and horror, so overcame the experienced Booth that the latter hesitated even to disconcertment for a time, and only by a strong effort of the will managed to maintain the action of the Ghost. It was declared by a writer in 1740 that Betterton himself, under the spell of his temporary living in the character, would actually turn pale at sight of his father's spirit, while his body would shake with genuine tremor.

All this fervor could be retained even as the years advanced.

On the 20th of September, 1709, at the age of seventy-four, he was playing the young Prince of

THOMAS BETTERTON.

Denmark; and, fortunately for us, Steele was present at the performance. In the *Tatler* he describes the acting : —

" I was going on in reading my letter, when I was interrupted by Mr. Greenhat, who has been this evening at the play of ' Hamlet.' ' Mr. Bickerstaff,' said he, ' had you been to-night at the play-house, you had seen the force of action in perfection : your admired Mr. Betterton behaved himself so well, that, though now about seventy, he acted youth, and by the prevalent power of proper manner, gesture and voice, appeared through the whole drama a youth of great expectation, vivacity, and enterprise. The soliloquy, where he began the celebrated sentence of " To be, or not to be ; " the expostulation, where he explains with his mother in her closet ; the noble ardor after seeing his father's ghost ; and his generous distress for the death of Ophelia, are each of them circumstances which dwell strongly upon the minds of the audience.' "

Only a few more times were his impersonations to please the town. On the 28th of April, 1710, he died, suddenly overcome by the violent eighteenth century remedies taken for gout. His wife lost her reason over her husband's death, and two years later followed him to the grave.

The February sun, four years after this sad event, saw an English soldier in the town of Lichfield rejoicing over the birth of a finely formed child.   Father and mother planned then a great business career for their offspring; neither of them inherited histrionic connection or taste, and the future stage nobility of the boy could not have been foretold, even in their dreams. Davy, they called him, Davy Garrick.

Soon the father died: and the boy, with his brother Peter, entered into the wine business. Then the mother passed away; and the young man, twenty-two years of age, looked seriously towards the theatre.   His wonderful *début* at Goodman's Fields, in the character of Richard III., set the town agog.   That was in 1741.   The next summer he was in Dublin; and there, to great applause, for the first time acted Hamlet, the gay Peg Woffington appearing as his Ophelia.

The die is cast: the great leader of the stage of the eighteenth century is at hand.

Garrick is a Shakespearian actor; and yet how rashly does he handle the play of the bard.   As manager he can revise the text, and he does so with an eye chiefly to his own advantage.   Laertes's character is changed; Ophelia's death is not made known to the audience; the Queen is reported to have gone insane; the King defends himself in a fight with the Prince, and then Laertes and Hamlet die of their mutual wounds; while a dying speech, originally given to Laertes, is found to win him too much applause, and so is turned into the mouth of Hamlet. Moreover, Osric and the Grave-diggers are completely out of the play.

The strength of the acting made England accept this mutilation. In fact, some years later, when John Bannister, playing the Dane for his benefit, restored the original version, an old actor whispered in tones of reverent horror, "Sir, if ever you should meet with Mr. Garrick in the next world, you will find that he will never forgive you for having restored the Gravediggers to 'Hamlet.' "

The accomplished Thespian, too, would not scorn stage tomfoolery. In the closet scene, for example, he had a trick chair with inbent, narrow, pointed legs, that, by its own weight, would fall with a crash to the floor when Hamlet started up at the appearance of the Ghost. Old Dr. Johnson thought Davy rather exaggerated terror in this scene.

"Do you think, sir, if you saw a ghost," quoth Boswell, "you would start as Garrick does in Hamlet?"

"No, sir," promptly replied the lexicographer; "for, if I did, I should frighten the ghost."

But, for all this, when we see how the scene affected Mr. Lichtenberg, we can readily understand the popular favor of the impersonation. It was in 1775 that that gentleman pictured in graphic language the first scene with the Ghost. Hamlet, Horatio, and Marcellus are awaiting the Spirit, Hamlet, with folded arms and hat drawn over his eyes, shivering in the cold air. It is so quiet that one can hear a pin drop at the farthest end of the play-house. Suddenly Horatio points out the Ghost. Swiftly turning, Garrick, with trembling knees, staggers back a pace or two, his hat falling to the ground, and his arms involuntarily extending to their full length, with the hands at the height of his head. With legs stretched far apart, and with mouth open, there he stands, as if electrified, while the expression of horror upon his face is so intense as to cause a repeated shudder to pass over the spectator. There is almost appalling silence on the part of the audience.

At last he speaks in trembling voice, "Angels and ministers of grace defend us;" words which, to use Mr. Lichtenberg's language (translated), " complete whatever may be wanting in this scene to make it one of the sublimest and most terrifying of which, perhaps, the stage is capable."

The mad scene comes on, and Hamlet, with fly-ing hair and with a stocking hanging half-way down the leg, and a red garter slipping towards the ankle, slowly advances, as in deep thought, with one hand upholding the chin, while the other rests the elbow of the supporting arm. His eyes are downcast as he paces forward in dignified man-ner. Removing his hand from his chin, but still letting the other hand support the elbow, he begins in a soft, yet clearly audible voice, " To be, or not to be."

" I pity those who have not seen him," cries Hannah More, after one of those impressive scenes. " The more I see him, the more I wonder and admire."

Have not you, a reader of Fielding, noted Par-tridge's criticism of Garrick in the play? " You may call me coward if you will, " he exclaims, " but if that little man there upon the stage is not frightened, I never saw a man frightened in my life. . . . Did you not yourself observe after-wards, when he found out it was his father's spirit, and how he was murdered in the garden, how his fear forsook him by degrees, and he was struck dumb with sorrow, as it were, just as I should have been had it been my own case? . . . He the

best player! why, I could act as well myself. I
am sure, if I had seen a ghost, I should have looked
in the same manner, and done just as he did."

But the nervous, impetuous Hamlet passes away,
and a slow, meditative Hamlet takes his place. It
is John Philip Kemble, the founder of another
school of acting, the ponderous, dignified school.
The Garrick version is thrown to the winds, and
the original Shakespearian tragedy returns. The
costume this new Hamlet wears is a dark velvet
court dress of the day ; with mourning sword swing-
ing at the side, and a heavy robe hanging from the
shoulders. A glittering star of a modern order rests
upon the breast of the Prince, while the symbol of
the Order of the Elephant is suspended from his
neck.

Mrs. Siddons has already won fame in London
town, and has brought her elder brother to Drury
Lane, there, on the 30th of September, 1783, to
make his *début* as the melancholy Dane. That
night, with excessive modesty, the *débutant* omitted
the advice to the players, on the ground that he,
a newcomer, ought not to utter such lessons to
others. After he had become a recognized member of the profession in London, he quickly restored
the lines.

JOHN PHILIP KEMBLE AS HAMLET (In Act V., Scene I).

Graceful, — "too scrupulously graceful," says one critic, — deeply studied (and, in fact, it is said he wrote out his part forty times during his study of Hamlet in order to keep it familiar in his mind), with grand declamation in the soliloquies and suggestive by-play, but yet cold and unimpressive, — is the general verdict. In the fencing scene, for example, the critical little liked the over-abundant complaisance and solemnity of bowing.

And yet Matthew Arnold, in after years, when summing up certain actors, would say, "All Hamlets whom I have seen dissatisfy us in something. Macready wanted person; Charles Kean, mind; Fechter, English; Mr. Wilson Barrett wants elocution. . . . Perhaps John Kemble, in spite of his limitations, was the best Hamlet after all."

Moreover, Tom Davies, writing in the olden day, could bestow this unstinted praise: "In the impassioned scene between Hamlet and his mother, in the third act, Kemble's emphases and action, however different from those of all former Hamlets we have seen, bore the genuine marks of solid judgment and exquisite taste. I never saw an audience more deeply affected, or more generously grateful to the actor who so highly raised their passions. Mr. Kemble is tall, and well made; his

countenance expressive, his voice strong and flex-
ible, his action and deportment animated and
graceful."

Indeed, we may well agree that Kemble's "sen-
sible, lonely" Hamlet was a worthy addition to
the stage.

One day Dr. Johnson was called on to settle a
point in Kemble's interpretation. The actor, with
tender but pronounced emphasis on the second
word in the query uttered to Horatio, "Did *you*
not speak to it?" used to imply that, most assuredly, Hamlet's dear friend must have questioned
the Ghost.

"What say you, sir?" said Kemble to the author-
itative scholar; "Steevens says I am wrong. Do
you agree with me?"

"To be sure I do," replied Johnson; "in that
phrase 'you' should be strongly marked. I told
Garrick so long ago, but Davy never could see
it."

Another point of difference between the two his-
trions manifested itself in the same act, when
Kemble, departing from all tradition, instead of
pointing his sword at the apparition, while following it, let the weapon drag behind him as he
advanced.

"And for my soul, what CAN it do to *that?*" exclaimed Kemble's Hamlet, as if rejoicing in the safety of his soul, as well as asserting its security; while Garrick merely brought out the latter point, by exclaiming, "And for my soul, what can it do to THAT?"

So in other ways the later actor diverted from the familiar readings of the day, and yet without radical innovations.

Stephen Kemble, in his old-fashioned gentleman's dress, with breeches and buckled shoes, and long auburn wig, attempted Hamlet; while still another brother, Charles Kemble (who, like his daughter, Fanny Kemble, believed that Hamlet was really mad), played the *rôle* occasionally. The daughter has left us this interesting, although undoubtedly flattering, description of the impersonation : —

"The great beauty of all my father's performances, but particularly of Hamlet, is a wonderful accuracy in the detail of the character which he represents — an accuracy which modulates the emphasis of every word, the nature of every gesture, the expression of every look, and which renders the whole a most laborious and minute study. My father possesses certain physical defects, — a faintness of coloring in the face and eye, a weakness of voice, — and the corresponding intellectual deficiencies, a want of intensity, vigor, and concentrating power. I have acted Ophelia three times with my father; and each time, in that beautiful scene where his madness and his love gush forth together like a torrent swollen with storms, which bears a thousand blossoms on its troubled waters, I have experienced such deep emotion as hardly to be able to speak. The exquisite tenderness of his voice; the wild compassion and forlorn pity of his looks, bestowing that on others which, of all others, he most needed; the melancholy restlessness, the bitter self-scorning — every shadow of expression and intonation was so full of the mingled anguish that the human heart is capable of enduring, that my eyes scarce fixed on his ere they were filled with tears; and, long before the scene was over, the letters and jewel-cases I was tendering to him were wet with them. The hardness of professed actors and actresses is something amazing. After this part, I could not but recall the various Ophelias I have seen, and commend them for the astonishing absence of everything like feeling which they exhibited. Oh, it made my heart sore to act it."

Henderson, in his three-cornered cocked hat, pleased some and displeased others. Macklin, too, had his friends. George Frederick Cooke tried to capture the *rôle* from John Kemble, but the public cried down his unpolished, sarcastic madman.

When Charles Mayne Young first essayed the *rôle* in London, he was so disconcerted by a hissing from the auditorium that he could scarcely proceed; that hissing, it was later found, came from his own father. Hamlet was the character in

whi h he made his metropolitan *début*. Twenty-
five years later, on the 31st of May, 1832, at the
age of fifty-five, Young saw his name for the last
time on a playbill, and then again it was opposite
the character of Hamlet. Macready was the Ghost,
Mathews was Polonius. This Hamlet was solemn,
yet somewhat vehement with its great show of ardor and animation.

Others, too, of the olden day played the *rôle*,
but to name the long list would require an ency-
clopædic history. The great impersonations alone
need be noted here.

There is Edmund Kean, on the 12th of March,
1814, appearing for the first time in London as
Hamlet, after having made a remarkable success in
other *rôles* during this first important metropolitan
engagement. Tenderness to Ophelia, says Dr. Doran, affection for his mother, reverential awe of his
father, and a fixed resolution to fulfil the mission
confided to him by that father, were the distinct
" motives," so to speak, of his Hamlet.

Edmund Kean did not use his sword to keep off
the Ghost, for whom he felt deep love rather than
dread, but instead introduced a novel bit of business by turning the point back against his friends
to prevent their stopping him from following the

vision. So, too, he introduced another novelty for those times, — the return to Ophelia's side, after his harsh words to the fair young girl, his tender imprint of a kiss upon her hand, and then, after a sad, loving glance at her face, his rush from the scene.

As for the mournfulness of his voice, it is said that in his boyhood his only friend, Miss Tidswell, would teach him the proper expression to the phrase, "Alas, poor Yorick," by recalling a sad affliction that had happened to his uncle, Moses Kean, and then having him say first, "Alas, poor uncle!"

Observant Hazlitt, while declaring that Kean's Hamlet too often showed a severity approaching to violence in the common observations and answers, yet commended the power and feeling of his action. The kissing of Ophelia's hand, this critic pronounced "the finest commentary that was ever made on Shakespeare. It explained the character at once (as he meant it) as one of disappointed hope, of bitter regret, of affection suspended, and not obliterated, by the distractions of the scene around him. The manner in which Mr. Kean acted in the scene of the play before the King and Queen was the most daring of any, and the force and an-

imation which he gave to it cannot be too highly
applauded. Its extreme boldness bordered 'on the
verge of all we hate,' and the effect it produced
was a test of the extraordinary powers of this extraordinary actor."

Of course admirers of Kemble's noble personality thought that his diminutive successor was very
insignificant in comparison; at least, they thought
so at first, if they were in the mood of Joe Cowell
when he originally saw Kean.

"Astonishing!" exclaimed Cowell, as he leaned
over to his neighbor Keeley in the pit, that night.
"Do you see the little fellow? Why, I was prepared to see a small man; but — compare him with
the princely person of Kemble, and he 's a perfect
pygmy."

Keeley, with his eyes on the stage, merely nodded
in response; but Cowell could not stop at this criticism. "This man's voice is objectionable," he continued. "His manner is tedious. His gesture —
Keeley, he 's a humbug, a veritable humbug."

But the play went on. The Ghost came in.
Cowell gradually grew more and more interested;
and finally, when Hamlet cried, "I'll call thee
Hamlet, . . . father," the sturdy admirer of Kemble
was completely won over, so touchingly were the

words uttered. Between his applauding and cheering of the actor, Cowell managed to whisper to his friend, "I 'm converted. It is admirable."

Even the widow of Mr. Garrick was so interested in the new Hamlet that she sent for him to call at her house, sat him down in her husband's chair, — which she declared should henceforth be kept solely for him, — and gave him points on the stage "business" of Davy.

"You are too tame in the closet scene," she said; "that is, you are tamer than was Mr. Garrick. Please to try it in more vehement a manner."

And the fiery little actor, though somewhat nettled by the criticism, not only did as she bade him, but thenceforth invariably acted the closet scene in Garrick's manner.

The young player never liked these comparisons with the heroes of old. "They insist," he would say, "that to praise me must necessarily detract from the fame of John Kemble. It is not so. Let every tub, I say, stand on its own bottom. Now, Kemble, I admit, was a great actor, but he never could have done this" — and, with a rush over the stage, he leaped into the air and turned a complete somersault.

The American stage had seen its first Hamlet

EDMUND KEAN.

EDMUND KEAN AS HAMLET (In Act I., Scene 4).

seventeen years after Garrick's original essay with the character in Dublin. On the 27th of July, 1759, in Philadelphia, Lewis Hallam the younger, advancing rapidly in the profession of his father, the founder of the American stage, was playing the title *rôle* in the great tragedy, while his mother of real life acted also the part in mimic life, portraying the Queen. Her second husband, Mr. Douglass, was the Ghost; and Mrs. Harman played Ophelia. Three years before the century closed, when the youth of 1759 was a man of nearly sixty, he was still acting the young Prince.

A most versatile player was Hallam, skilled in the gymnastic pranks of the harlequin of pantomime, admirable in comedy, and particularly entertaining in negro characters, and satisfactory in tragedy. He was a good dancer and a good fencer, besides possessing a mobile, attractive face, marred only by a slight cast in one eye, the result of an accident while learning to handle the foils.

The night of May 11, 1773, Josiah Quincy, being in New York, attended the theatre, and there saw tragedy and comedy both acted, liking not the former, but enjoying the latter. Yet in both he found Hallam well sustaining his *rôles*. That was the night Mr. Quincy confessed in his diary that while, "as a citizen and friend to the morals and happiness of society, I should strive hard against the admission, and much more the establishment, of a play-house in any State of which I was a member," yet he was so gratified with the evening's experience that personally he believed "if I had staid in town a month I should go to the theatre every acting night."

The theatre which Mr. Quincy attended on that evening was long famous as the home of the noted early productions of the metropolis of this country. It was not the first play-house of the city, but it was the first to obtain permanency. Before 1766 no town in America had possessed any but temporary homes for the play-actors. That year saw erected in Philadelphia the Southwark Theatre, a rough, homely, bright red brick-and-wood affair, whose best seat (for view of the stage) was in the gallery. In December, 1767, there was opened the first permanent home of the drama in New York, the John Street Theatre, a red building standing some sixty feet back from the street, and reached by a covered walk of rough wood. The dressing-rooms were in an adjoining shed. When the house was filled, the management's gross receipts were eight hundred dollars.

In the first American play produced in New York ("The Contrast" by Judge Tyler of Vermont), the character of Jonathan described, in quaint but probably truthful language, the general impression made upon the spectator on first entering this playhouse. "As I was looking here and there for it," quoth Jonathan, "I saw a great crowd of folks going into a long entry that had lanterns over the door, so I asked the man if that was the place they played hocus-pocus. He was a very civil kind of a man, though he did speak like the Hessians; he lifted up his eyes, and said, 'They play hocus-pocus tricks enough there, Got knows, mine friend.' So I went right in, and they showed me away clean up to the garret, just like a meeting-house gallery. And so I saw a power of topping folks, all sitting around in little cabins just like father's corn-crib."

Here it was that "Hamlet" was produced on the fourth day after the opening performance; and here it was that Lewis Hallam acted the Dane until, in 1798, the building was turned into a carriage factory, and then, the same year, demolished.

Up to the days of Kean, the stage of this country saw (besides Hodgkinson and Moreton) Cooper and Fennell, both of whom were essentially actors

of the early part of this century, although the
former played Hamlet, and the latter was acting
in New York, in that very year, 1797, when the
son of the founder of the first organized American company was still playing Hamlet — so brief
is the history of our stage. The first American-
born Hamlet was John Howard Payne, who at the
age of seventeen was acting the great *rôle* at the
Park Theatre in New York.

Payne saw Cooper playing the Dane in London
in the year 1817, and, writing home, declared that
in his opinion, while the American player (for such
he had then become) was not as great an actor
as Kemble, Cooke, or Kean, yet in natural grace
he led them all; while he was unmistakably "the
best Hamlet on the stage," being far less rude than
Kean, if not so startling in the part, more natural
than Kemble, if not so grand. " I shall never forget
his finished style of bowing to the audience," said
the author of "Home, Sweet Home," alluding to
the dignity of Cooper's deportment; "it acted like
mysterious magic over all, and at once made the
audience his personal friends."

As has been said, however, Cooper lost caste
with English play-goers after he had abandoned
them for America; and their sentiments were prob-

ably accurately voiced by " Anthony Pasquin "
(John Williams), when he wrote : —

"Where, where, is young Cooper, that Tyro so vain,
Who Hamlet re-kills, who's so often been slain?
But my memory urges, he'll vex us no more,
As he's sought with a troop the transatlantic shore,
Since our mummers believe, like some wine, (what a notion!)
They'll be more in request by their crossing the ocean."

HAMLET.

THE same year that Edmund Kean first played Hamlet in America (1820), Junius Brutus Booth also presented the character here. The acute, profound, spiritual melancholy of the elder Booth left an impression which time never effaced from the minds of those who saw him. What though some people scolded because his arms were awkwardly held close to the side, and maliciously asserted that his legs were bandy and his voice nasal; they all had to admit the intellectual acting of the born player. His rendering of the soliloquies of the tragedy was especially fine, without a sign of straining for startling points, but with a sustained interest that made harmony throughout all the play.

If ever a generous tribute was paid to an associate, it was in the year 1831, when Booth, then manager of a Baltimore company, gave to the vis-

iting Englishman, Charles Kean (his inferior as an
actor), the *rôle* of Hamlet, and himself assumed the
part of the Second Actor. The lines that fell to
the splendid impersonator were few; but he uttered
them with such expression and with such superb
elocution that the audience rose as if inspired by
one thought, and cheered him to the echo.

When this eminent, but sometimes eccentric, actor
was travelling through Kentucky, he took a freak
one day to pass himself off as Fontaine, a notorious
horse-thief in those days, when horse-thieving was
a capital crime. A couple of rustics, to whom he
imparted this mock information, immediately saw
visions of great rewards, and proceeded to take
him back to Louisville. In his best-natured manner the pseudo Fontaine consented to accompany
them.

In the town, however, he was recognized by the
sheriff, who asked what the trouble was. Booth
doubled the joke on the countrymen by declaring
that one of them was Fontaine. But just before
they were locked up, by a singular coincidence,
the real Fontaine was brought in as a prisoner.

Booth had a curiosity to visit the man in jail,
and queerly enough a sentimental friendship sprang
up between the two. One day Booth spoke of the

difficulty he experienced in always procuring a human skull when he played in "Hamlet." Then and there Fontaine made his will, bequeathing his head, after he had been hanged, to Junius Brutus Booth.

The elder Booth never obtained the memento, as he left Kentucky before Fontaine was executed; but, when Edwin Booth was playing in Louisville, Dr. Morris presented him with the skull, and told him its story.

The incident recalls the adventures of George Frederick Cooke's head. One day when "Hamlet" was staged at the Park, in New York, a theatre hand rushed to the office of Dr. John W. Francis, begging for the loan of a skull for the last act. "Alas, poor Yorick!" The only skull the doctor possessed was that of his old friend Cooke; so once more the actor, without the soul, assisted in a theatrical performance. In connection with this story I may add that never, so far as I am able to find out, did Cooke himself play Hamlet in America.

But another tragedian is appearing on the stages of the two countries, William C. Macready. In America he drew more money with Hamlet, his own favorite *rôle*, than with any other part; yet his constant use of the handkerchief, with its ac-

companying weeping and fretful tones, his somewhat fussy manner, and his lack of sympathy with
the character, were marked for disapproval.

Then, again, he had that wretched custom of prolonging his words. " To-er be-er, or not-er to-er
be-er " was almost as bad, in its effect, as Charles
Kean's catarrhal soliloquy, " To be or dot to be,
ch'dat is the queschdion."

That Macready had a loving regard for the wonderful character is shown by a story related by
Henry Irving. A friend of Sir Henry was with
the older tragedian on the night he last played
Hamlet; and as the curtain fell, and the actor laid
aside his velvet mantle, he was heard to mutter
almost unconsciously in Horatio's words, " Good-
night, sweet prince." Then, turning to Irving's
friend, Macready continued, " It is only now that
I am just beginning to realize the sweetness, the
tenderness, the gentleness, of the character."

When in America Macready had a peculiar taste
of the independent spirit of the country. He had
warned the King to die at the side of the stage,
so as to leave the centre (the point of advantage
for effect on the spectators) to Hamlet. But, instead, His Majesty deliberately dropped right in
the place where Hamlet had planned himself to die.

"What-er do you mean-er by such conduct?" cried the angry tragedian, as the curtain fell.

"Well, Mr. Macready," coolly replied the wearer of the purple, "we Western people don't know much about kings, except that they have a habit of doing as they like; and I thought, as I was King, I had a right to die wherever I blamed please!"

Another story, which, however, may be taken with a grain of salt, was told by the actor Harley to his English friends. It was, in effect, that Macready, when remonstrating with his American Guildenstern for pressing too close to him on the stage, sarcastically remarked, "What, sir, you would not shake hands with Prince Hamlet, would you?" and was totally overwhelmed by the quick democratic reply, "I don't know; I do with the President."

The *pas de mouchoir* in the play scene was what called from Forrest that fatal hiss of which mention has been made in the Macbeth chapter. In his diary the Englishman describes his experiences that night: —

"Edinburgh, March 2 (1846). — Acted Hamlet with particular care, energy, and discrimination. On reviewing the performance I can conscientiously pronounce it one of the very best I have ever given of Hamlet. At the waving of the handkerchief before the play, and 'I must be idle,' a

man on the right side of the stage hissed! The audience took
it up, and I waved the more, and bowed derisively and
contemptuously to the individual. The audience carried it,
although he was very stanch to his purpose. It discomposed
me, and, alas, might have ruined many; but I bore it down.
I thought of speaking to the audience if called on, and spoke
to Murray about it, but he very discreetly dissuaded me.
Was called for, and very warmly greeted. Ryder came and
told me that the hisser was observed, and said to be a Mr.
W—— who was in company with Mr. Forrest.

"March 3. — Fifty-three years have I lived to-day. Both
Mr. Murray and Mr. Ryder are possessed with the belief
that Mr. Forrest was the man who hissed last night. I begin
to think he was the man."

How odd the gaunt, awkward tragedian must
have looked as Hamlet on this occasion is easily
surmised when one pictures his costume. The waist
of the garment over the dirty looking satin shirt was
nearly as high as his arms; his hat had a plume, as
one man said, " big enough to cover a hearse ;" his
black silk gloves would have fitted a coal-heaver's
hands; and his long, skinny neck extended in a
most homely way above his low collar.

One day Macready, turning to his friend Westland Marston, exclaimed, " No man is able to play
Hamlet completely until he has reached an age
too old to look the character !" This illustrates
the thought the actor put into his interpretation.

Phelps, who never really looked like Hamlet, was very apt to quiz Polonius in a comic vein, and, indeed, to give the whole turn of the acting at times a droll rendering that would arouse laughter. One night, however, at Sadler's Wells the humor came in spite of the actor. Under the theatre ran an old waterway; and on the evening in question the Ghost, a substitute actor, ignorant of the traps of the floor, went down the wrong hole. There was no "Swear" heard from below, as the text demands.

In an anxious undertone Mr. Phelps leaned over and called, "Mr. Mellon, Mr. Mellon! why don't you 'swear'?"

"How the divil can a mon swear when he's up to the neck of him in watther?" came the unexpected, loud response from below,—and the audience roared.

"Rest, rest, perturbed spirit," quoth Hamlet, in the words of the play, and not, we may be sure, without a twinkle in his eye,—and the audience saw the point, and laughed all the harder.

Charles Kean, "the son of his father," could not certainly be called an imitator of Edmund Kean in Hamlet, since he never saw the latter in the *rôle*. Perhaps, however, it would have been better if he had, since his own interpretation, seek-

ing to catch the romantic flavor, missed it just
so far as to become melodramatic. It was his first
performance of note in London that won any degree of popular favor; but though it had many
beauties, yet, for all that, one can hardly class it
as a permanently successful interpretation. An
American actor has described it roughly as "a tis-
sue of bustle, rant, and posturing."

James E. Murdoch, whose stage career extended
over many years, insisted that no actor ever absolutely lost himself in his part, and, as an illustration, would narrate his experience as Horatio to
Charles Kean's Hamlet. In the midst of an important scene, when, to all outward appearances,
the player was absorbed in his character, he suddenly whispered to his Horatio, "Good Heavens,
what noise is that?"

"It's only the ticking of the green-room clock,"
replied Murdoch, in a similar aside.

"What a nuisance!" responded Kean. A few
minutes later, in an irritated undertone, he queried,
"Can't they stop that confounded thing?"

And yet, all the time, he was expressing out-
wardly the emotions of his stage character, and
never giving to the audience the slightest sign of
annoyance or of interruption.

Henry Irving and Wilson Barrett, the latest of
the English Hamlets, offered interpretations of rad-
ically differing nature. The latter was essentially
of the melodramatic order, dealing in sensational
" new readings " and in constant nervous action;
in short, his was a Hamlet made over to suit his
own stage characteristics. His Prince was a youth
of twenty, a fiery, impetuous, determined hero, eloquent and flashing enough, but without depth.

Irving's troubled, pathetically bitter Hamlet, of
sensitive disposition, was thoroughly a student and
a gentleman. Nothing could be more strongly expressed in his portrayal than his love for Ophelia,
his warm-hearted friendship for Horatio, and his
filial affection for his mother, — thus illustrating
the tender side of the Prince's nature.

" Very human," declared Lady Hardy, after seeing the performance, " a genuine human being, with
the faults and the frailties that we all have. A
courteous gentleman is this Hamlet; he is neither
wholly mad nor wholly sane, his mind is clouded
and ill at ease." There was grace and there was
charm, but, on the other hand, there was lack of
passionate, tragic force.

The first time Irving tried the *rôle* of mystery
was in June, 1864, when he was in the stock com-

pany at Manchester. Ten years later he gave the part in London, and won such attention as to carry the character for two hundred nights in succession. He had never seen Macready in the part; and, as Kean had retired from the London stage in 1859, Irving probably had never seen that player in the *rôle*. On the 30th of December, 1878, a day of triumph was at hand for the actor; then for the first time he stood before the London public as manager of the Lyceum Theatre, as well as its chief performer, and then he again appeared as the melancholy Dane. With him, as Ophelia, was Ellen Terry; while, it is interesting now to note, Mr. Pinero, the noted playwright of to-day, was also in the cast.

"To produce the Hamlet of to-night," declared Mr. Irving, when called before the curtain, "I have worked all my life, and I rejoice to think that my work has not been in vain."

Picturesque, truly, is his hero, unlike in appearance any other Hamlet the stage has seen. His slight but yet nervously strong frame is surmounted by a long, deeply lined face, not handsome, but yet, with its broad forehead set off by curling black hair, its large, half-melancholy, half-fiery eyes, and its intellectual cast, a face not to be forgotten. He

HENRY IRVING.

wears above his black silk tights a rich loose jacket trimmed with fur, and ornamented with a gold chain hanging from neck to waist. A strong face, say you, the face of a student.

One night, while playing Hamlet, — Irving himself told the story to a friend, — something was flung from the gallery to the feet of the actor. It was a small gold cross, having its sides engraved with the words, "Faith, Hope, and Charity," "I believe in the forgiveness of Jesus," "I scorn to fear a change." The actor picked up the emblem, and placed it in his jacket. Later he learned that it had been thrown to him by a poor woman who was carried away by his acting, and who wanted Mr. Irving always to wear this cross, an heirloom of her family. So it hung for years — perhaps hangs to-day — from his watch-chain.

To the mind of Salvini the first part of Hamlet was sustained the best by the English leader. The Italian, when acting in London in 1875, was advised to play the part. He went to the Lyceum to see Irving in the *rôle;* and as he noted at the outset the "sublime" efforts of the English actor, with his "mobile face mirroring his thoughts," and his perfect shading and incisiveness of the phrases, he declared to himself at the end of the second

act, "I will not play Hamlet! My manager can
say what he likes, but I will not play it." As the
play proceeded, however, he modified his opinion,
finding that the English actor's mannerisms and
lack of power prevented him from doing full justice to the passion of the Dane when it had assumed a deep hue. Salvini then left his box, saying,
" I can do Hamlet, and I will try it."

But the public, as the Italian himself admitted,
regarded his form as too colossal for the mystery-
driven Prince; and though Robert Browning could
declare in his letter to Salvini, in 1875, that during
the play " the entire lyre of tragedy resounded
magnificently," the other spectators, for the most
part, frankly acknowledged it was not Shakespeare's
Hamlet.

Another hero of the play from abroad was Rossi,
an excellent actor in many ways, but an interpreter
of Hamlet who could apply realism so strongly to
poetry as to make a vivid, spirited, hot-blooded
Prince, sad, but yet intense and melodramatic, out
of a mournful, dreamy, pathetically blighted personality. On no night would he act the part exactly the same as he had on the previous night, —
in fact, he intended to avoid so doing, as he did
not believe in an actor having a set method or

arrangement of gestures and tones, — so that his Dane was always novel and unconventional.

As for Hamlet's madness, one day, in conversation in Boston, during his American tour of 1881, Rossi concisely expressed his views on that point in these words: "Hamlet's madness is feigned, but with this qualification, — he always has a penchant for acting the lunatic, for raving as the madman; he always has a fondness for displaying his violent notions to the world; and so, as insanity is a convenient cloak for his plans, he falls all the more readily into it. His is the insanity of the man who reasons, the lunacy of *raisonnement*."

Meanwhile the American stage had witnessed, besides several of the Hamlets already mentioned, the shrewd manager-actor William Pelby; light and airy James W. Wallack; the tall, commanding W. A. Conway; experienced Thomas Hamblin; the dashing younger Wallacks, Henry and J. W. Jr.; the popular Boston Hamlet, John R. Duff, whose wife was one of the best of Ophelias; Edward Eddy; George Vandenhoff, who made his first appearance in America in 1842 as Hamlet to the Ophelia of Sarah Hildreth, afterwards the wife of General Benjamin F. Butler; James Stark; Wyzeman Marshall; McKean Buchanan; James E. Murdoch, who first acted Hamlet in 1845; Edwin Adams, John McCullough, Bandmann, Bogumil Dawison, Barnay, and scores of others of lesser note. The world to-day is interested in only a few.

Though neither Forrest nor Davenport made a success of the deep character, yet we must give a passing glimpse at their interpretations. Forrest was a philosophical Hercules, a robust, ponderous Hamlet. When he first played the part, at the age of twenty-one, he adopted the general idea of assumed madness; years later he made the Prince actually mad. Davenport's Hamlet was quiet and tender, but was never popular, and never regarded as among his best parts.

Let me here relate a story of Forrest's experience with an incapable Horatio. In vain had the latter tried to satisfy the eloquent-voiced star in delivering the line, " I warrant it will," after Hamlet has said, " I will watch to-night, perchance 't will walk again."

" No, no," roared the tragedian, as Phillips, the actor in question, delivered the words with the wrong emphasis, " Speak it this way, sir." And Forrest himself gave the line in his own resounding way.

The subordinate tried. In vain. Once more

was the lesson repeated. Still Phillips failed to satisfy the leader.

"Great Heavens!" Forrest angrily cried, "can't you say it this way?"

"No, sir, I cannot," coolly responded Mr. Phillips. "My salary is eight dollars a week."

"We're not here to discuss salaries," cried the enraged Forrest. "Can you, or can you not, speak that line this way;" and again he repeated it.

"No, sir," calmly replied the other once more; "if I could deliver it that way, my salary would not be eight dollars a week, but five hundred dollars a night."

Forrest saw the point. In spite of his anger he smiled, as he turned to the manager, and exclaimed, "Let Mr. Phillips's salary during this engagement be doubled at my expense!"

But, alas, that night, Phillips, excited over his raised pay, forgot himself, and snatched directly from Hamlet's mouth the second phrase, "Perchance 't will walk again," repeating it himself. In a rage Forrest rushed off the stage at the end of the scene, crying, "I'll give a hundred dollars per week for life to any man who will kill that Phillips!"

The experience Forrest had with Barry Sullivan was of a different nature, yet equally spirited.

The Britain, a harsh, melodramatic Hamlet, was playing in Philadelphia, and Forrest, in the audience, showed to all around him how much he despised the innovations of the new actor (his alteration, for example, of the line "I know a hawk from a hernshaw" to "I know a hawk from a heron — pshaw!"). Sullivan might well resent the insult; but he waited his time, and in the second act, as he took Guildenstern and Rosencrantz aside, he pointed his finger straight at Forrest in the box, and, in the words of the text, exclaimed with emphasis, "Do you see that great baby yonder? He is not yet out of his swaddling clouts." And the audience cheered and hissed, admired the quick wit, but resented the attack.

Now Edwin Booth advanced to the front, and both Forrest and Davenport, as Hamlet, were thrown completely into the shadow by the thoughtful, melancholy actor, to whom for years to come the character was unconditionally awarded by all American players as essentially his property.

It was for this latter reason that Charles Fechter's novel portrayal came under stronger discussion than even its own peculiarity would have aroused. Fechter's pale, woe-begone Norseman, as Charles

CHARLES FECHTER AS HAMLET.

Dickens called him, shook his head of long, flaxen, curly hair, threw tender glances from his fine eyes, and with sympathetic voice expressed the tones of a romantic Prince. He would not mouth nor rant; but, as his acquaintance with the English language was acquired in his mature years, he was necessarily imperfect in his speech.

Some praised this Hamlet, called him an artist; others condemned and called him a mountebank; both sides were forcible. To one, the quick, passionate Hamlet, lacking completely in repose and dignity, was repulsive in conception; with the other, that very impetuousness thrilled to the tips of the fingers. He was brutal to the Queen, ferocious with Polonius, and continually on a rush in every scene; but yet his personal magnetism warmed the hearts of thousands of admiring spectators. The veteran actor, Dion Boucicault, once said, in conversation, that a deaf man would have revelled in Fechter's Hamlet; meaning that his picturesque appearance would win the eye, but his inadequate rendering of the text would offend the ear.

It was early in the year 1870 that the French educated actor — for to France he owed only his youthful bringing up, being by birth a native of London and the son of a German father and an

English mother — made his American *début* at
Niblo's Garden, New York, and on the 15th of
February he first showed us his Hamlet. His
initial stage experiences had been in Paris; but on
Oct. 27, 1860, he had appeared in London as a
professional English actor, choosing for his *début*
the same play in which he first greeted Americans,
Falconer's version of Victor Hugo's "Ruy Blas."

Long before Fechter was presenting his pathetically pretty Hamlet, the magnificent Prince of Edwin Booth had won the hearts of Americans. That
allegiance never ceased; and even to-day, when the
great actor has been in his grave for several years,
only a few daring young players venture to tempt
comparison with the glorious recollections of a
noble impersonation.

As far back as 1852 young Booth received his
first suggestion of undertaking the part. It was
on a summer's day in Sacramento, when Edwin,
then less than twenty years of age, appeared before his father clad for his benefit in the black
velvet garb of Jaffier in "Venice Preserved."

In his customary moody, thoughtful way, Junius
Brutus Booth gazed for a long moment at his son,
and then suddenly exclaimed, "You look like Hamlet. Why don't you play it?"

"Perhaps I will, — if I ever have another benefit," responded the younger man, thinking possibly, in the light of their present unsuccessful engagement, that such an opportunity was not very near at hand.

But the chance did come shortly afterwards; and so well was this Hamlet received by the California audiences, that the actor no longer hesitated to adopt the part as a leader in his *répertoire*. In 1857 he first performed the character in New York on the stage of Burton's Theatre.

At that time Booth's Hamlet had much more fire and enthusiasm than it presented in later years, when the intellectual had been made to predominate over the physical; it was brilliant, impetuous, and forceful. The very glitter of his acting won the favor of the spectators. When, for example, he threw the pipes far into the wings, as he cried, "Though you may fret me, you cannot play upon me," the house applauded liberally. But, as time went on, the studious actor saw that, if he abandoned all such striking but artificial methods, and adopted the melancholy, philosophical style, he would approach nearer the ideal.

I recall the note he wrote me regarding his favorite scenes. "I have no preference for any one

character as a whole," he said, "but like best the
quieter passages of 'Hamlet,' 'Lear,' and 'Macbeth.'" Then he added that his favorite lines
were: "If it be now, 't is not to come; if it be
not to come, it will be now; if it be not now, yet
it will come; the readiness is all. Since no man
has aught of what he leaves, what is 't to leave
betimes?"

As Booth changed, the audiences changed with
him, and still applauded freely. They could not
fail to be entranced with the graceful, dignified,
and natural interpretation. It was, indeed, sombre
in tone, but yet so pleasing in its freedom from
all attempt at theatricalism, so interesting in its
clear and incisive diction, and so fascinating in its
weirdness and absorbing in its awe-inspiring mys-
teriousness, that art seemed therein to have reached
its closest touch with nature. Booth's Hamlet
actually lived. With his death, for a time, Hamlet
died.

In that interesting, and at the same time touching, brief memoir of the elder Booth which the son
himself penned, is an explanation given of the eccentricities of the father, an explanation that brings to
the mental eye, in part, a view of Edwin Booth's own
conception of the hero of the tragedy of thought.

"To comprehend the peculiar temperament with which my father charmed, roused, and subdued the keenest and the coarsest intellects of his generation," wrote Booth, "one should be able to understand that great enigma of the wisest, Hamlet. To my dull thinking, Hamlet typifies uneven or unbalanced Genius. But who shall tell us what genius, of any sort whatever, means? The possessor, or rather the possessed, of it is, as in Hamlet's case, more frequently its slave than its master; being irresistibly, and often unconsciously, swayed by its capriciousness. Great minds to madness closely are allied. Hamlet's mind, at the very edge of frenzy, seeks its relief in ribaldry. For a like reason would my father open, so to speak, the safety-valve of levity in some of his most impassioned moments. . . . My close acquaintance with so fantastic a temperament as was my father's so accustomed me to that in him which appeared strange to others, that much of Hamlet's mystery seems to me no more than idiosyncrasy."

Not only was Edwin Booth's own acting polished in its entirety, but it was finished in all its details. On one occasion, when following the Ghost, Booth by chance turned the hilt of his sword towards the retreating spirit figure; and then recognizing the symbolic force of such a presentation of the cross formed by the handle and the guard, adopted the action for all future performances. That the audience might note the significance of the skull of Yorick, "the fellow of infinite jest," Booth had a tattered fool's cap attached to one of the skulls tossed up from the grave, and that was the selected death's-head for the apostrophizing.

Talking one day with Henry Tuckerman of New York, Booth received from that gentleman the suggestion that he follow the example of the old actors, and stand while delivering the soliloquies. At the very next performance Mr. Tuckerman observed the player seated, as before, when he began the lines, "To be or not to be."

"Surely," said the observer, "he cannot now rise with propriety or grace."

But just as Hamlet finished the words " to sleep, perchance to dream," the Dane seemed, in a moment of deep thought, to look far away into that mysterious abode of death, and then, with his face showing an awful realization of the future, rose as if driven by the horror of the mental vision while he cried, " Ay, there's the rub! "

" Yes," declared Mr. Tuckerman, "he has caught the inspiration in that reflective pause."

In 1860 Booth married Miss Devlin, and the next year visited England, there to meet with the discouraging reception narrated in another chapter. In England his only child, Edwina, was born; but shortly after this, when the family had returned to America, Mrs. Booth died. Now the actor, in association with J. S. Clarke and William Stuart, leased the Winter Garden Theatre, in New York, and in November, 1864, began a notable run of one hundred nights of " Hamlet," the longest run that that play, or any other Shakespearian drama, had ever enjoyed up to that date.

It seems that, when the play was first staged for this run, the promoter of the engagement, William Stuart, was confident that it would go for six months; but, as the rehearsals progressed, he changed his mind, and decided that two months was all it could hold out, and finally came to the conclusion that a four weeks' season would satisfy him. Booth himself was then entirely unused to such lengthy runs, and, as he himself said shortly afterward, was heartily sick and weary of the monotonous work.

" Let us change the bill," he said to Stuart; " this incessant repetition is affecting my acting."

But Stuart, happy over the money that was pouring into the coffers, cried, " No, no, my boy ! Keep it up! Keep it up ! Never mind if it goes on for a year; keep it up ! "

" And so," naïvely said Booth, when telling the story, " we kept it up."

The citizens of New York planned to give the actor a commemorative "Hamlet" medal; but circumstances delayed the presentation of this testimonial until the 22d of January, 1867.

Going from New York to Boston, Mr. Booth was there playing, on the 14th of April, 1865, Sir Edward Mortimer in "The Iron Chest." In Ford's Theatre, Washington, on the same evening, the terrible tragedy that touched the whole nation was acted. Immediately Booth cancelled his engagement, and, grief-stricken to the heart, retired, as he then thought, forever from the stage.

But friends induced the actor to return; and on the 3d of January, 1866, he made his reappearance on the stage of the Winter Garden Theatre, playing Hamlet. There were angry citizens outside the play-house, hissing and hooting, and threatening to shoot; but inside there was a more judicious and representative body, which encouragingly greeted the actor, on his entrance, with three times three

EDWIN BOOTH AS HAMLET.

hearty cheers, and banished his troubled spirits with applause and floral tributes.

One evening, about a year later, Hamlet was obliged to act with his arm in a sling; for on the night before, during the performance of the "Apostate," at Baltimore, Charles Vandenhoff, acting Hemeya, overcome with the excitement of his part, neglected to notice that his dagger was not blunted, and furiously struck the Pescara of the evening again and again with the sharp blade. Fortunately, Booth had raised his hand to his breast to ward the blows, and so he escaped with life. But the three thrusts through the hand caused him to faint from pain, and necessitated his abandoning his engagement for a while after that week. In "Hamlet," on the night after the encounter, he fenced not ungracefully with his left hand.

At this time Mary M'Vicker was acting with Booth; and on the 7th of June, two years later, the two were married. In November, 1881, the lady died. Booth meanwhile passed through the strain of the history of his own finely conceived, but ill-fated, Booth's Theatre, in New York, and for a second time visited England.

Of his subsequent "Hamlet" productions, none (barring the great Wallack benefit of May 21,

1888 [1]) was more notable than those in which he united, in succession, with Salvini as the Ghost, with Modjeska as Ophelia, with Lawrence Barrett as Laertes.

For the last time in his life Booth trod the stage on the 4th of April, 1891 (at Brooklyn), and the play then was "Hamlet." The house was crowded to its utmost capacity, and Mr. Booth responded to the enthusiasm of his audience by playing as if inspired. Yet he did not for a moment speak, or seem to think, of the occasion as being his farewell to the stage.

Miss Annie Proctor (Queen Gertrude), taking

[1] Hamlet	Edwin Booth.
Ghost	Lawrence Barrett.
King Claudius	Frank Mayo.
Polonius	John Gilbert.
Laertes	Eben Plympton.
Horatio	John A. Lane.
Rosencrantz	Charles Hanford.
Guildenstern	Lawrence Hanley.
Osric	Charles Kochler.
Marcellus	Edwin H. Vanderfelt.
Bernardo	Herbert Kelcey.
Francisco	Frank Mordaunt.
First Actor	Joseph Wheelock.
Second Actor	Milnes Levick.
First Gravedigger	Joseph Jefferson.
Second Gravedigger	W. J. Florence.
Priest	Harry Edwards.
Ophelia	Helena Modjeska.
Queen Gertrude	Gertrude Kellogg.
The Player Queen	Rose Coghlan.

the call with him after the closet scene, said, as they retired behind the curtain, "Mr. Booth, I hope this is not the last time you will ever play."

"Oh, no, I think not," he answered; "I shall take a good long rest, endeavor to regain my health, and then resume the old work."

The scene of that same afternoon in Montague Place was wholly a surprise to Mr. Booth. He dressed quickly after the curtain fell; in fact, was among the first of the company ready to leave the theatre. He passed directly to the stage-door, and the rest heard a tremendous cheering immediately following his stepping from the building. Every one hastened to the door, there to see Montague Place filled with a great throng which had gathered to have one last look at the idol of the stage. Hats and handkerchiefs were waved, men, women, and children cheered, and police assistance was necessary to make a passage for Mr. Booth from the theatre to the carriage. Booth himself seemed nearly overwhelmed by this unexpected farewell. He only lifted his hat, bowed with a smiling and appreciating modesty, and was soon borne away from his enthusiastic friends.

Mr. Booth's associate, Lawrence Barrett, had died; and it was for this reason the surviving

actor cancelled his engagement. On the 7th of
June, 1893, he himself passed to that undiscov-
ered country from whose bourn no traveller returns.

Mr. Barrett had attempted the melancholy Dane,
but not after becoming associated with Booth. "No
one," said he, in those later years, to the writer,
"will attempt Hamlet while Edwin Booth is alive;
the part is his, and his alone." Barrett's impersonation was restless and rapid, and, though intellectual and vigorous, could not be accepted as an
ideal. It is said that in his life he acted every
male character in the tragedy excepting the First
Gravedigger and Polonius. When first he assumed
the title *rôle*, in 1855, the management thought
best to tempt the country audiences by giving a
more popular name to the play, and so billed it as
"The Grave Burst; or, The Ghost's Piteous Tale
of Horror."

Of the younger actors of to-day, the earnest, energetic Joseph Haworth; the picturesque, passionate Alexander Salvini, son of the elder actor of that
name; the well-experienced Louis James; the reserved Robert Mantell; the conscientious but metallic
Beerbohm Tree; Edward S. Willard and Creston
Clarke, — have all essayed Hamlet.

It is believed that Mrs. Patience Blaxland Rignold (mother of George Rignold) was the first actress to undertake the part of Hamlet, playing the character in Birmingham, England, at her own benefit, in the early part of this century. Among other women in the *rôle* have been Mrs. Bartley, Mrs. Barnes, Mrs. Battersby, Charlotte Cushman (who never played the part of Ophelia), Eliza Shaw, Fanny Wallack, Clara Fisher, Miss Marriott, Mrs. Emma Waller, Rachel Denvil, Susan Denin, Mrs. F. B. Conway, Julia Seaman, Adele Belgarde, Winnetta Montague, Anna Dickinson, and Mrs. Louise Pomeroy.

Few are the play-goers who have seen Shakespeare's "Richard III." on the stage. It has been Colley Cibber's version that the masses have witnessed, almost without exception, since the year 1700, when the adaptation first caught the reflection of the footlights.

Colley Cibber was a character, indeed. Born in 1671, he acted with Betterton ten years before the seventeenth century ended, and lived to play with Garrick, and to continue an active figure up to the year 1757. His first night was not successful, but yet he unexpectedly gained money by it.

"Who is that fellow?" cried the great Betterton angrily, enraged at the blundering way in which the youth entered the scene, and disturbed the harmony of the whole play.

" 'T is Master Colley, sir," replied the prompter.

" Fine him five shillings," bade the famous actor.

" Why, sir, he has no salary," responded the man of the play-book.

" No salary, eh ? Then put him down for ten
shillings a week, and fine him half of that at once.
He shall pay a forfeit."

And thus Colley obtained his first money in his
chosen profession.

He progressed slowly, for all the players and
managers seemed to distrust his ability, until finally,
writing a satiric play of his own, " Love's Last
Shift," with a special part in it for himself, that
of a fop, Sir Novelty Fashion, he made a decided
impression.   More plays followed from his pen, —
" She Wou'd and She Wou'd Not; " " The Careless
Husband," with its famous coxcomb and libertine,
Lord Foppington, for Cibber's own character — Lord
Foppington being his old friend, Sir Novelty, advanced in rank ; the " Nonjuror " adapted from
Molière's " Tartuffe ; " and other plays that in their
day were famous.

A rake and a toady, a gambler and a tyrant, a
gay old beau to his death, he yet rose to the top
of his profession so far as popular success as a comedian was concerned, and became the Poet Laureate
of England.

When Shakespeare's original " Richard III." was
produced, Burbage was the hero. After Cibber put
forth his version, every player courted the con-

COLLEY CIBBER.

glomeration from his pen, rather than the text of
the master. Certain it is that no other adaptation
of any play of Shakespeare equalled in merit that
of Colley's. Into the text comparatively few new
lines were introduced, but those that were in-
terpolated gained ever the applause of the galleries.

"Off with his head — so much for Buckingham!"
" Richard's himself again!" How men have cheered
and women applauded those lines for twice one
hundred years!

What cared the pittites if a part of " Henry VI."
and a bit of " Henry IV." and a slice of " Richard
II." and some lines from " Henry V." were shoved
into this " Richard III."? The dovetailing was very
ingenious, and the play was made entertaining. As
for the actor, he rejoiced at the multitude of " points "
offered him, the numerous telling lines with which
he could bring down the house, and the striking
situations for the hero and his foes. It was hard
work, a constant bustle and rush from first to last
— but, ah, the applause!

Cibber himself was never esteemed remarkable
in the *rôle* of the crook-back monarch; in fact, the
audience always laughed when he tragically called
" a horse, a horse;" but in his day he saw a great

impersonator of the character fight on the bloody field of Bosworth.

That was a memorable night, the 19th of October, 1741, when David Garrick, billed (not strictly with accuracy) as "a gentleman who never appeared on any stage," came forward in the historical play of the "Life and Death of King Richard III." at the little play-house in Goodman's Fields.

The audience, grown accustomed to the monotonous sing-song declamations of the drawling actors of that day, were astounded when this little man presented a natural Richard, a live, human, genuine plotting duke and scheming monarch, full of dash and full of passion. Recovering from their astonishment, they were delighted; and before long Garrick had become the craze. The young actor faced with confidence the splendidly dressed gallants and ladies, who deserted now the fashionable theatres to see the little wonder at Goodman's Fields; but he quaked somewhat when told that Pope, critical Pope, was there in a box one night watching his acting.

"When I was told that Pope was in the house," said our Richard, "I instantly felt a palpitation at my heart, a tumultuous, not a disagreeable, emotion in my mind. I was then in the prime of youth, and in the zenith of my theatrical ambition. It gave me

a particular pleasure that Richard was my character
when Pope was to see and hear me. As I opened
my part, I saw our little poetical hero dressed in
black, seated in a side-box near the stage, and view-
ing me with a serious and earnest attention. His
look shot and thrilled like lightning through my
frame, and I had some hesitation in proceeding from
anxiety and from joy. As Richard gradually blazed
forth, the house was in a roar of applause, and the
conspiring hand of Pope shadowed me with laurels."

Pope's word, indeed, was very commendatory. "I
fear the young man will be spoiled," he exclaimed,
"for he has never had his equal as an actor, and
will never have a rival."

Sarcastic old Cibber, made supremely jealous by
Pope's praise of the new player, contemptuously
remarked to his friends, "You really should see
Master Garrick. He is the completest little doll
of a figure, the prettiest little creature you can
imagine." But generous people agreed with Pitt,
that "he was the only actor in England."

For thirty-five years Garrick ruled the stage. Five
nights before his last performance, his crook-back
monarch made love to a handsome Lady Anne, then
closing most disastrously her initial season on the
London stage. This was Mrs. Siddons. The poor

woman, destined to become the greatest actress of
her day, met with the disapproval of the critics in
those early performances at Drury Lane, and on this
especial June night of 1776 was pronounced "lamentable." Yet there was reason for her seemingly
negligent acting, since, in her flurry over her selec-
tion, above all the other ladies of the company, for
the leading character, she utterly forgot Garrick's
strict injunction that, whatever she did, she should
always stand so that he, in addressing her, could
face the audience, and in consequence was given
such a glare of anger and disgust from the jealous
actor, that she nearly fainted on the stage. Moreover, little David, spurred to his best, put such
tremendous ferocity into his acting, that the young
girl at times was actually frightened.

Mrs. Siddons's brother, John Kemble, could not
make his Richard III. equal that of his rival, George
Frederick Cooke, but the latter himself, in his drink,
often played queer games with the character. One
night, for example, after his "indispositions" had
become the talk of the town, and the play-goers
were beginning to get tired of the announcements
of Mr. Cooke's illness, the actor stumbled and hesitated, mumbled and misread completely the very
first soliloquy of Richard. The pittites would not

stand that, so early in the play. They hissed and jeered and hooted. Maudlin Cooke, seeking again the familiar excuse, staggered to the front, laid his hand on his chest as if to indicate illness there, and blunderingly blurted out, " My old complaint, my old complaint." The audience aptly applied the words in a manner differing from his intention, and with derision howled him down.

With his prominent nose and chin, he looked something like Kemble when dressed for Richard. " Yes," said Charles Mathews, commenting on this fact, " he has, too, a very finely marked eye, and upon the whole, I think, a very fine face. His voice is extremely powerful, and he has one of the clearest rants I ever heard. The most striking fault in his figure is his arms, which are remarkably short and ill-proportioned to the rest of his body, and in his walk this gives him a very ungraceful appearance."

" He disturbs my acting," declared Kemble, in Dublin, jealous of the player during their first season together; " I can't act Hamlet when the Ghost is so drunk that he forgets his lines, nor Richard when Henry is staggering over the stage."

That was too much for the high-spirited George Frederick. " I'll show him that he can't play some of the greatest parts when I undertake them," he exclaimed; and, true to his word, played Richard at Covent Garden, on the 31st of October, 1800, with such fire and energy that Kemble, in the audience, saw he had met a dangerous rival; and soon afterwards, when the praises of the critics showered upon the Irish-born player's head, Black Jack relinquished Gloucester completely to his now acknowledged rival.

Dunlap voiced the popular idea when he said of Cooke, "His superiority over all others in the dissimulation, the crafty hypocrisy, and the bitter sarcasm of the character, is acknowledged by every writer who has criticised his acting."

This Richard performance, in the fall of 1800, was the beginning of Cooke's London engagements. His contract was for three years, at six pounds a week the first season, and an increase of one pound each subsequent season.

Every one anticipated a glorious opening of Cooke's second season in London, when Richard was again announced, and hours before the doors of the play-house opened a crowd had gathered to seek early admission. But the management had been hunting in vain for the reckless fellow, and now, perforce, was obliged to issue a notice that some accident must have happened to Mr. Cooke, and the bill therefore would be changed. It was again his " old complaint." Not until five weeks later did the man turn up.

In America, Richard was Cooke's first character. Acted in New York, on the 21st of November, 1810, it brought him added reputation and added dollars. But before long the metropolis, disgusted at his habits and at his insolence, rejected him. How could they continue to admire a stranger, who, when informed that President Madison was coming from Washington especially to see the player in his most noted character, could insult their country by declaring, " If he comes, I'll be hanged if I play before him. What! I, George Frederick Cooke, who have played before the Majesty of Britain, play before your Yankee President? I'll not do so. It is degradation enough to play before rebels; but I'll not go on for the amusement of a king of rebels, the contemptible king of Yankee-doodles."

He found no displeasure, however, in drinking wine with his new acquaintances — when he did not prefer to appropriate all the liquor to himself.

Dr. Francis visited him after one of his drinking-bouts, and found the talented player finishing up a thirty-hour spree at a table covered with decan-

ters, all empty except those that were utilized for
candlesticks. It was early in the afternoon, but
the candles were blazing in full strength. With
much difficulty Cooke was persuaded to go to the
theatre that night; and, though all were fearful he
would be so exhausted from his dissipation as to
be unequal to playing Richard with any force, yet
the verdict, after the curtain fell, unanimously pronounced the performance one of the best the actor
had ever given. Some twenty-four hours after this,
Cooke threw four hundred dollars into the hands
of poor beggars, and then — went to sleep.

The actor's art was very cleverly shown in the
impression Cooke made upon Dunlap, the manager
and author, when first they met. Dunlap could
not see the slightest marks of intemperance or
the least signs of eccentricity in the neat, soberly
dressed gentleman, with the powdered gray hair,
who greeted him at the hotel. And when the
curtain rose at the theatre, and the visiting player
stepped to the front, his new acquaintance noted
with admiration the picturesque and proudly noble
bearing, the elevated head, the firm step, and the
eye beaming fire. "Why," cried the experienced
man of the play-house, "I saw no vestige of the
venerable, gray-haired old gentleman I had been

introduced to at the coffee-house; and the utmost effort of my imagination could not have reconciled the figure I now saw with that of imbecility and intemperance."

At that time Cooke was fifty-four years of age, and was earning twenty-five pounds a week. Two years later his dissipation and his life were at an end.

With Edmund Kean the scheming Duke had an equally interesting association. In his early days the audiences sometimes hissed the player in the character because, forsooth, in his natural style of acting, he disregarded the listeners, making them, as the critics of Guernsey sapiently said, of no more account than if they formed the fourth side of a room in which he moved! But his violent temper gave them tit for tat, and temporarily silenced their sibilant condemnation by turning pointedly upon them the words of Richard, " Un-mannered dogs! Stand ye, when I command!"

"Apology?" cried the fiery young fellow, when the pittites yelled for a show of humiliation after this emphatic rendering of the text, "take your apology from this remark; the only proof of intelligence you have yet given is the proper application of the words I have just uttered."

This, of course, was before he came to London and won that glorious triumph in the "Merchant of Venice." Shylock brought him recognition; and Richard, following immediately afterwards, placed him in the front rank.

"It was the most perfect performance of any that has been witnessed since the days of Garrick," cried one critic; while another placed its advance over Cooke's as "an immeasurable distance." Some wiseacres, like the men of Guernsey, found his action "too natural," — for it was a return to Garrick's school that Kean inaugurated, in contradistinction to the heavy Kemble declamatory school, — but the most of the writers felt that with them now was a new genius, to whose ideas, however novel, respectful attention should be given.

The actors suddenly grew civil. Scornful Rae, playing Richmond, deigned to ask the little man, "Where shall I hit you, sir, to-night?"

"Where you can, sir," was the curt and significant reply. And Rae's arm grew weary long before he succeeded in making the fatal blow against the fierce, wiry, energetic fighter.

In that final scene it had been a trick of Young to hurl his sword at Richmond, as a last fruitless expression of rage from the dying monarch. Kean improved on that, by making weak though angry passes with his unweaponed arm as he fell back to death. In the earlier scenes the biting sharpness of his sarcasm, and the audacity of his hypocrisy, were studies of life, and remarkably effective. The spectators admired the graceful and striking poses as he leaned against the pillar; they noted the high breeding he seemed to show, and the humor of pleasantry he expressed above the wickedness of the character; and they wondered especially at his skill in turning swiftly from fierce, passionate utterances to familiar tones without making an unnatural, ineffective transition.

Lord Byron had been loth to accept the methods of the young player, but after Richard his admiration could not be left unexpressed. He hurried to the actor, as a mark of appreciation, an elegant sword and an embossed box of much value. "By Jove," Byron cried, "he is a soul. Life, nature, truth without exaggeration or diminution. Kemble's Hamlet is perfect; but Hamlet is not nature. Richard is a man, and Kean is Richard."

Mark the contrast of his last years, when Dr. Doran saw him as Richard at the Haymarket. "The sight was pitiable. Genius was not traceable in that bloated face; intellect was all but

quenched in those once matchless eyes ; and the
power seemed gone, despite the will that would
recall it." Occasionally he would burst out as
grand as ever, but his action was continually
hampered through the necessity of using a stick
for support, while, last of all, when Cooper, as
Richmond, dealt the final blow, he had to grasp
King Richard's hand and gently lower him to the
stage to prevent a fall that would have been dangerous to Kean in his condition at that time.

This was the end of that Richard who, in former
years, had fought "like one drunk with wounds,"
as Hazlitt said, presenting a picture of preternat-
ural and terrific grandeur, while he stood, after
his sword had gone, with hands outstretched as
if, though deprived of weapons, he yet by the exercise of his powerful will could fight the battle
on to victory.

In America Edmund Kean had seen fit to antag-
onize cultivated audiences in a most unnecessary
manner. In the early summer of 1821, when the
season was dull, the Englishman, in spite of the
protest of the local manager, opened a Boston engagement. For two nights he played to slim
houses. On the third night "Richard III." was
billed, but only a handful of people were in the

auditorium when the time came for the curtain
to rise. Arrogantly Kean declined to play; and,
though all present urged him to fulfil his obli-
gations to the public, he refused, and left the
theatre. Shortly after he had gone, more people
came, until the house was comfortably filled with
an audience that included many men of high standing in the city. Word to this effect was sent to
Kean's hotel, but still he obstinately refused to
change his position. The next day he hurried
from the city to await the coach from Boston in
a neighboring town.

The Bostonians arose in their indignation, and
hotly condemned the visitor for his discourteous
action and his unmanly retreat. The papers took
it up, and one sheet even printed the following
(the phrase " literary emporium of the New World "
being the very words used by Kean during his
previous engagement in Boston, when honor after
honor had been showered upon him) : —

ONE CENT REWARD.

Run away from the " Literary Emporium of the New
World," a stage-player calling himself Kean. He may be
easily recognized by his misshapen trunk, his coxcomical,
cockney manners, and his bladder actions. His face is as
white as his own froth, and his eyes are as dark as indigo.

All persons are cautioned against harboring the aforesaid vagrant, as the undersigned pays no more debts of his contracting, after this date. As he has violated his pledged faith to me, I deem it my duty thus to put my neighbors on their guard against him.

PETER PUBLIC.

New York sided with Boston; and Kean was obliged to write several letters to managers and to the newspapers, endeavoring to explain that he had withheld his services simply because they were not appreciated. Even then the popular indignation would not be stemmed; and soon Kean found it best to abandon all thoughts of further engagements in America at that time, and to sail for home.

In 1825, after his domestic disgrace in England, the actor again visited America, and here issued a most humble and piteous appeal for pardon. When he attempted to open his engagement in New York, with Richard, there was manifest opposition, though not sufficient to stop the play. But in Boston his appearance brought disaster. The Bostonians within the theatre hissed and pelted him with missiles until he left the stage, and then they even refused to allow the mimic tragedy to proceed without him. The mob outside stormed the windows and doors, and made almost a genuine tragedy by attacking the audience, — apparently for no reason except to create a disaster, — driving the occupants of the house out of the windows, and wrecking the chandeliers, seats, and all else within reach. The riot act was read twice by a justice of the peace, but without avail. Early in the fight Kean escaped, and immediately left the city.

Thomas Abthorpe Cooper once met a reception in England less disastrous than Kean's, but of the same emphatic nature. Though an Englishman by birth, he had identified himself with the American stage; and when he attempted to play in his native land, during a return visit there, his Richard was given such a storm of hisses and groans that he was obliged to retreat. "Off with him!" "No Yankee actors here!" cried the Manchester Britons, referring to his adoption by the country across the water.

All these years since 1700, Colley Cibber's version of the tragedy had held the stage. But the conscientious, student-like Macready was now at hand; and through his influence Shakespeare was restored in part in 1821, though only for two performances, as old Colley's adaptation quickly returned, to remain the prompt book of the tragedia s (with the exception of Phelps) down to the time of Henry Irving and Edwin Booth. Even when Macready introduced the novelty of an approach to Shakespeare's own work, he was obliged to retain the Cibberian lines that always brought down the house.

> " Off with his head! so much for Buckingham!"

> " Hence, babbling dreams : you threaten here in vain.
> " Conscience, avaunt! Richard's himself again."

It was with the tragedy of the wily Plantagenet that Macready, two years before, had saved Covent Garden from failure, replenished its treasury so that the company could be paid, and for himself turned the crucial point in a career that marked him famous. He shrank from the initial attempt, fearing that his figure was ill-adapted to essay a rivalry with Kean, but the management persisted in announcing him.

What was the result? "The pit rose to a man, and continued waving hats and handkerchiefs in a perfect tempest of applause for some minutes. The battle was won." So wrote Macready in his record-book. The performance was uneven, and in some scenes tame, but yet often was novel. There was apparent an assumed sincerity in the courtship

scene with Lady Anne, instead of the sarcastic
touches with which so many players sought and
gained effect. While Kean's characterization was
sombre and reflective, Macready's was bold-faced
and ardent. At the same time the latter player
would occasionally turn Richard's lamentations into
actual whining.

Charles Kean gave an animated Richard that
was, perhaps, less stagey than any of his other
heroes. Its earnestness may be surmised from the
incident that once occurred at Exeter, England.
Travelling with the player was his favorite dog,
a big Newfoundland named Lion. During the
performances the animal was usually locked in
the dressing-room; but on this particular night he
nosed the door open, and, hearing his master's
voice in loud tones upon the stage, bounded between the wings straight into the scene of Bosworth Field. There were Richard and Richmond
engaged in their deadly fight. Lion saw the
situation at a glance. His master was under.
With a growl he dashed upon the victorious Richmond, and without trouble drove that terrified
gentleman-at-arms off the stage, flying in dismay
from the big sharp teeth of Richard's defender.
The king, left to himself, had to fall back and die

without a scratch. Then Lion, returning before the curtain could fall, placed his paws gently on his master's prostrate form, and lovingly licked his face. The house roared. What Kean said is unknown; but he ungraciously refused to let gallant Lion share the call before the curtain, though the cries for "the dog" filled the theatre.

It was as Richard III. that Kean introduced him-self to Americans, at the Park Theatre, New York, on the 1st of September, 1830.

In the spring of 1845, Samuel Phelps, at Sad-ler's Wells, presented "Richard III." in its Shake-spearian form; and in 1877 Henry Irving repeated the experiment, for such it was. To the deformed monarch Irving gave a princely air, chivalric grace, and a force of intellectuality that made the *rôle* an attractive study, even though it lost, in his in-terpretation, the needed strong relief for the tragic scene in the final act.

In America, although the real interest in the theatre began with Hallam's company, yet there were irregular performances before the day of that organized troupe, and one of the earliest produc-tions known was that of "Richard III." Addi-son's "Cato," produced at Philadelphia in August, 1749, holds rank as the first play of which we have any record in this country, although there were performances — but of what drama we know not — as early as 1732. In the spring of 1750 the Philadelphia company came to New York; and there, in a room on Nassau street, on the 5th of March, brought out for the first time in America the "Historical Tragedy of King Richard III., Wrote originally by Shakespeare, and altered by Colley Cibber, Esq." Furthermore, the advertisement announced, "Tickets to be had of the Printer hereof. Pitt 5s., Gallery 3s. To begin precisely at Half an Hour after 6 o'clock, and no person to be admitted behind the scenes." The entire money capacity of the house in those days was $127.

The interpreter of Richard was one of the managers of the company, Thomas Kean, a writer by profession, but an actor by choice. Further than this brief record, nothing can be found of the original crook-back monarch. The second Richard was Robert Upton, of whom I have spoken in the Othello chapter. We will pass by Rigby and Hallam and the other early impersonators, to look at the more familiar men of the stage who gave especial emphasis to the hero of the play. Several of these have been noticed in the descriptions of the Englishmen who visited these shores.

The elder Booth, whose name is so closely associated with the American stage, gave his most interesting performance of Richard in England. That
was on Feb. 12, 1817. A year or two before this
he had secured his first London engagement, but
had then, ungraciously, been cast only in small
parts, while his salary was but two pounds a week.
In 1817, however, he was put forward at the same
theatre, Covent Garden, in the leading *rôle* of
Richard.

Every one noticed at once the resemblance to
Kean, both in appearance and in acting; and many
pronounced the impersonation an imitation. "He
has the eyes, face, and walk of Kean, the same
stamp of the foot, the same voice, except in its
vehement tones," cried one attendant of those days,
adding emphatically, "when we entered the box
at Covent Garden, and heard Mr. Booth in the
scene with Lady Anne, we really were doubtful
whether we had not mistaken the house, and wan-
dered into Drury Lane."

The public demanded repetitions of the play.
But the manager tried, in a niggardly spirit, to
keep the newcomer's salary down to five pounds a
week; and, as a result, Booth ordered his name
from the bills. Then Kean, in a carriage, hurried to

Mr. Booth's lodgings, induced him to drive to the rival theatre, and there prevailed on him to sign an engagement. Of course a controversy arose. Meanwhile, at old Drury, Booth acted Iago to Kean's Othello, but was refused the chief characters in other plays where Kean had made successes. So the younger player once more changed sides, and returning to Covent Garden, there appeared again as Richard.

The complications thus caused led to a tumult of disapprobation that effectually prevented a word of the actor's being heard, and to the end the play went through in dumb show. More rioting followed on succeeding nights, and by many it was claimed that these occurrences led to Booth's abandonment of the London stage. However that may be, it is certain that in April, 1821, he came to America with his young wife, whom he had married three months before, and here, on the 6th of July, at Richmond, Va., opened his New World career as Richard III.

This engagement at Richmond was broken for one night by a performance at Petersburg. Mr. Russell, of the Petersburg Theatre, had seen Booth in Richmond, and had returned home with an enthusiastic verdict regarding the new actor. At that time a great many people thought that the announced Booth must be an impostor, as they did not believe the English actor could have landed so quietly in the United States.

N. M. Ludlow, who was well known as a manager in former years, was present at the rehearsal and performance in Petersburg. At that morning rehearsal he stood at the head of the stairs, in the rear of the stage, when up to him rushed a rather overgrown boy, of some sixteen years in age, with roundabout jacket covered with dust, and with a cheap straw hat thrust back from his perspiring forehead.

"Where is the stage-manager?" queried the newcomer.

"Over there," replied Ludlow, pointing to Russell; and then, to the former's astonishment, he saw Mr. Russell turn, hurry forward, and, seizing the hand of the "boy," exclaim, "Ah, Mr. Booth, I am glad you have arrived. We were fearful something had happened to you."

Ludlow could scarcely believe his eyes and ears. He thought the manager was playing a joke on the company; for surely this little fellow could not be the great Mr. Booth of whom Russell had said, "He is undoubtedly the best actor living."

But, as the rehearsal went on, it was noticed that, although the stranger ran through his part very carelessly, he seemed to be perfectly familiar with all the business of the play. It may here be stated that the dust covering the actor's clothes was due to his having walked the entire distance from Richmond to Petersburg, twenty-five miles, when he found he had missed the stage-coach.

There was a strange feeling behind the footlights that night as the first acts of "Richard III." progressed; for Booth not only neglected to recognize the applause of the audience when he entered, but also walked through the early scenes with the utmost indifference, and without the slightest effect.

Old Benton, who was playing King Henry, exclaimed in astonishment to Ludlow, "What do you think of him, sir?"

"Think," replied Ludlow, "just what I thought before; he is an impostor." And everybody else agreed that, if he was not an impostor, certainly Mr. Booth's reputation had been misstated. The great scenes which George Frederick Cooke had made prominent, such as the meeting with Lady Anne, were completely slighted.

Every one felt disgusted.

Then came the fourth act, the scene with Buckingham, where Richard hints at killing the princes. From that moment there was a complete change in the actor's interpretation. Fire, enthusiasm, energy, and spirit gave magnificent strength to those final scenes; and when at last the curtain fell, the actors exclaimed, one to another, that even their idol, Mr. Cooke, was completely eclipsed by the grand performance; while the auditors thundered their applause in a most significant manner.

Booth's dying scene was said to be frightful, his eyes dilating and glaring in terrible manner, and the perspiration actually rolling down his forehead from the earnestness and vigor of his performance. Often in "Richard III.," as in other plays, he introduced his eccentricities, and on one occasion carried his fight with Richmond to such an extreme that he drove the frightened associate player off the stage, out of the theatre, and down the street, pursuing him sword in hand all the way.

Edwin Booth, the son, had good cause to remember his first experiences in "Richard III." They were crucial. On the night of Sept. 10, 1849, he appeared, clothed as Tressel, before his father, in the dressing-room of the Boston Museum. It was to be his first appearance on the stage, and the *début* had been planned without consultation with the elder Booth.

With his feet perched on a table, the experienced tragedian sat, critically scanning the looks and dress of his trembling son, then a handsome, romantic lad of only sixteen years.

"Humph," he said, "you play Tressel. Now, sir, who was Tressel?"

"A messenger from the field of Tewksbury," was the reply.

"Very well. How did he make his journey?"

"On horseback, sir."

"Where are your spurs, then?"

In dismay Edwin looked down at his boots to note that he had certainly forgotten this realistic accoutrement.

"Here," said the father, "take mine."

Not another word was uttered. Immediately after the short scene on the stage, Edwin hurried again to his father's room, and there saw him still nonchalantly smoking his cigar.

"Give me my spurs," was his only remark. Not a word of comment. And never, through his life, did the elder Booth tell his son how he had hastened to the wings, and there followed with greatest attention and with apparent satisfaction every move of the *débutant*. Edwin learned it from others.

In 1851, when in New York, Junius Brutus Booth was announced for "Richard III." at the National Theatre, but, in spite of all protests from his son, refused to go to the play-house. He gave no reason whatever, except the absurdly fictitious reason that he was ill.

"What will they do?" cried Edwin, in despair at this latest freak of his eccentric father. "Who can take your place?"

"Act the part yourself," gruffly replied the senior; and when the young man reached the theatre with his apologies, he found the manager there ready to make the same suggestion. Unwillingly Edwin allowed himself to be over-persuaded, and went upon the scene. At the close the applause was so great that the youthful actor was obliged to come before the curtain.

In after life Edwin asserted that he had reason to believe his father was in the audience that evening, but never a word did that father utter, after the performance, to show that he had seen it.

The beginning thus made was auspicious, and yet Booth's first engagement after this was to play for six dollars a week in any part that might be proffered him.

A rough toiling tour through the West brought hard experience to the youth.

Then, returning to the East, Booth, no longer the "younger," since the elder Booth had passed away, made his initial appearance in Baltimore as the humpbacked monarch, and a little later met the beautiful Mary Devlin, to whom he was afterward married. His first New York appearance, also, was as Richard; and on that occasion, May 4, 1857, Lawrence Barrett (as Tressel) first appeared on the same stage with the actor with whom his professional career was destined to be so intimately connected. Barrett has described the Booth of that day as a "slight, pale youth, with black flowing hair, soft brown eyes full of tenderness and gentle timidity, and a manner marked by shyness and quiet repose." "He took his place with no air of conquest or self-assertion," adds Mr. Barrett, "and gave his directions with a grace and courtesy which have never left him."

Of Booth's acting as Richard, it is sufficient to say here that it was not of the old school that took so literally the man's description of himself; it was not a malformed, scowling murderer of the deepest dye, but, instead, showed above the physical infirmities and mental perversions a sharp intellectuality that removed him from the melodramatic field. Other characters, however, were more to Booth's liking, and in his later years playgoers saw little of his Gloucester.

The last of the Richards, Mr. Mansfield, came before the public in 1889. With elaborate care, the enterprising young actor made his first important step into Shakespearian drama. Gifted with a thorough education and with refined tastes, Richard Mansfield adds to these acquirements a versatility and a cleverness in impersonation that have enabled him to play all manner of *rôles*, from the humorous burlesque Ko Ko in the " Mikado," to the repulsive, realistic old *roué* in " A Parisian Romance." His " Richard III." discarded Cibber, for the most part. His Gloucester was shown at the outset as a cool, gay youth of nineteen, reckless, brave, and ambitious, and later on as the haggard, shattered, conscience-stricken tyrant of thirty-three, thus giving opportunity for marked contrast in appearance. At the same time Mansfield, like Booth, threw away the stilted, declamatory methods so common to the early Richards, holding in mind Napoleon's words to Talma, " The

RICHARD MANSFIELD AS KING RICHARD III.

greatest kings do speak like ordinary mortals."
The physical deformity of the king was merely
suggested.

A long list of other Richards could be mentioned, from James Fennell to Joseph Haworth,
and including Edwin Forrest, E. L. Davenport,
G. V. Brooke, James Bennett, Barry Sullivan,
J. W. Wallack, John Wilkes Booth, Lawrence
Barrett, John McCullough, Thomas Keene, Frederick Warde, and Louis James; but in this chapter
the chief aim has been to present interesting features connected with the heroes of the more notable players. We will let this volume, also, simply
record the fact that there have been female Richards, including Mrs. Henry Lewis, Miss Marriott,
and Charlotte Crampton, as well as the prodigy
heroes of whom William Henry West Betty, Clara
Fisher, Jean Margaret Davenport, and the Bateman
sisters were leaders.

INDEX

www.ingramcontent.com/pod-product-compliance
Lightning Source LLC
Chambersburg PA
CBHW030819110726
47900CB00006B/1672